Vengeance

Roger A. Price

First published by Endeavour Press Ltd in 2017.

'For my grandchildren Jakub and Julia'

.

Chapter One

Jack Quintel didn't need to be here, he'd requested his usual proof of death, but as he hadn't used this killer before, he wanted to see it for himself. It took him a while to find a spot among the trees, and he was conscious of not flattening too many bluebells that were everywhere at this time of year. He knew the killer Charlie was no mug, nor was the target, Jim Reedly. If all went well Quintel planned to use Charlie again. The last thing he wanted was for him to realise he'd been here checking up on him; after all, he'd asked for his normal, if not unusual, evidence that the job had been done. He just wanted to satisfy himself, and watch the killer's craft. Enjoy the show. It was starting to go dusk so that would help; he just hoped Reedly wasn't late home and it became too dark - he knew that wouldn't bother Charlie, but he was beginning to wish he'd brought a pair of night-vison glasses.

It took a couple of minutes to settle himself as he took in the surroundings. The house was a fairly new build, but a grand affair nonetheless, detached in its own grounds with a tree-lined private driveway – the privileges of rank. Its location was handy though, Fulwood was an established district of Preston and had more than its share of such houses – especially on the eastern side of the city where a lot of the newer builds were situated. It wasn't far away from the industrial unit Quintel had hired, or had had hired for him. That was in a traditional brown field estate behind a newish built Asda supermarket. Perfect; as it backed onto the M6 motorway. Quintel always liked an emergency egress from anywhere he used; he was cautious, he had to be.

Quintel passed the time trying to fathom out where Charlie would be. He guessed somewhere where the car would stop, somewhere near the house-front. He could see a turn-around in front of the property which would seem to be the obvious place, but he couldn't see Charlie, which wasn't entirely surprising, given the circumstances. He just hoped his suspicions were ill-founded; it was not that easy finding a good assassin. You couldn't just type 'killer wanted to join enthusiastic team' into an internet search engine, well, not without a world of trouble landing on you. It was just that he had learned long ago not to ignore his hunches; he wouldn't have reached his forties if he had.

The setting sun was dropping behind him now so he made sure he had good cover behind the oak trees. A peaceful vista, which was about to be shattered. He couldn't help but inhale the spring fragrancies which were all around, in what was soon to become a place of carnage – he enjoyed both.

Quintel heard a car's engine about the same time as he saw its headlights – weak in the twilight - as they struggled to stretch down the drive. A silver BMW 6-series crackled along the gravel road and pulled up in the turn-around, with its back to Quintel. Game on. The engine was cut and the lights were turned off. Quintel could see the back of the driver's head, and it looked like Reedly – greying hair around a tanned bald spot. The rest of the car looked empty.

Seconds passed, and Reedly hadn't moved. What was he doing? He'd soon find out if his hunches were right, or whether it was just paranoia. It was too easy to get over-distrustful in his line of work; he'd never met a decent villain who didn't suffer from it at some time or another.

Then Quintel heard a dull crack coming from in front of the motor. Not the sound of a suppressed round, but the noise a reinforced windscreen makes when submitting to one. He saw the back of Reedly's head slump forward, and Quintel let go of his breath. He could now see the shattered windscreen, and then he saw Charlie approach from side-on, from beyond the trees on the other side of the road, rifle slung over his shoulder. He watched as the man dressed in black leaned into the BMW and started to manhandle Reedly's body from the driver's seat. He watched Charlie as he dragged the cadaver out onto the path, and then beyond the tree-line and out of sight. Quintel knew what would happen next and didn't need to wait around. He'd leave Charlie to finish off and clean the scene, he'd see him later. It looked as if he'd been wrong about Charlie; it had been a clean, no-nonsense job, nicely done. No, he'd seen what he'd come to watch; the slaying of Jim Reedly. Time to make himself scarce while Charlie busied himself in the opposite wood.

6

Chapter Two

It was almost dark as Quintel arrived at his industrial unit; its brickwork looked even more orange than normal in the mixture of illumination cast from the last seepage of the sun's glow, together with the strengthening glare of the street lamps. A contact had taken out a short-term lease on the two-storey building on his behalf. It had a workshop on the ground floor with three offices above. Quintel had only used it for a couple of days and now Reedly was dead, he didn't plan to hang around. It was situated at the rear of the small modern industrial estate and was far enough away from its nearest neighbour so as to ensure privacy. Quintel had parked his hire car in front of another unit 100 metres away. There was no CCTV at this point according to his man, Jason, and in any event he wouldn't be returning to the motor. It had been hired a few days earlier by his contact on a nicked driving licence, and he'd always worn gloves when using it. His contact would return it to the hirer tomorrow as arranged.

Jason was the one person he trusted, a brutish man who had worked with Quintel for years. His name didn't fit his character. As he approached the front doors Jason was there to greet him.

'Any problems, Boss?'

'Sweet, all done.'

'Charlie?'

'Sound, though I was hoping for a head shot – more dramatic.'

'He do him in the chest?'

'I guess so; he never got the chance to get out of his motor, just slumped forward.'

'Sounds like a pro, central body mass – bigger target. Heads are easy to miss.'

Quintel just nodded as he entered the building and passed Jason, he knew what he'd said was right; he'd have just loved more of a show.

Thirty minutes later, Quintel was behind a desk in the largest of the three offices with Jason stood next to him. On the desk was a briefcase with 10,000 pounds in it in used notes. The door opened and Charlie walked in, holding a plastic carrier bag.

Jason spoke first. 'You park where I told you?'

'Yes, where there is no CCTV, I'm not an idiot.'

'Just doing my job.'

Charlie stopped in front of the desk, and looked at the briefcase as he spoke. 'Is that what I think it is, Mr Quintel?'

Quintel nodded, and then dipped his brow towards the carrier bag. 'Is that what *I* think that is?'

'Yes.'

'Now, let me see yours first,' Quintel said, and then watched as Charlie reached into the carrier bag and pulled out a small translucent plastic bag. He briefly held it up in front of him as he faced Quintel, before quickly putting it back inside the carrier bag. 'Not so fast, Charlie, I want to savour the moment.'

'Look, Mr Quintel, you've seen it and I've got to get going to make sure I'm where my alibi says I am, and in any event, it's grossing me out.'

Quintel produced a white cardboard plate from the desk drawer and placed it on the empty desk top.

'Planning a picnic?' Charlie asked.

'I want you to empty that bag onto the plate, before you take the briefcase. No offence Charlie, but we've not worked together before and the last man who tried to pass me off with a leg of lamb is now keeping the bottom-feeders in the Irish Sea happy.'

'None taken,' Charlie said as he pulled the dull plastic bag out again and emptied its contents onto the plate. 'Voila,' he said as a bloodied heart plopped onto the platter.

Quintel stared at the grisly item, and after a few seconds Charlie reached forward towards the plate.

'Not so fast, Charlie,' Quintel said, adding, 'Jason, grab him.'

Jason jumped behind Charlie and before he'd any time to react, had bear-hugged him and kicked his legs from under him. Charlie went down with a thud. Quintel was always impressed with the big man's agility.

Jason quickly searched Charlie, who was now face down on the floor and starting to remonstrate.

'Clean,' Jason said, as he stood up with his right boot on the back of Charlie's neck.

'Cuff him, and stand him up.'

Seconds later Charlie was back on his feet with his hands plasti-cuffed behind his back, with Jason stood slightly behind him.

'What the hell do you think you are doing, Quintel?'

'I could ask you the same, Charlie.'

'Look man, I don't know what your problem is, but I killed the man, as directed, and there's his bleeding heart – no pun intended.'

'I have to agree Charlie, the kill looked sweet,' Quintel said, enjoying the confused look on Charlie's face, 'you see; I was in the woods watching.'

'Well, you know the job's been done then.'

'The trouble is Charlie, what you've brought me here is a pig's heart.'

Charlie hesitated before he answered, and Quintel saw uncertainty in his eyes.

'Look man—'

'No bull,' Quintel interrupted, before Charlie could continue.

'Ok, it's a pig's heart,' Charlie said, continuing, 'but you saw the kill. I just didn't fancy cutting his heart out, it would take ages and cause a lot of mess, so I thought I'd bring you this instead, just to make it easier, not to rip you off or anything.'

'I'd like to believe you, Charlie.'

'How did you know?'

'I got the nickname "Butcher" not because of my sunny outlook, but because as a youth I worked in an abattoir for a while. Though it does no harm for people to think otherwise.'

'I'm sorry, Mr Quintel, it was unprofessional of me, but I just wanted to get out of there as soon as I could, you can understand that, surely?'

'If that was true, then why did you move the body into the woods, if not to remove the bastard's heart?'

Charlie didn't answer.

'Unfortunately, I left as you were dragging the body from the car; I wished I'd stayed a bit longer now.'

'Why is that?'

'Because I've got a funny feeling, if I had, I'd have seen Reedly walk out of that bloody wood.'

'Wait, no way, you saw the hit. You said so.'

'I saw his windscreen shatter, that's all. If I ask Jason to go have a look now, what will he see?'

Charlie suddenly threw himself backwards into Jason, knocking him off balance. He turned and started to run for the door, but his head looked too far in front of him and without free arms to counterbalance he went down hard. Before he could get up Jason was on him, again impressing Quintel with his sprightliness.

'Bring the bastard back here.'

'Yes, Boss.'

'And hold him down, this time.'

Quintel watched as Jason dragged Charlie by his collar and slammed him face down on the end of the desk.

'Please, Mr Quintel, I'll make it right, if you let me,' Charlie said, as he turned his face onto one side towards Quintel.

'Hold his head still.'

Quintel waited until Jason had finished. He stood astride Charlie, one hand on his neck, forcing it against the table, and the other on his head, keeping his face flat.

'And how the hell do you propose to do that? Not only is the bastard still alive, but he now knows he's at risk, so will be almost impossible to get at. What did you do, blow us out for a double pay day?"

'No, no nothing like that, they were on to me, made me go through a mock-up, said I'd get some sort of immunity.'

'I learned many years ago to trust my premonitions, which is why I brought this with me,' Quintel said, as he produced a short-handled machete from behind his desk. He moved around to the end of the table.

'No, for God's sake, I've got a family, I'll do—' Charlie started to say.

Quintel's axe cut off his sentence and nearly severed his head. One fast downward hack was all it took to achieve both. Quintel and Jason sprang backwards, away from the resultant jet of blood, like demonic acrobats. Quintel smiled, he'd not lost all his butchering skills.

Chapter Three

Vinnie Palmer changed cheeks as he made himself comfortable in the driver's seat of his small white van. He'd been parked up near the large Asda superstore for a couple of hours now. He was in a layby far enough past the store so as not to attract any attention from their security, but not so far into the estate as to draw notice from the main industrial estate's staff. Though recces done over the last couple of days showed the main site only had one security man, and he seemed to spend most of his time sat in his office doing the crossword or whatever. And in any event, he had his cover story ready if approached – a travelling rep, he'd pulled off the M6 motorway and parked up for a while as he was far too early for his next appointment, a bogus company in Preston.

He could of course just pull out his detective inspector's warrant card and badge, but this was an undercover operation and he didn't want to trust anyone he didn't have to, safer that way. Though having seen the security bloke from the main site earlier, he wasn't expecting to be disturbed.

He was quite enjoying himself, apart from his aching backside. Normally, he was only brought in when bodies started turning up, but this job was different; a threat to kill and a chance to intervene before the murder was committed. That didn't happen too often.

He kept his gaze on the building he had seen Charlie enter a while ago, but two things were starting to bother him; the failing light; as he would start to stand out more once the daylight was gone; a man sat in a van in the dark would raise a question in anyone's mind, even with the site security bloke. Especially after he'd been here too long for his cover story to hold up.

Secondly, he'd seen the main target – Jack Quintel, drive into the site some time ago, followed thirty minutes later by Charlie Parker - who should have done what he had to and have been out by now. Normally, on a job like this the Special Ops department would have run the job on the ground, but due to the high profile nature of the intended victim – Jim Reedly – Vinnie's boss Harry Delany had asked him to cover it.

But it was passing dusk now; something must be wrong, time to ease his backside and go and take a closer look. Then his phone went off which made him jump. Vinnie grabbed it, hoping it was Charlie, but the screen said "Harry". He took the call. 'Hi Boss, there's no change here, Charlie is still in there.'

'How long?' Harry asked.

'Too long. He said he would show Quintel the pig's heart, grab the dosh and that would be that. I'm going to take a closer look.'

'Ok, but be careful, and keep me informed,' Harry said before ending the call.

Once out of the van, Vinnie stretched his six foot frame as he made his way to the rear of the vehicle. He was still fairly fit, which he should be for a man in his thirties, but he'd never been any good sat idle in surveillance vehicles, it just adds up to back and bum grief. This was just one reason why he preferred working homicides.

He was already wearing his Glock 17 handgun in a shoulder holster under his suit jacket; he just needed to change the coat. Once he was sure he couldn't be seen he opened one of the back doors to the van and changed. He locked the vehicle before walking away with his yellow reflective jacket and white hard hat on. He'd chosen to wear a black business suit as the trousers wouldn't look out of place under the high-viz coat. One could always dress down, when you needed to; but you couldn't dress up. An idiom he'd always respected.

With a torch in hand Vinnie made his way straight to the rearmost building. He was hoping he could help extract Charlie from whatever drama he was in, covertly, by bundling in as a night security patrol starting his round. That way, Charlie could get out without the whole job being blown. If it was too late for that, then he'd just go noisy. His sudden change of character would buy him a few seconds to call for back up. He was no expert when it came to these sorts of jobs but he'd met a few police undercover operatives in the past, and Charlie looked the real deal to Vinnie, so he was still hopeful the delay wasn't a problem.

As he neared, he could see that the main entrance to the building was open; one of the two main doors was slightly proud of the other. He also noticed a light on upstairs in the middle office. Previously gathered intelligence told him that there should only be Quintel and his minder in there with Charlie. Vinnie was about fifty metres away now and felt his own pulse starting to rise, though he tried to keep a calm visage in case he bumped into anyone. Years of experience had taught him how to foul himself while appearing to enjoy it. He also knew that a calming demeanour had a mirrored effect on others, too. The misreading of a potential threat to an adversary could save your life in the moments of advantage it could give. He unzipped his jacket halfway to speed up his access to the Glock. He glanced up at the lit window, the blinds were drawn, but then he saw something which made him stop to re-evaluate. The blinds were horizontal and they had just moved. He watched as they rolled up, disappearing as black smoke belched through the space against the glass.

Vinnie started to run; he was twenty metres from the double doors when an explosion ripped through the upper floor. The shockwave hit him and propelled him backwards across the grass frontage. A weird sensation of being stopped, picked up, and then thrust backwards against his will. He felt a hot air-blast race over his face as he landed hard on his back. A moment later he put his hands over his face as broken glass peppered him. Seconds passed and he realised the glass shower had stopped. He pulled his hands away from his face; they had protected it but at a small cost as blood ran down his arms from what seemed like a hundred tiny stab wounds across their backs.

He gathered his senses as he rose to his feet. Then a second explosion hit. Not as violent as the first, but as Vinnie instinctively tried to turn his back to the building the effects hit him side on, and decked him where he stood. He was straight back to his feet this time and could see that the ground floor was ablaze. Entry via the front was impossible, as flames roared through the entrance in their hungry pursuit of oxygen.

He dialled three nines on his phone as he ran down the side of the building, alerting the emergency services. At the back he could see an open rear fire-door and instinctively looked across the grass away from the building. After 150 metres or so the flat turf disappeared downhill, towards the embankment of the northbound carriageway of the M6, and out of sight. Vinnie thought he glanced two figures vanishing into the darkness beyond the building's security light's reach. He went cold at the thought. Maybe there were three but he'd only seen two? Momentarily unsure what to do, he turned back to go to the rear of the building, but could see thick black smoke rolling out of the open fire-door. The building was becoming engulfed, and he knew he wouldn't last seconds inside without breathing equipment; he'd been in similar situations before, years earlier when he'd been in uniform. It always shocked him how quickly the thick acrid smoke would cause your windpipe to constrict as if some invisible hand had your throat in a vice-like grip. Most fatalities in building fires were caused by the smoke, long before the flames got to work. But he also knew he would have to try. He ran through the doorway but immediately faced a furnace. The whole building was alight now and the flames darted and danced at him, forcing him back outside with spear-like jabs. It was like looking into the gates of hell, but not being allowed in.

Back outside he gasped for air as the invisible hand let go and he turned back towards the darkness but saw no one. He prayed Quintel and his thug had taken Charlie with them, albeit under duress, because if they hadn't and he'd been left inside, Vinnie realised he would already be dead.

What the hell had happened in there?

Chapter Four

The shockwave from the first explosion hit the back of Quintel about the same time as the heat. Perversely, it propelled him forwards, helping him cover the ground more quickly, while still keeping his footing. He didn't look around. Jason was ahead and he saw him disappear down the embankment. Quintel made it over the edge as he heard the second set of charges detonate. He was over the verge before the blast reached him. Slipping and sliding down the grass he came to an abrupt halt as he reached the hard shoulder as Jason stopped him falling into the main carriageway. He instinctively looked around but could see no attention from the passing traffic, which was light.

It was fully dark now, and this section of motorway had had its lighting turned off, some pathetic attempt to save money by the local council no doubt. But the benefit was his; he doubted if anyone had seen either of them coming down the bank. He jumped into the front seat of the waiting Ford Mondeo. He knew Jason had arranged for its delivery only ten minutes earlier to limit the chances of any passing filth picking up on it; he'd even had a made-up sign put on the front windscreen with the words, "Awaiting Tow Truck" written on it. Jason took the cardboard sign and threw it onto the back seat before retrieving the electronic key from above the driver's side sunshade.

'You were right, Boss, to be worried about Charlie after all,' Jason said.

'I wish I hadn't been. This will balls-up our plans a bit now. Reedly will be tucked away somewhere all nice and safe. We'll have to leave him for a while. It puts us back, and I hate disruptions.'

'So what do we do now, Boss?'

'Just get us out of here. Reedly will wait; in fact I rather enjoy the thought of him shitting himself. I'm more concerned at how they knew of our plans? And what else they might know?'

'Does that mean you want us to postpone things?'

'We can't, even if we wanted to, Jason. No, we press on; we've just got to be extra careful from here on in.'

Jason accelerated onto the main carriageway, and they were soon approaching Junction 32 of the M6, where the M55 – Blackpool – motorway commenced.

'Head to Blackpool, Jason, we can book into a hotel and stay anonymous there.'

'Yes, Boss.'

As Jason got busy with the driving, Quintel thought back to how they had come across Charlie Parker. He had been recommended by a supposedly solid bloke. 'The guy who put us onto Charlie?'

'Dempster. Yeah, don't worry, Boss. When I get a chance he's gonna get a visit.'

'No doubt, Jason, but the problem I'm wrestling with is this: Was Charlie just a chancer who went to the filth, or...,"

'The filth themselves? I know, Boss, I've been wondering the same, but after Dempster gave us Charlie's details I did some digging around.'

Quintel was impressed, he hadn't asked Jason to do that, as he hadn't seen the need. Initially he never intended to let Charlie walk away from the gig; that was until he witnessed the job being "apparently" done. He'd been so impressed, the thought of letting him live and using him again had taken root. Until he'd seen the pigs heart.

'What did you find out?'

'That Charlie Parker existed. He was a mean bastard who was muscle for hire with no scruples.'

'So what went wrong?'

'Either Dempster went straight to the cops and they provided an undercover cop posing as Charlie before we'd first met him, or...,'

'Or Charlie himself saw a way to get two pay days, and blew us out.'

'We won't know which until I get hold of Dempster.'

'Either-way we are partly compromised, though the cops' knowledge of us will be very limited and they'll have no idea of our agenda. I don't see why they shouldn't just think it all begins and ends with Reedly.'

'Makes sense, Boss.'

'In fact, how do you fancy earning some extra cash?'

'Sure, what is it?'

'Can you still shoot straight?'

'I keep it up, and if I'm thinking right; I told you I could have done Reedly.'

'I know, Jay I just wanted some distance between the target and us. But we carry on.'

'Ok, Boss, but I thought you said Reedly would have to wait?

'I did, but that could change; there's a reason sometimes that I only tell you stuff when you need to know it; it's not that I distrust you, it's to protect you, now I need to make some calls, so just drive, will you.'

Quintel wouldn't make the same mistake again. He'd done it for the right reasons, rather than not valuing Jason's abilities. He knew he'd spent six years in the army, and he trusted him as much as he'd ever trusted anyone. It was more about distance, keeping them away from the smelly end of business, but needs must now, and it would be the lesser of the risks. He hoped the real Charlie had been the one to do the dirty on them off his own back. That way they could use Dempster again, he had his uses as a local dirt bag – come – dogsbody. The two cars they'd used today being a prime example. But if it was Dempster who'd betrayed them, then he'd pay a heavy price, and not just with his life; a message would need to be sent into the criminal community.

Overall though, no real harm had been done. Reedly would be harder to get at in the short term, but his end would still come, and he could spend the time in-between adding to his grey hairs. There was a still lot to do.

Chapter Five

Vinnie met Harry Delany at Preston Central Police Station at 7 am the following day; it was a newish built nick in the city centre with a purpose-made incident room, which made a pleasant change from having to set one up in a gym or in whatever space one could, which was the norm.

Vinnie's injuries were limited to superficial cuts to the back of his hands and arms, and by the time he'd left the local hospital, he couldn't be bothered driving back to his home in Manchester so he'd booked into a city centre hotel. It wasn't as if he'd had anyone waiting for him since he and Lesley had split up.

It was his first time working in Preston. Since he joined Greater Manchester Police's Major Incident Team, the police forces of the north west of England had formed a jointly staffed Regional Homicide Unit, a further collaboration between forces made necessary by all the budget cuts. Harry reckoned it was just another step on the way to amalgamating all forces into larger regional outfits. Like they had in Scotland.

He hadn't slept well, especially after he'd received Harry's call while he was at the hospital. It hadn't taken the Fire Brigade long to find poor Charlie's body. According to preliminary findings, he'd died from severe neck wounds, but the fuller details wouldn't be known until after the post mortem examination. And as of now the body was still in situ in what was now a huge crime scene. At least he'd died quickly, before the smoke and flames got to him, Vinnie thought, and then immediately felt guilty for thinking such a thing.

He'd spent most of the time since wondering what had gone wrong. And what, if anything, he could have done differently.

Having found the incident room on the ground floor, Vinnie soon found the SIO's – Senior Investigating Officer's – office. He pulled up a chair and waited for Harry. He knew he was already here as his jacket was on the back of the chair behind the desk; he'd probably been here most of the night.

Vinnie stared through the glass walls at all the activity going on in the main spacious office as terminals and office furniture were being arranged. He usually loved the feel of the frenetic activity that always happened on day-one of a murder investigation, but not this time.

He saw Harry's portly figure and ruddy face as he walked across the floor toward the office. He kept getting stopped but eventually he made it there, entered and closed the door behind him. Vinnie felt a feeling of relief as the ambient noise dropped to a background level.

'How are you, this morning?' Harry asked.

'I'm fine, I told you on the phone last night.'

'I know you did but I just thought I'd ask.'

'Thanks, but more importantly, what about Charlie's family?'

'He was single and unattached as you know, so his parents are next-of-kin. I had the task of going to see them last night with the chief from Lancs.'

'How did that go?' Vinnie asked, immediately regretting the stupidity of the question.

'They're in bits, and they want answers.'

'Sure. How did we not see this coming?'

'A question I keep getting asked by all the senior-ranked soothsayers.'

'Most of those dozy bastards have spent all their lives behind ever increasing desks, having never met an angry man,' Vinnie said, feeling the emotion in his voice.

'Now, now Vinnie, we have to tread carefully.'

Vinnie knew this, but hated those who had never been anywhere near a difficult or dangerous operation and then suddenly thought they were experts simply because they'd achieved a certain rank. He knew the operational strategy had been to go through with the mock execution and then on "proof of death" get the payment and leave. That way, Quintel and his goon friend couldn't try and claim "agent provocateur" later at court by alleging that they only went along with the killer/undercover officer. Or that he had been the leading figure or the driving force behind it all, as was often the case in contract killing undercover sting court cases.

'What about the strategy, not to have an arrest team ready to go straight in at the meeting and arrest them all?' Vinnie said.

'You questioning our strategy?'

Vinnie instantly realised how his question had sounded, and held his hands up in the air, before adding, 'Of course not, Harry, I was just paraphrasing what we might be asked.'

Harry's hackles seemed to descend before he carried on. 'Yes, I've already had that one from the Lancs chief. I had to explain the rationale to follow rather than arrest.'

Vinnie knew that the evidence against Quintel and his goon was in the bank, but as they didn't know who was behind the threat to Reedly's life, they had decided to postpone their arrests in the hope that a surveillance team would be able to follow them away from the meeting with Charlie, and lead them to the top man. If they jumped too soon, there would still be an ongoing threat to Reedly.

Of course, Vinnie knew that the strategy hinged on the assumption that Quintel and his goon were just middle men. 'But what if Quintel is the man behind it?'

'He might be, but until we know for sure we can't risk it. If we pull them in and they say jack shit, it'll leave the main player out there to start over.'

Vinnie knew all this of course, but sometimes asking the questions out loud helped the thought process. That was one of the difficulties with undercover jobs; no black or white, but lots of grey. He moved on. 'How did the surveillance team get on? he asked, more in hope.

'That was the chief's next question. And unfortunately they hadn't planned on the bad guys leaving the estate from the rear; they must have had a car waiting on the hard shoulder of the M6.'

Vinnie had guessed as much. He'd have heard by now had it been any different. 'We should have thought of that.'

'That's what the chief said.'

'What about the car that they didn't leave in? The one they'd left parked in the estate being watched by our surveillance team.'

'PNC – Police National Computer – says it's a local rental. As soon as they open I want you down there.'

'Not a problem, Harry, but how do you plan to run this whole job?'

Vinnie knew that with a murder investigation, once all the detectives had been drafted in from divisions, the job would be run as one team with no secrets. But this job was very different. Not least because of the sensitivities surrounding the intended target, but also because an undercover officer had been deployed and now had sadly lost his life.

'We'll keep the undercover side of it to ourselves for now, and get the detectives to follow the initial clues to try and capture all the evidence at the scene, and to trace Quintel and his sidekick.'

'Obviously they all know that Charlie was a cop on duty, but not exactly why he was there, I guess.'

'It won't last long, Vinnie, but the longer we can hold back on the undercover side of things, the longer we can keep the details of the operation, and therefore the identity of the intended victim, a secret. We don't know why Charlie was rumbled; so we don't know what other dark forces are in play.'

Vinnie knew it wouldn't take too long before it became known in the incident room that Charlie was operating undercover, and then all the obvious questions would follow. He just nodded.

'Which is why we are against the clock, and you can't use any of the normal detectives to help you. We need to find these bastards quickly, of course, but you need to find out who is behind it. I'll give you all the help I can, but am restricted in that I've got to deal with the reactive side of the investigation, act as head of the enquiry and keep the bosses happy.'

'Are you saying what I think—' Vinnie started to ask?

'I'm saying, use whatever resources you have to, Vinnie, but start on that hire car first.'

'What about the intended victim?'

The deputy chief constable of Manchester, Mr Jim Reedly, has been whisked away to a safe location, but leave him to me, for now. We need to have a lengthy chat as soon as I can arrange it, and see if he can help us anymore in identifying exactly who this Quintel and his mate Jason are, and what the motive is? We still have no idea why.'

'Ok, Harry.'

'You go and grab some food; I'll join you in the canteen shortly, after I've briefed the troops and got them all out on their inquiries.'

Chapter Six

It was nearly 8 am by the time Harry returned to the canteen. Vinnie had just finished a chest-clutcher – or Full English Breakfast, as the menu called it. He'd forgotten just how hungry he was; he hadn't eaten in twenty-four hours. Harry joined him at his table as he finished using a paper napkin. 'I got you a brew, but it'll be cold now, sorry.'

'No worries, I've no time.'

'How'd the briefing go?

'Ok, I've sent most of the team up to assist at the crime scene, the quicker we can get Charlie's body moved, the better. Then the HOLMES2 system can start spitting out some actions.'

Vinnie knew that HOLMES was an anagram for "Home Office Large Major Enquiry System" set up after the advent of computers to ensure effective cross-referencing of information gathered during an investigation. It had been first brought in in the late seventies after the 'Yorkshire Ripper' murder enquiry. The mass murderer had been in the system several times before he became a suspect. Back then it had all been done using index cards. Hard to imagine that today, he thought.

'Ok, Harry, I'm off to see the hire company now,' Vinnie said.

'That's what I came to tell you, don't bother. They've just rung in to report one of their motors missing. They thought it was an overdue return, but it looks as if it had been nicked from the company's overflow car park two days ago. They only realised when they found the key-drop box screwed. Uniform are there now, as is a local detective, and CSI are going to have a look at the box, but don't expect too much.'

'Any other keys gone?'

'Nope, just one set and one motor.'

'CCTV?'

'Yes, but a well-aimed brick nullified it.'

'Damn.'

'Damn indeed.'

'Look, I've to go and front a press conference soon, why don't you have a sniff around up at the murder scene instead?'

'Will do, Harry.'

Twenty minutes later Vinnie pulled up back at the industrial estate. The place displayed an uncomfortable calm in the daylight. There were numerous white-suited CSIs busying about, and one fire brigade tender was still on site, presumably damping down any smouldering ashes. As for the building itself, Vinnie didn't hold out much hope of anything forensically significant coming out of it. More than half of what was combustible was gone. The main frame of the place was evident in an array of twisted metal girders. A uniform cop with a clipboard got out of a marked police car as Vinnie approached on foot; the cop was obviously maintaining a Scene Log.

Vinnie showed the officer his warrant card and then said, 'No need to show me on the log, I'm not going to get in the way by going in, I just want to have a mooch around the back.'

The cop nodded, but Vinnie noticed his pen-hand move across his board nonetheless. Before he headed to the rear of the premises Vinnie reacquainted himself with the main site. It was mid-size with around thirty or forty units on it, all newly built, and most appeared to be used as office spaces and admin blocks. At the north end of the estate was a porta-cabin which was used by the security staff. He was tempted to speak to whoever was there, but didn't want to take any chances. It would just be his luck that whoever had been on duty the night before was on a quick change to a day shift and may have seen Vinnie in his yellow jacket and suddenly recognise him. But to be honest, he knew there was virtually no chance of that. He'd kept a constant lookout for the guard last night and never saw anyone. Just better to be cautious; and in any event as soon as HOLMES2 was running and spitting out actions, one of them would be for someone to interview the security guard. It would seem strange if a DI had already done so.

Fifteen minutes later, he walked around the inner service road of the site and had not seen anything of interest. Not that he would know anything was of interest until he saw it. Detective work was often about hunches, seeing things which were apparently innocent until other information changed that. One of Vinnie's strengths had always been the ability to review things once discarded as of no interest, but through new eyes in the light of new information. It was probably why as a DC he'd often been picked to do the Exhibits Officer's job on major incidents; continually going over old ground. Boring, repetitive but essential.

Back where he started, he was about to head to the rear of the burnt out building when his phone rang. He was pleased to see the screen light up with the words "Christine Jones". It lightened his mood. Christine was a local TV investigative reporter working mainly for independent regional TV stations and had been instrumental in helping him on his last job – catching the escaped killer Daniel Moxley – he couldn't have done it without her. Especially after he'd managed to get himself suspended; she'd been the public face of his inquiries and got a pretty good scoop at the end of it. They'd been out for a drink a few weeks afterwards, and he intended to ask her out again, he enjoyed her company and she was switched on. He pressed the green icon to accept the call. 'Hi Christine, I've been meaning to give you a bell, how's it going?'

'Yeah, yeah, cut the crap. But seeing as you ask I'm fine. Look, you're not in Preston, are you?'

Vinnie knew that Christine sometimes had a difficult relationship with the detectives. They thought she got in the way of investigations sometimes, and he used to subscribe to that; but knew better now. She was just good at her job and often got to the story before the cops did. He wasn't surprised by her question. 'How did you know?'

'No crystal ball this time. My editor asked me to leg it up to Preston from Salford to cover a new murder investigation press conference. It was given by Harry Delany, so I wondered if you were on the case.'

'You wondered right, but I thought you were doing some deep exposé type investigation?'

'Even knowing that much could get you killed, Palmer, so be careful what you say. Walls have ears as well as sausages, and all that.'

He smiled at what she had said, she clearly loved playing the reverse cop-like strategies, it was partly what got up the noses of some of his contemporaries; but not Vinnie. 'Ok Sherlock, I'm just up at the fire scene, where the poor victim lost his life.'

'I was just about to head up there; can you wait for me and show me around?'

Vinnie agreed and arranged to meet Christine in the Asda café on the entrance to the site. He had a cappuccino waiting for her when she arrived fifteen minutes later.

'So, what were you intending to bell me about?' Christine asked, before she'd sat down.

She had a natural way of disarming Vinnie by asking not so much random, but unexpected questions, or just questions at unexpected times. After a slight pause, he said, 'Oh nothing, just a catch up chat. Anyway, to business, what did Harry tell the press?'

'Don't you mean what did Harry not tell us,' Christine said with a smile.

'Probably, but do I have to ring him?'

'Of course not,' she answered, before going on to elaborate.

As expected, Harry had told the press that the fire had been started deliberately, and that a man had died in the fire, but no more, other than to add that the two men thought responsible had been seen running away from the rear of the premises by a witness, and it is was highly likely that they made good their escape in a waiting vehicle which may have been parked on the hard shoulder of the M6 northbound, somewhere between junctions 31A and 32, and if anyone had seen bla, bla, bla, they should get in touch.

Christine finished by asking, 'Anything to add, Vinnie?' followed by, 'My first job is to try and find the witness; I thought I'd start with site security, unless you can point me in the right direction?'

'Nothing to add, but I can save you some trouble. I'm the witness, but I can't tell you why, not yet anyway.' Vinnie saw Christine raise an eyebrow, but she didn't say anything.

'Look, I'm about to have a look around the rear of the place, in the direction that the two figures went last night, join me if you want, but the building itself is off-limits for now.'

'Fair enough,' she said, 'there's an outside broadcast unit on its way so it would be good to get a feel for the place before they arrive.'

Ten minutes later, they were around the back of the building. Vinnie had noticed from his earlier walkabout that all the CCTV on-site pointed to the front of each building, and it appeared the same at the rear. It was the first time he had seen the back of the building in clear daylight and as he looked out across the grass towards the motorway's sounds Christine asked which way the two shadows had gone, exactly. He pointed towards the edge of the embankment 150 metres away, which led to the M6.

As he set off towards it, he looked at the building's only neighbour to their left and hadn't realised how far set back it was, probably about thirty or forty metres. When they reached level with its rear, Vinnie stopped and stared to his left at a further building, at its back. It was obscured by its larger neighbour and positioned about a further twenty-five metres behind it. In distance, it was roughly halfway between the motorway embankment and the back of the burned-out building.

'I'm guessing you didn't know that was there?' Christine asked.

'No, it's totally hidden from view. It looks like an annex from the main building in front; come on let's take a closer look.'

Five minutes later they had circled the small one-storey brick building. It had no windows but a glass front door facing back towards the estate. There was a gravel path linking it to the rear of the main building which hid it.

'Did you notice the CCTV,' Christine said, smiling.

'I did, come on.'

Vinnie had seen the usual cameras at the front of the building looking towards the glass, double-door entrance. And as there were no windows in the annex, he hadn't expected to see any at the rear. But not only where there two cameras on the building's rear wall, one on each edge, but they were facing outward – towards the motorway.

As he walked to the front door, Vinnie pulled his warrant card out. On opening the door, he could see a small reception area of about ten feet by ten feet, a small counter to the left which had a door behind it, and a further closed door was to their right. He rang the bell and two minutes later a portly man in his sixties appeared through the door behind the desk.

'Yes?' the man asked.

'I'm DI Palmer and this is a colleague,' Vinnie announced, showing the man his ID while giving Christine a wink.

'How can I help you?'

'We are investigating the fire around the corner and noticed you have outward facing CCTV at the back,' Vinnie said.

'That's right,' the man said, and before Vinnie could ask why, the man continued. 'We got done once before, or should I say the last owners did. Bastards smashed their way in through the rear wall, must have taken them half the night, and then they pissed off down the M6. No one saw anything, apparently, so they had those cameras installed. A bit late if you ask me.'

'What do you actually do here?' Vinnie asked.

'We just keep all our company's records here, it's just a depository now, its design is ideal for that, which is why my company bought it,' the man said, before going on to explain that his company kept paper records and files for the few remaining clients that still needed to hold onto non-digital records.

Vinnie suspected that the CPS or legal chambers would no doubt use facilities like this.

'What was the place used for when the break-in happened?' Christine asked.

'It was several years ago, but it used to be a holding facility for cash-in-transit deliveries, but as I say it's just full of paper records now. I'm surprised you don't already know all this.'

Vinnie explained that they were from Manchester, but no doubt the locals would know the history.

'Talk about right and left hands,' the man muttered.

Vinnie ignored the comment and watched as the man leaned down and opened a drawer and pulled out a DVD case.

'You'll be wanting this, then,' he said, as he passed the case over. 'I've been expecting you. It's a copy of the whole twenty-four hours covering the fire, all yesterday and through the night. I've obviously not had time to look at it so I don't know if it's any use.'

Vinnie thanked the man and asked, 'Is this the only copy?'

"Fraid so,' the man answered. 'The system re-records over itself every forty-eight hours, which is why I changed the disk sharpish this morning.'

Vinnie thanked the man again and said that at some time later someone would call back and take a statement from him.

Back outside, Vinnie turned to Christine. 'Well, I'm off to find a DVD player.'

'I'll help you,' she said.

Chapter Seven

'Damn, there's no DVD player,' Vinnie said, stood at the end of the double bed in his hotel room. 'Just the flat-screen TV.' He'd reckoned it might be quicker than trying to grab some equipment in Preston nick while the chaos of getting the incident room fully operational was still in progress. Plus, he'd agreed to let Christine help him as two sets of eyes were always better than one when watching CCTV; things could be easily missed. It was amazing how tiring and boring it could be.

'Try the TV itself, sometimes they're a combo?' she said.

Vinnie examined the TV more closely and could see a DVD slot in its side. 'Nice one, Christine,' he said, before turning the set on and pushing the DVD into the slot.

'Evidentially, we should really make a working copy of the DVD to protect the original,' Vinnie said, pausing as he spoke, but the delay in finding not only a DVD machine but one that makes copies, and a technician to do it in order to ensure integrity sufficient to satisfy a court, would take ages.

'Taking a little look won't harm, will it? she asked.

'I suppose not, we can use anything we see as intelligence and enter it into the evidence chain later.'

'I won't tell if you won't.'

Vinnie thought further for a moment. Strictly speaking he should do as he'd suggested, all his cop instincts were telling him this. But at this stage they were only seeking the information from it; if there was any. He decided to press on.

'If there is anything of value on it, surely only then does it become evidence and need preserving?' Christine offered.

'Strictly speaking, that's true. If there's nothing on it then it just becomes unused material. Let's see what we've got.'

Once the DVD started to play, it showed two views, each taking up half the screen and each with the same view. It was daylight, and the view was away from the premises they had visited, showing grass which eventually fell away. A further field was visible in the distant foreground.

'It's obviously a dual-camera system, but both showing the same thing,' Vinnie said, adding, 'Probably a zoom operated infrared motion detector on the second lens.'

Christine looked at him, and he explained further.

'This is basic kit. The first lens shows the view, but if anything disturbs the motion detector, the second lens zooms onto it. You get the close-up but keep the overall view to contrast it against.'

'Doesn't sound too basic to me,' Christine said.

'Trust me.'

'Oh, I do.'

Vinnie fast-forwarded the disc. There was no date or time stamp on it but as they knew the fire went up at dusk, he could use the failing light to guide him.

Twenty minutes later, the light was clearly going and he pressed play on the remote. He kept leapfrogging until the second half of the screen suddenly went into zoom mode. A flash of brilliant light was soon followed by another. He assumed the explosions had caused the zoom to kick in, but he backed the disc up anyway and pressed play again.

'There,' Christine shouted.

Vinnie lent in towards the TV and could see the image of the backs of two men running from the right of the screen across the grass towards the embankment. They were shadowy and not too clear, even when the flashes appeared, which were only for an instant. They weren't much help, as they tended to white-out the view. Certainly no way could the figures be identified from this footage, but he knew it must be Quintel and Jason. The two shadows neared the edge of the grass where the embankment started. 'They'll disappear in a mo, and then that'll be that I'm afraid.'

Vinnie sighed as a moment later the zoomed view returned to its previous state, but then a new view appeared from the second half of the screen. This time it had the footer of "Camera Three" under it. This new view showed the two fugitives slipping and sliding down the embankment towards the hard shoulder of the motorway, one after the other.

'Where's this feed coming from?' Christine asked.

'That post,' Vinnie shouted as he glanced at camera one's view - the overview - and could just make out a tall white post at the edge of the grass. 'Brilliant.'

Returning to the view from camera three, both men could be seen approaching a family sized saloon parked on the hard shoulder. The larger of the two – he assumed to be Jason – got in the driver's side, and the other – Quintel - got in the passenger side. Then car lights came on and the vehicle started to drive forward, then the camera three view went blank. Seconds later the TV screen returned to the joint overview position and the footers changed back to "Camera One" and "Camera Two".

'Damn, what just happened?' Vinnie said.

'I can guess,' Christine said, before going on to explain. She reckoned that the motion detector on camera three – the one on the post – probably would only be activated once camera two had picked up motion heading towards it.

'I see. It would probably be in some sort of sleep-mode until alerted by the system of something coming towards it, or by a near-motion incident coming from the other way. Otherwise every time a car drove past on the motorway, the system would be kicking off.'

'Makes sense, but why did it have to shut off right at that point?' Christine asked.

'Come on, let's go through it again.'

Vinnie orientated the remote control and then re-ran the DVD once more, and then again using the pause function until he was happy they had it on hold on the very last frame from camera three. It showed the car driving away with its lights on: including the rear number plate light.

'Look,' Christine shouted, and then ran to one of the bedside tables and returned with hotel pen and paper.

Vinnie leaned in and could see that the rear number plate was visible for the first time. He hadn't noticed it on the live playbacks. 'It's on the very last frame,' he said as he looked up to see Christine scribbling.

'Got it,' she said.

'Brilliant,' Vinnie said, 'I'll get it checked on the PNC – Police National Computer - then I can go and pay the owner a visit.'

Just then Vinnie's mobile started to ring. It was Harry. He put a finger to his lips and looked at Christine before he took the call.

'Good timing, Harry, I've got something.'

'Where are you now?'

'Five minutes from the nick.'

'Good, will it keep until you get here?'

'Sure, Harry, is everything ok?'

'I've just had a very interesting chat with Jim Reedly, albeit only over the phone.'

'And?' Vinnie asked.

'I think he's bullshitting me, see you in five.' The line went dead.

'Everything all right?' Christine asked.

'No, Harry thinks he's being rubber-dicked, I'd better get back.'

'I'm sure Detective Superintendent Harry Delany would never use that expression,' Christine said, grinning.

'You're probably right, but I'm working on him.'

Vinnie took the piece of paper from Christine, who said she needed to meet her camera crew back at the scene anyway, and record a short piece-to-camera in time for the lunchtime news. Vinnie said he'd ring her later, and they both headed out the hotel.

Chapter Eight

Vinnie walked into Harry's office just ahead of him and closed the door behind them. As Harry sat down behind his desk Vinnie noticed a smaller one at right angles to it that hadn't been there earlier. It had a desk phone and computer terminal on it.

'That'll be yours, Vinnie, and I'll give you a key for the door before you leave.'

Vinnie nodded, before trying out his new chair and turning to face Harry.

'I take it things didn't go too well with Reedly, then?' said Vinnie, feeling like he needed to say something to start Harry off.

'You could say that. I had to remind him that not only had he *not* been assassinated, but that the man mainly responsible for ensuring so had been.'

'How do you mean?'

'I rang him hoping to set up a face to face, but DCC Reedly didn't seem to want this, so I persevered over the phone. I was trying to find out why hitherto unknown villains such as Quintel and Jason-whatever, would want to kill him.'

'He's always claimed not to know anyone by their known names or descriptions,' Vinnie said.

'I know that, which was one reason why we thought there were others involved.'

Vinnie nodded.

'But after poor Charlie's death, I was hoping he would revisit it and try to help all he could, but all he seemed bothered about was that we catch them quickly as we had "already cocked-up by letting them escape".'

Vinnie understood why Harry was wound up, it wasn't as if they hadn't run their strategy past Reedly before the mock execution, which he'd willingly agreed to.

'Plus, he seemed to show a total lack of concern about Charlie Parker,' Harry said, adding, 'Maybe he should have accompanied me to see his parents last night.'

Vinnie shuddered at the thought of that task. "Death Warning Messages" as they were called were one of the job's worst tasks. He recalled each and every one he'd ever had to deliver, all of them vividly and indelibly stamped in his memory.

'He said he'd try and think again, but due to his seniority it had been many, many years since he'd been operational, so was struggling to think it was linked to any cases he had been involved in.'

'A fair point, Harry, I bet it's twenty years since he felt his last collar.'

'And that's what worries me. What if this is not job-related? What if he's been shagging, or whatever? But then it's all a bit extreme. The whole set up is too organised.'

'If he had been a naughty boy, then the aggrieved would probably want the pleasure of sorting Reedly out himself, that's what usually happens when that's the motive.'

Harry nodded, before carrying on, 'Plus, as soon as I put the phone down to you I got the chief of Lancs' office on the blower.'

Vinnie didn't believe in coincidences so knew whatever came next wouldn't be good news. Harry explained that he was now not allowed to ring Reedly without first going through the chief's office, and when he'd asked why he'd been told it was an order.

'That's a bit over the top,' Vinnie said.

'It gets worse. I've been told by his office to say that Charlie Parker was just passing the building, when he saw someone breaking in and went in to investigate before meeting his doom.'

'For Christ's sake, Harry, those bastards nearly cut his head off. Not the sort of attack carried out by your usual interrupted burglar.'

'That's what I said, and then I was told that the official line would be that Charlie is suspected to have died from smoke inhalation, and received severe neck injuries by - as of yet – unknown cause, but if pressed, I have to suggest that possible falling girders or similar might have caused the injury, either post death or whilst incapacitated.'

Vinnie was all for keeping Charlie's undercover status, and therefore the operation, a secret, but this was going to the extreme. 'Won't the home office pathologist have something to say about that?'

'He's already been put on a confidentiality contract, apparently, and he's not even seen the body yet, let alone examined it,' Harry said.

'What about giving out misleading information which could undermine any future court case against those bastards responsible?'

'That's why I've been told to use words like "suspected, unknown and suggest". And I've been told to do it before the post mortem examination, and to refuse comment once the PM's been done.'

'I see, get the bullshit out there before the PM and never correct it.'

'Exactly,' Harry said.

'You're right, Harry, we are being rubber-dicked.'

'What?' Harry asked, so Vinnie explained the expression.

They both sat in quiet contemplation for a couple of minutes before Harry asked Vinnie what his news was, so he told him.

'That is a piece of luck. I'm going to need you under the radar even more now until we get a clearer picture of things,' Harry said, before elaborating.

Harry told Vinnie that he would have to play along with the chief's office's orders for now, and ensure the investigation was limited to the recovery of evidence from the scene and the attempt to trace Quintel and Jason. He would open a sensitive policy log and record the CCTV DVD in it and indeed all of Vinnie's enquiries. Statements from witnesses such as the depository man could be actioned later when they knew what was going on. Vinnie was to keep Harry fully briefed and he would have to operate alone.

A twinge of guilt prodded Vinnie regarding Christine's involvement so far, but he decided not to tell Harry. Now was not the time to add to Harry's stress. He could see his ruddy complexion already turning purple, and he'd noticed that he'd already given his head an overarm rub, which was another sign of stress. 'What do you think is going on?'

'Someone has spent a lot of time thinking through this cover story, and not just to protect the covert side of things, and in any event, that would be our job, not the chief's office, so it looks as if he's being advised by outside influences.'

'Granted,' Vinnie said, 'and not by his staff officer, either.' Vinnie knew the uniform chief inspector who wiped the chief's butt. Vinnie had always thought that even that particular task was one that no doubt stretched his normal abilities as it were. 'It can only be about the true motive.'

'My thoughts too,' Harry said.

'That would in-part explain Reedly's lack of compassion about Charlie. Not that I'm excusing his callous behaviour, because I'm not. But it would explain his single-minded concern with catching Quintel and Jason – if that is their real names, even.'

Harry nodded, and his face seemed to be turning more pink-like once more.

'But surely motive will have to come out during any court case once we do catch them?' Vinnie added.

'They are probably taking it one step at a time; dynamically risk managing things, if you like. But I know when I'm being lied to, and Reedly was lying, no question. And something else, too.'

'What?' Vinnie asked.

'He was frightened, very frightened, as if he knew the threat was not only continuing; but was only going to get worse.'

Vinnie said he'd get the car checked on the PNC and follow that lead, while Harry prepared himself for his next press conference later in the day.

Chapter Nine

Jack Quintel wasn't too impressed at having to share a room with Jason, but he'd advised him that a downmarket bed and breakfast was less showy and far less traceable than booking into the usual standard of hotel that he would use. Plus the bored looking youth on reception was happy to take cash as he barely looked up from his wank mag, or whatever shite he'd seemed mesmerised by.

He'd had a shower to get the smell of smoke off, him having already left his overcoat in the boot of the car prior to checking in. Jason had done the same with his, but had reckoned they could have both been on fire and the dozy youth on reception wouldn't have noticed.

He'd just finished a call on his phone as Jason came out of the bathroom with a towel wrapped around him.

'Was that The Man again?' Jason asked.

'Yes, he's a little more chilled now. He can be an excitable fucker, but I've calmed him,' Quintel answered.

'I didn't know you had such a disarming nature, Boss.'

'I don't, unless there's money involved.'

Jason just grinned as he dressed.

'How well do you know Blackpool?'

'I can get around,' Jason answered, 'done a few stag dos here over the years. Why?'

'Well, until you've had your little chat with Dempster, I don't want to use him, for obvious reasons, so I've rung a contact who knows people around here, and he's given me a name and address.'

'Another motor?'

'No, the one we have will do for now, but we are going to need other hardware if you are going to earn your pay rise,' Quintel said, noting the expression on Jason's face. He carried on, 'I've taken a further call while you were cleaning all your important little places, and target number two will be on the move the day after tomorrow.'

'That's quick.'

'I know it doesn't leave a lot of time, though we've done most of the pre-planning effectively already.'

Jason nodded as he finished pulling his sweatshirt down over his jeans. Quintel knew that Jason had spent time in the Signals whilst in the Army, and had impressed him with the reconnaissance he'd previously done. But he'd keep the target's identity to himself until the last minute. Safer that way.

'I just hope the name you've been given is not a tosser.'

Quintel shot Jason a severe look.

'Don't get me wrong, Boss, I mean because it's come to you third hand.'

Quintel said, 'Explain?' as he felt his flash of temper subside.

'Well, you don't know the guy is what I mean, and sometimes these tossers have shit sticks for weapons, and expect proper cash.'

'If you need to break anything to get to the good stuff, do it. We don't have time to piss about.'

'Fair enough, Boss, I'll just put my trainers on and I'll be with you.'

'Then we can grab some food and kip, it could be a busy day tomorrow; we'll need to make the final arrangements for Friday. And if all goes to plan, this will put the shits right up that worm Reedly. Things might be turning out for the best after all,' Quintel finished.

*

Vinnie thought about what Harry had told him as he drove to the car rental firm who had hired out the family saloon that Quintel and Jason had fled in. He'd been a little surprised to learn it was from a different firm to the other one. Both were national outfits, but at least this one hadn't reported the car stolen.

He'd known Harry on and off for several years, but it was only recently that he had worked with him, when they'd been chasing the escaped murderer Daniel Moxley, and as wound up as Harry could get, Vinnie trusted him and his judgement. If he said that Reedly was holding back, then holding back he was. But at least this gave Harry the excuse to cut Vinnie loose on his own. He'd just have to be careful how he went about it. That was when a certain idea started to form, but it would depend on how he got on at the car rental place. Knowing his luck, Quintel could have dropped the motor off at any of the companies national outlets, no doubt wiped clean or worse.

It was late morning by the time he walked into the car hire firm's Preston city centre office. Parking was a nightmare in the centre of

37

Preston and Vinnie couldn't be bothered finding a car park so had abandoned his car on double yellow lines with a two-penny piece on the dashboard. It was many years since he used this ruse and he was unsure if it still worked. It was supposed to tell any passing traffic warden that the plain car parked illegally was that of a copper on duty. Hence the two-penny coin. A one-penny would also have done, but obviously not a silver coin. But back in the day the traffic wardens had come under the command of the local police whereas today they were council run, so it was a risk; the days of getting out of parking tickets were long gone unless you had a big blue light on top.

Ten minutes later Vinnie retrieved his coin, grateful that there was no ticket on his car, though he still didn't know if the old ruse had worked or not. The really good news was that the rented car was still out on loan - it had been hired two days ago by a local. Vinnie rang Harry and gave him the details for intelligence checks. He'd also managed to obtain a still photo printout from the company's CCTV showing the hirer. It wasn't too clear as the white male had been wearing a baseball cap, but the bloke who'd given it to him had been the same guy who had dealt with the hirer, so was able to add to the description.

Harry rang back after only a couple of minutes to say that the driving licence used to hire the motor had been stolen from a local burglary over twelve months ago. He should have expected this. He told Harry about the CCTV still and description and said he'd head straight back in to see if any of the local cops could put a name to it, he wouldn't hold his breath.

*

Quintel kept seeing new strengths in Jason that he'd never known were there. True, he had used him for years, but he himself was new to this line of work. If all went well they could make quite a name for themselves, and become very wealthy. Their current client was paying serious money for what was relatively straight forward stuff. He should have made the switch years ago. Importing drugs was just getting harder and harder, taking longer and longer, and with greater risks. Their current work was as easy as robbing kids, which was where it had all began a long time ago.

No, Jason seemed happy with the sawn-off shotgun and the Glock17 handgun they had bought, together with ammo. Though the little toe-rag

38

they had traded with in a bedsit on a side street off Blackpool's Central Drive wouldn't be able to count the money for a while; well, not until his fingers were better.

As Jason had predicted, the little turd who called himself Shocka – whatever the fuck that meant – had tried to sell them some crap that had clearly spent time submerged. That had plainly annoyed the big man. Quintel had thought he was going to give him a slap there and then, but no, it was when Jason had asked about oil, when he flipped.

'I wouldn't have thought about that, Jay,' Quintel had said afterwards as they'd walked away, heading towards the promenade.

'They drill it in into you in the Army, Boss,' he'd replied.

Quintel smiled as he lay in bed the following morning and replayed the scene in his mind. Jason asking "do you have any oil"? And Shocka's reply, "If you want bum lube you've come to the wrong place". Though, after all they were in Blackpool, Quintel had thought.

'I hope your contact won't be upset, Boss?' Jason had said.

'Don't worry about that, the cheeky shite got what he asked for, anyway, he can probably only count to five as it is. And we still left the correct amount of cash behind – minus Insult Added Tax of course – we're not thieves.'

Jason had grinned, and Quintel had asked, 'What about the oil, anyway?'

'We'll manage, it was more for the Glock than the sawn-off and the one we eventually got hold of looks brand new.'

'Excellent,' he'd said, and then they'd dumped them in the motor and headed off to eat.

Back to the present and Jason walked out of the bathroom and said, 'Is that a grin or a grimace, Boss? Last night's curry repeating itself?'

'No, I was just admiring your work last night. It was a grin,' Quintel answered before throwing back the quilt. They had better get going; they had a busy couple of days ahead.

Chapter Ten

'Hi Christine, how did your filming go?' Vinnie asked into his phone.

'Straightforward enough, thanks.'

'Are you in any rush to get back to Manchester?'

'No, my editor wants me to keep covering Preston; though at some stage I need to get back to other work.'

Vinnie's interest in this secretive exposé Christine was working on was piqued, but he wouldn't pry just yet, especially as he needed her help, his earlier idea was a goer now. 'Look, do you fancy meeting up for a late lunch? I've got a proposition to put to you.'

'O - Kay,' she replied slowly, adding, 'but remember the last time that happened you nearly ended up getting me killed.'

The Moxley job, still fresh in Vinnie's memory. 'True, but what a scoop you got.'

'That's not fair; you mentioned the scoop word. Now, I've got to know.'

Vinnie smiled as he gave Christine directions to a restaurant on the outskirts he'd noticed near the motorway junction when he'd first arrived.

*

Fifty minutes later, they had both eaten a club sandwich with fries, and Vinnie was enjoying relaxing in Christine's company. Over lunch, he'd told her about Harry being stonewalled and him sending Vinnie out on his own agenda until they knew exactly what they were up against.

'What, you mean like, corruption?' Christine asked.

'Could be, but I'm not sure it's that, but there is certainly a hidden level to this,' he answered. Vinnie then told her about his trip to the hire firm.

'Bummer,' she said.

'Well, then my luck changed. One of the local criminal intelligence officers recognised the face and description, said he's called Warren Dempster, a local petty thief who lives on one of the outer estates, not too far from the murder scene, though I don't think that's too relevant.'

'He's not Quintel or Jason then?'

40

'No, too scrawny, and anyway he's not an assassin. When he's not robbing the locals of their DVDs he's known for hanging around the big boys' tent.'

'What do you mean?'

'"Delusions of his own self-worth" is how the intel officer put it. Apparently, he gets used by the serious villains as a gopher, though he apparently likes to think of himself as some kind of quartermaster, a Mr Fix-it.'

'Ok, so where do I come in?'

'Well, I could just go straight in and lock him up, but he'd no doubt just say he was paid to hire a car by some unknown shadowy figure, or even worse, just sit there and go "no comment" on interview. And we'd be no nearer Quintel or Jason, in fact they'd probably get tipped off that we'd pulled Dempster.'

'What about the burglary, where the licence came from?

'My, aren't you the Miss Marple,' Vinnie said, noticing a flash of red in Christine's cheeks. He carried on, 'Only kidding, no you're right to some degree, he'd probably say he was given the licence by whoever had propped him to hire the motor, we'd charge him with burglary of course, but he'd probably only get done for handling. Hardly much of a threat.'

'Ah, I see, so what do you want me to do?'

Vinnie grinned, he'd remembered on the Moxley case they had gone on the knocker – door-to-door – and where he'd usually get told to fornicate with himself, it amazed him how much further Christine had got coming from the press angle. "Vanity interviewing" she'd called it, saying how everyone wants their fifteen minutes of fame at some time. He reminded her of this and then added, 'Seeing that this Dempster has such an ego, I thought if you went in with the investigative reporter angle, and say how you'd been pointed in his direction as he was known and respected as the local "go to man" he might slip up and come out with some intel we can use. We can always revert to plan A and lock him up later. What do you say?'

'Sounds like fun. And can I use anything I get?'

'When it's safe to do so without compromising the investigative side of things.'

Christine didn't answer right away; Vinnie knew this was always a difficult point between the press and the police, each with very different agendas. He broke the impasse. 'It worked well last time. Look at the scoop you got.'

'There you go mentioning the S word again. Ok, I'm in but I'm not waiting until after some court case, Vinnie Palmer. If we get something we can use, then redact it if you must but I'll need to give my editor something in the next twenty-four hours. I can always use the "unnamed local resident says" routine.'

'Fair enough, but what's with the "we" bit?'

'Because if we are doing this, then you get to be my bitch. Sorry, I mean junior reporter.'

A short time later Vinnie drove onto the council estate where Dempster's last known address was. According to the intel officer, Dempster spent a lot of time in a Labour club which adjoined the estate. He told Christine he'd drive around to locate where the club was and Dempster's address before they made an approach. Get a feel for the place, just in case this was a bad idea.

The place had seen better days, but he'd certainly been in far rougher areas. He tried to remember to drive around at normal speed; cops' natural default was to crawl around such streets, taking in all around them. It was probably what made them stand out as cops.

Glancing up ahead he could see the rundown Labour Club, no doubt Dempster felt more at home there than he did at home. His sort usually did, probably had his own stool at the bar. The concrete fronted building looked the same age as the council estate it edged, probably built in the 60's, when such estates were shooting up everywhere on the outskirts of towns and cities. Idiotic social engineering thinking of the time thought it was a good idea to house all the problem families on these estates among decent families who needed housing help. It was a disaster for those decent folk and for everyone else as towns and cities grew outward and eventually enveloped these estates.

Vinnie knew from his early years as a foot patrol cop, just how problematic and deep rooted some of these problem families were, all shoved into the same streets. He guessed it was still the same; the only difference being that it would now be son, or grandson, of the people he used to deal with causing most of the problems. Do-gooders who claim criminals aren't subjects of their environments are all talking rubbish. Sure there were exceptions to any rule, but it was mostly rubbish.

'Let's leave the club for now,' Vinnie said. 'It'll be more difficult to pull off the scam in that environment.'

'I'm glad you said that, look Vinnie, I've been thinking, as chivalrous as you no doubt are, and as much as I am looking forward to abusing you as my intern, it might be better if I approach Dempster alone.'

Vinnie was about to argue when Christine carried on, 'If it all comes to nothing, and you need to revert to a cop, it's better for me that he's taken me on face value. Not that I'm bothered, but it may save complications later.'

Vinnie knew that she was probably right, but was concerned about her safety, probably more than he would normally be. He pulled up outside a rundown terraced property with a small overgrown front garden with an unusual centre display consisting of a faux leather three-seat sofa.

'Here we are, look I'll go with that, but I want you to have my number ready to text on your mobile, so that all you have to do is press send. That can be your signal that you need some help, and I'll be straight in after you, agreed?'

'Ok, James Bond, agreed.'

'Exactly what are you going to tell him?'

'Not sure until I open my gob,' she said, before flashing her perfect teeth at him as she opened the car door.

Chapter Eleven

Vinnie couldn't help admiring Christine's legs as she strode confidently down the weed covered garden path and knocked on the front door. A couple of minutes later it was opened by a spotty white man in his late twenties with long, dark, unkempt hair. Vinnie immediately recognised him as Dempster from the mugshot he'd seen in the nick. He also recognised him from the car rental company's CCTV still photo. He was wearing the same stain riddled AC/DC T shirt. Idiot.

Dempster opened the door wider and Christine disappeared inside. The door then closed. Vinnie glanced at the phone in his hand, and then weighed up the front door. It was half-glazed at the top, and the bottom half was made of wood with peeling red paint. It had black streaks within it which Vinnie was sure would be rot of some kind. He'd never known the difference between dry and wet rot. But rot was rot and a well-aimed fart would have that door off its hinges, he thought.

He relaxed a little and looked at his watch. She'd been in there two minutes. He'd already agreed with himself that if she wasn't out after ten, he'd ring her anyway to check up; he'd stand the bollocking she'd no doubt give him later. But he didn't have to wait that long; at nine minutes the door reopened and Christine came back out.

She got back in the passenger seat and said, 'Let's get out of here,' as she searched her handbag for something.

'Everything ok?

'Yes, I'm just looking for my perfume to mask the scent of that smelly cretin.'

Vinnie smiled as he drove off, but something caught his attention in the rear view mirror when they were about thirty metres away. It was Dempster leaving. He was walking away in the opposite direction so Vinnie pulled over and adjusted his door mirror angle so he could watch.

'What is it?' Christine said.

'I don't know what you said in there, but he's just left, and I don't believe in coincidences.'

Christine quickly filled Vinnie in as he watched Dempster walk down the long road in the opposite direction. Apparently, he'd lapped up the "go to guy" routine and said he was "indeed the man to know on the estate" but he couldn't help her as "he'd no idea how the fire had started, or who could have done it".

Then Christine had mentioned that for the right information there might be some cash in it.

'How did that go in?' Vinnie asked as he did a three point turn in the road. Dempster was a safe distance ahead of them now so Vinnie moved the car forward slowly, maintaining the gap.

'He turned a bit then; his eyes lit up at first, but then he scowled and asked me if I was a cop?'

'Obviously not an avid watcher of the regional news.'

'Said he was no grass, if I was a cop. I tried to reassure him, but I'm not certain I did. I could see this moral dilemma raging behind his eyes – dosh versus being a grass – he eventually said, he might be able to find out but he "wasn't sure that I wasn't a cop". So I left him, said I'd call back in a day or so.'

Vinnie knew that Dempster was the type to grass up his own mother if he thought there was a tenner in it for him, but guessed the difference here was that he knew he was involved, albeit in a minor role, so if he grassed up Quintel and Jason it could no doubt rebound on him.

'What do you think he's doing?'

Vinnie didn't answer straight away as he watched Dempster near the T junction at the end of the road. On the right hand side, the corner was cut off by a triangle of grass, and in the middle of it was a phone box. 'You must have touched a sore spot,' he said as he started to accelerate.

'How come?' Christine asked.

'He's heading for that phone box.'

'He could be ringing the police to see if I am a cop?'

'He could do that from his mobile. There's only one reason villains use phone boxes, and that's to make dirty calls.'

'What do we do now?' Christine asked.

'We have to stop him. How do you fancy confirming his fears?'

'Suppose so.'

Vinnie pulled up sharply by the kerb and got out as Dempster was opening the glass door to the phone box. He turned to face Vinnie. 'A word, Warren?'

'Who the fuck are you? Another reporter?'

Vinnie told him and saw Dempster look over his shoulder towards the car.

'Fucking knew it. Reporter, my arse.'

'A word, Warren, that's all, before you make any phone calls that may end your life.'

'What the...,' Dempster said, before he let the phone box door go, and started to walk towards Vinnie.

'Not here, jump in the back seat, and we'll go for a drive,' Vinnie said, adding, 'or else you are on your own when Jason comes after you.' He knew he was taking a risk using Jason's name, but by the look of fear in Dempster's eyes, it had done the trick.

'Five minutes,' Dempster said, 'but for fuck's sake get me off the estate quickly.'

As Vinnie approached the driver's side he noticed that Christine had moved across and was now at the wheel. Nice one. He clambered into the front passenger seat and turned to face Dempster who was hunched down in the rear.

'Where to? Christine asked.

Dempster directed her off the estate and onto a major A road named Ribbleton Avenue. It headed east out of the city.

'I knew you were no reporter, man,' Dempster said.

'You're a smart lad, Warren, but look, we thought we'd try a covert approach, didn't want your neighbours knowing you'd had the old bill at your door.'

'I appreciate that, man.'

Vinnie noted a change in Dempster's tone and attitude, but wasn't sure why. He knew Dempster had sorted out the transport for Quintel and Jason, but didn't know if he actually knew anymore about what was going on, he'd have to tread carefully. 'Look, I'm going to level with you. We know you sorted out the motors for Quintel and Jason.'

'Says who?' Dempster said.

'Says this print out,' Vinnie said as he showed Dempster the photo. 'You've not even changed your T shirt.' Vinnie could see the recognition register in Dempster's eyes, even if it wasn't really clear that it was him in the picture. That was the thing about seeing a photo of yourself; you always recognised yourself, even if it wasn't clear to others.

After a pause, Dempster said, 'Look, Jason is a mean bastard, and he gave me no choice with the motors. Anyway, it's not a crime to rent a car.'

'It is with a knocked-off driving licence, especially one which has come from a burglary,' Vinnie said.

Dempster then made the obvious comments about being given the licence by Jason, but Vinnie pointed out that the use of the licence was still a crime.

'Why haven't you nicked me then?'

'You'll have to face that later; it'll be either a minor fraud or Burglary, or both. Depends.'

'On what?'

'On how helpful I tell the CPS you've been.'

'Look, I'll stand a handling charge, because I honestly didn't do the break – burglary – but I'm not having a poncy fraud.'

Vinnie knew he had to be careful that he didn't turn the conversation into an interview, which would be highly improper, with Dempster being the suspect. 'Just tell us what you can about Quintel and Jason, and we'll do what we can for you. It's them we are interested in, not you.'

'First up, I don't know any Quintel geezer, only that mad bastard, Jason.'

'Go on,' Vinnie said.

'Look mate, I've done what you've asked so far, can't we call it quits?'

Vinnie had no idea what he meant, and caught a quizzical sideways glance from Christine too.

'You don't know who I am, do you?' Dempster said with a renewed confidence in his voice.

Vinnie decided not to try to bluff him. 'No, I don't know what you're saying.'

'Fuck me, you lot, talk about left and right hands and all that shit.'

Vinnie didn't say anything, so Dempster carried on.

'I'm the daft twat who introduced your undercover cop to Jason. The one that got barbequed.'

Chapter Twelve

Four hours later, and Vinnie had just taken the head off a pint of lager in a boozer near his home in Stretford, Manchester, as Christine was returning from the Ladies. It was a quiet, traditional backstreet boozer which was presently quiet. Give it a couple of hours and it would start to get busy. They had dropped Dempster off and Christine had jumped out to pick up her own motor and cover Frank Delany's teatime press update, before doing a short piece to camera for the evening news. This was the first time they had had any chance to talk.

'Bet you weren't expecting that little tester from Dempster, were you?' she said as she sat down next to Vinnie.

'Not in a million years.'

'What does it mean? Apart from the fact that my scoop is getting even more scoopier.'

Vinnie had been weighing this question up since he'd dropped her off. He knew that those who handled informants were always kept separate from any investigation teams, and for good reason. The firewall between the two worlds existed to provide security for those who acted as informants, and to provide scrutiny of their use without compromising the investigation team. As SIO on the ground, he knew that intelligence existed about Jason trying to hire a hitman, but not how it had been obtained. A snout was the obvious first thought, but it could just have easily come from a listening device, or even a phone tap, though now he knew where and from whom. Just knowing now gave him huge problems, and Dempster's handlers would not be overjoyed to learn that their source had outed himself, and had become criminally involved by the hiring of the motors. The whole thing was turning iffy. 'I'm not sure, is the short answer. But it's bound to have an effect at any subsequent court proceedings against Quintel and Jason. We'll have to show the judge everything in private, and he may allow the case to proceed, or he may not.'

'How come?'

'Well, first off, Dempster will have to be prosecuted for the offences he's committed, but under the circumstances CPS may agree to just caution him.'

'Seems fair to me, he did say that Jason gave him no option.'

'True, but I think his days as a snout will have come to an end, not least because he outed himself to us.'

'But we are not going to say anything, and he thinks I'm a cop.'

'Until he watches the news for the first time.'

'Don't worry, as of tomorrow, it's hair up with glasses on in front of camera; and hair down and no specs on with you.'

Vinnie took a second slurp from his glass as Christine continued. 'What did Harry say?'

'He says if we believe Dempster in that he was under extreme duress to arrange the motors for Jason, and it was the first time he'd done it, then he can't see a problem with the CPS. He also says the dedicated source unit won't actually confirm or deny if Dempster is on their books, but as we know he is, he won't be for much longer. It'll be their job to approach the judge before any trial and try to satisfy him or her that Dempster wasn't more involved.'

'Do you believe what Dempster told us?'

'I think so, but I'm not sure. I know it sounds implausible that he wouldn't even have Jason's mobile number, but it could be true about him leaving messages for Dempster at the Labour club, and any telephone number to ring was either a phone box, or he had to wait at his phone box, where we picked him up, for a call.'

'What leans you toward believing him?'

'Because I made him recite the phone box's number and checked later. He knew it off by heart. But the real test will be if he rings us after they contact him again.

Christine just nodded as she took a sip of her white wine, before asking, 'Well how did he know what number to ring when we stopped him?'

'I asked him that as we dropped him off and he said he didn't, he was just going to try the last one he'd been given, and before you ask I've had it checked, it's just another phone box.'

They both sat quietly for a couple of minutes as they finished their drinks, before Vinnie filled the void. 'Are you on this story tomorrow as well? You are making a great partner.'

'Why thanks, kind sir. But no, I'm having to do more work on my exposé job. I'll get someone else to cover Preston, it'll not do any harm to keep my face off camera for a while, and to be honest I don't do too much of the daily news stuff nowadays. More the feature stuff, but I'm always happy to fill in, as and when.'

Vinnie tried to hide his disappointment by just smiling and thanked Christine for her help earlier. It was time to head home to a microwave meal and a couple of bottles of French lager before an early night. He was tempted to dump the motor and ask Christine if she wanted to make a night of it, but now was obviously not the moment, and they both had busy days ahead.

*

Christine watched Vinnie leave the car park of the pub before she drove off in her own car. She had enjoyed today, and had enjoyed Vinnie's company. She'd seen the side glances he'd been giving her, which she'd enjoyed. The first job they'd worked on together had been all frenetic over a couple of days, and she'd hardly had time to catch her breath, let alone look at Vinnie that way. She had started to ask herself the question, and she didn't mind. A good sign.

She drove off in the opposite direction, towards Salford and her new flat. It was handy for the Media City down on the Quays, not that she'd had much time to enjoy it since moving in a couple of weeks ago. Her mind then drifted back to the exposé she was working on, she was getting excited about this and had been tempted to tell Vinnie a little about it. After all, he'd taken her into his confidence totally, and she felt a little bit guilty about that. But no matter, she'd no doubt put that right soon enough. She might have to; she might need his help.

Chapter Thirteen

Quintel never agreed with the idiom that revenge is a dish best served cold - he just knew that to serve it properly, carefully, and without issue usually meant that cold it had to be. If he'd had his way Jim Reedly would have eaten his hot. The hotter the better; as per his client's wishes. But he'd let caution overstate its need when he'd hired Charlie; he'd overcomplicated things by trying to create distance between himself and his target. It was a mistake that had cost him, one he wouldn't make again. After all, he had Jason with him who was more than capable. Ok, Reedly's afters would have to wait now he was aware of the threat, but Reggie Carstair would be different. Quintel couldn't imagine why Carstair would be aware of the attempt on Reedly, especially after only forty-eight hours, and even if he was, he wouldn't make any connection, imaginary, or otherwise.

Like Reedly, Carstair was a northerner, although he still spent most of his time in London milking the private circuit like all the other greedy bastards - but he still headed north for the weekends. It was then when he was most vulnerable. Thanks to Jason's skills they had followed Carstair over a few weekends up the M1 and M6 motorways to get a feel for his habits. In fact, they could have intervened several times ad hoc, but the client wanted things doing in his order. And he was the paymaster.

During those reconnaissance runs Jason has stressed the need to stay far behind Carstair's 4x4 and to do the fact finding in stages. They knew that Carstair would leave the M6 at junction 29 at Bamber Bridge, south of Preston, before heading to his home in rural West Lancashire, but Jason had still insisted on doing the surveillances up the motorway, saying that Carstair might make a regular stop on the way which might identify opportunities.

The weeks of reconnaissance had paid off. Carstair had a following escort vehicle with him until he left the motorway, and then he finished the short journey home on his own as the escort headed back south. It was typical of the man's arrogance. In London you couldn't get a cigarette paper between him and his bodyguards, but once back home, he didn't need them, or so he obviously thought. Jason was unsure whether the security Carstair had was his own or not, but it didn't matter to them.

The second part of the reconnaissance had been to get ahead of Carstair on his Friday trips home and only follow him when he left the motorway. It was a short journey of twenty minutes or so to his private estate. The luxury house was in its own grounds set well back from the public road, similar to Reedly's place in nearby Fulwood, north of Preston. Quintel also knew that the property wasn't protected by local plod, God bless the cuts.

It had occurred to Quintel that they could take over the address on a Friday morning, and just wait until Carstair walked through the door – how much fun would that be? But he knew it carried too many risks, he just liked the idea.

They'd spent yesterday rechecking the route from the motorway to Carstair's home address, no problems. And today they had purposefully kept away from the area, it had been a long day, but the fun bit should start soon. Quintel glanced at his watch. It was nearly 8 pm; he hoped that all the prior reconnaissance would be worth it, especially after what had happened with Reedly. The exact timings were the only variable in Carstair's routine, the time he actually left the capital could vary by several hours. Today, he'd left later than expected according to Quintel's paid watcher in London, but no matter, it was still light and would be for an hour. They had found their spot and had been parked up for about twenty-five minutes when Jason spoke.

'Long range view of a possible contact on the 4x4,' he said as he sat up in the passenger seat and leaned into the small binoculars he was using.

'I was bothered he'd stop for a piss, and with the bastard setting off late we would lose the light and have to abort for another week,' Quintel thought out loud.

'Me too, Boss. Wait one…Yes it's a definite contact on the vehicle, with only a driver on-board.'

'The bastard?'

'Can't see with the low sun bouncing off the windscreen - can you move to the junction, Boss?'

They were parked in a narrow lane and normally Jason would do all the surveillance driving, but not today. Quintel had already started the engine after Jason said he'd clocked the vehicle and slowly drove their hire car towards the T-junction with the A59 Longton bypass. It was a dual-carriageway stretch of road which led from Preston into West Lancashire and eventually to Liverpool. Quintel knew that this stretch only lasted a couple of miles before it returned to a single-carriageway, so he'd have to be sharp. Though one advantage of the lateness of time was that the road was now relatively quiet.

'Go Boss, go. Confirming that the target is driving the vehicle,' Jason said as he put the small binos into a nylon bag at his feet.

Quintel joined the main road without stopping, and quickly put his foot down in the two-litre saloon; he could see the rear of the 4x4 ahead of them.

'Once he starts braking for the roundabout keep your foot down and brake as late as you can before the junction, but without causing a scene, Boss. We'll make ground on him that way without him realising.'

Quintel didn't reply, he knew this, he also knew what came next, but he'd forgive Jason in the rush of the moment.

'Once he's cleared the roundabout, we only have half a mile of dual-carriageway left.'

Quintel didn't reply.

The 4x4 was held up at the roundabout as a tractor bumbled around it. It allowed them to catch up nicely. The 4x4 cleared the junction after the tractor left at a different exit and they followed the 4x4 straight on. They were right behind him now on the inside lane, not too close, but not too far away either. Their speed levelled off at fifty.

Before they had even joined the dual-carriageway Jason had climbed between the front seats and was now in position by the rear nearside window.

'Ready? Quintel asked.

'Ready,' Jason answered, as Quintel looked at him via the driver's mirror.

He could see Jason putting the stock of the three-quarter length shotgun into his right shoulder. Quintel turned his attention back to the road as he pulled out to overtake and slowly started to pass the 4x4.

'Not too fast,' Jason said.

Quintel checked the speedometer – fifty-five – perfect, and edged alongside the 4x4. He heard the window motor start to whirl behind him, letting road noise flood in, and felt his pulse quicken. He was desperate to look sideways, but Jason had stressed he should not. According to him if you even glance at someone when you pass them they will notice and instinctively look at you. A second's warning could make all the difference. He resisted the urge, ceding to Jason's skills from his past life. But before they were level, Quintel was deafened by the boom from Jason's weapon going off. He couldn't believe how loud it was inside the car.

'Go Boss, as hard as you can.'

As Quintel floored the accelerator he allowed himself a glance to his left. He could see that the driver's window of the 4x4 was gone, as was most of Carstair's head Well, he assumed it was Carstair's head as he hadn't actually seen it beforehand; he'd have to take Jason's word for it. The grisly sight excited him.

The shoulders of the body were leaning to their left and the car was starting to veer that way too. He'd asked Jason about this earlier; how he could be so sure that the 4x4 would veer left and not to the right, into their path? Jason had told him to be prepared to step on it to get out the way, as a precaution, but emphasised that the force of the shot should drag the body and steering wheel away from them. It made sense. He seemed to know his stuff.

As Quintel powered towards the next roundabout he checked his mirrors for following traffic –there was none. He also saw that the 4x4 had hit the nearside embankment and flipped, he realised how much he'd underestimated Jason in the past. He was much more than just a bouncer; he felt another twinge of guilt about that. And now that he'd proved himself, he'd definitely give him a pay rise, and endeavour to use his entire skill base in the future. At least this job had gone sweet; the client would be pleased.

Chapter Fourteen

Christine Jones had spent the first half of Friday catching up and clearing her emails. She wasn't due to meet her contact until late afternoon at the earliest. She'd been working on this particular story for some time and her editor had kept reminding her of the need to get the balance right. The armed struggle by the Provisional IRA may have ended with the start of the peace process, but there was still plenty of hardliners out there that would never give in until Northern Ireland was back under southern Irish rule. And she knew that that would never happen whilst the majority of the population of Northern Ireland wanted to remain as part of the United Kingdom. The fact that the majority were Protestant by religion only antagonised the other side of the secular divide.

What she had found interesting through her research was the alleged way in which the police service had changed, and not just in name but in structure. The Royal Ulster Constabulary, as it was before the peace agreement, had been staffed by a largely Protestant workforce, and now it was split into two as the Police Service of Northern Ireland (PSNI), and the Northern Irish United Crime Squad (NIUCS). Both had far more Catholics among their numbers than the RUC ever had. Surely, a good thing.

She'd made the mistake of saying as much during an earlier visit to the Province where she'd sought comment from officers from both sides of the divide. One particular officer had vehemently informed her that he now felt unfairly treated - that it was politically correct to encourage and support Catholic officers to progress over Protestant ones. Or so it seemed.

As far as she could tell, each police force had equal standing. The PSNI covered everywhere at a local and regional level, whereas the NIUCS – or Nyucks as it was pronounced - operated only on a regional level, tackling serious and organised crime. The splitting up of the old Royal Ulster Constabulary had clearly been done for political reasons. She'd also come across the same biased accusations among local politicians. What was hard to establish was whether there was indeed, any fact to this, or was the bias being fuelled by false perceptions of those with unmovable beliefs on either side of the equation. She would dearly love to find evidence of this one way or another, as it would greatly enhance her documentary. Whether she ever would, she wasn't sure.

Christine hated watching documentaries which asked a great question in its title and premise; only to find out an hour later that the question remained unanswered. She needed to dig deeper, and her interview with today's contact just might provide a lead into this, or so she hoped. It had taken a lot of time, many phone conversations and many promises from the programme's producers to get to this stage; the first physical meeting. She was quite nervous, but also excited by the prospect. It wasn't every day a retired assistant chief constable broke ranks and spoke to the press; or an unretired one for that matter.

*

Seven-thirty, the text had said, and her contact was already ten minutes late. Christine was starting to get fidgety as she forced herself to only sip from the large glass of white wine in front of her. Nerves always quickened her thirst but she was determined to stay clear-headed; if today went well, then this could be the first of many meetings, and her current angle aside, who knew where it could lead. She checked her watch once more before calming herself. It was only ten minutes past, it just seemed so much more because she'd been ridiculously early.

She'd arrived at the bar at seven. It was a non-descript pub situated down one of the many side streets off Deansgate in central Manchester. Most of these backstreet boozers had long gone, or been replaced with trendy wine bars, but this was one of the few that remained. She was sat in the front snug which was largely empty, except for a homeless looking sort in a large brown overcoat who was engrossed in the Racing Post and had made his half pint glass of what looked like coke last longer than her wine. She was sat in the far corner with several tables between them. Her back was to a rough brick wall and she had a good view of the outside through the large bay window, and sight of anyone entering the pub, as they who would have to pass the open doorway that connected the snug to the rest of the pub.

She saw a middle-aged man in a lightweight raincoat pass the window on a beeline for the front door. It was his ramrod straight back and mien that caught her attention. Seconds later he passed the snug doorway as he entered the bar proper. She waited, one minute, two, but he didn't show himself. It was now seven-forty-five. She sighed. The man with the Racing Post got up to leave. He picked his coke up, and she figured he must be going into the main bar, but he hesitated in the doorway. Christine watched as the man looked both ways before turning around and then walked back into the snug. But he didn't stop at the table where he'd been moments earlier, but headed straight to Christine's and sat to one side of her.

'Would you allow me to introduce myself, Christine; I'm Paul Bury, ex-RUC and NIUCS ACC.'

Christine just stared at him as he took the smelly overcoat off and slung it over a chair by the next table. He must have seen by her expression what she was thinking, as he then answered her unasked question.

'Bought it off a tramp for thirty pounds, call it an act of charity, but I had to be sure you had come alone, and didn't receive any *unexpected* visitors, I hope you don't mind?'

Having got over her astonishment, Christine answered, 'No, not at all, I was just a little surprised.'

'You have to remember that during the troubles one learnt to be extra careful about everywhere one went. Can you imagine never standing with your back to a room full of strangers, always with your back to a bar when in a pub; never the other way around? Looking under your car every time you approached it? I learnt to be a cautious man and although times are different now, some habits are hard to break, that's for sure.'

Christine accepted his explanation for what had seemed at first as a little eccentric, and then thought about what he'd said. No, she couldn't imagine it.

'I've done my homework on you, as you have no doubt done the same, and that's why I've agreed to meet you. As you know the press and the police have had a turbulent relationship at times, so they have, but you seemed to be one of those who report fairly.'

'It works both ways,' Christine started, feeling the need to stand her corner, but without wanting to sound over-defensive; it reminded her of some of the chats she'd had with Vinnie. She continued, 'In fact I currently have an excellent working relationship with a local detective inspector.'

'I know you have, and if he'd have been a tosser, I wouldn't be here,' Bury said.

Christine was a little taken aback by this, and wondered how far into her life Bury's "background" had encroached.

'Look, I can see the surprise in your eyes, but please take no offence, you have to realise that during the troubles I worked in SB – Special Branch – so I'm a bit of a covert policing specialist, you might say.'

She smiled as she said, 'Yes of course. Does all the sneaky-beaky stuff still go on?'

'Yes, but it's massively scaled down. After the peace agreement, the new chiefs wanted to leave the past behind and slashed some of the covert departments in both new forces. Most unit heads in the newly partitioned NIUCS – Northern Irish United Crime Squad - were past their retirement dates and encouraged to leave and enjoy the fruits of their efforts.'

'Did the same happen in the PSNI – Police Service of Northern Ireland?'

'Not sure, but it did in NIUCS, that's for certain.'

'And you think there was another agenda?'

'Not at first; it made sense to downsize these units and as the officer in overall command of Specialist Operations at NIUCS I understood this. I even questioned my own tenure, but was told that I was needed to oversee the transition.'

'Please go on.'

'I soon started to feel side-lined. Decisions were being made on unit heads replacements, and I wasn't being involved in the selection processes.'

'That does sound strange. May I ask what religious persuasion you are?'

'I've never been too persuaded by any religion, but technically I guess I'm a Protestant. And that is partly the issue. I noticed that all the unit head replacements were Catholic. Don't get me wrong, I'm not one of these stanch secular types, I'm married to a Catholic lass, and at first welcomed the influx of Catholics at these new senior levels in this new force.'

'But?'

'But, one or two of them seemed to have Republican leaning tendencies – forget the religion, that's irrelevant to me.'

'So, you think there is positive discrimination in favour of Catholics, some of whom are still Republican in their political affiliation.'

'Without doubt. But it might go further than that,' Bury said, with obvious caution in his voice.

Christine didn't pry straight away. She let the pause hang, hoping it would weigh on Bury. She smiled as sweetly as she could, but eventually broke the impasse herself. 'As previously promised, anything you say to me is in confidence and you will have total control of the final edit. That said, I don't want you to tell me something you are not comfortable with. Tell you what, why don't I get a round in?'

'You have to understand,' Bury said, with a measured tone she hadn't heard him use hitherto; 'the units under my command were covert ones, undercover officers, touts, and suchlike. The access the heads of these specialist units had was total. And things started to go wrong.'

'What sort of things?' Christine said, trying to hide her excitement. This could be a whole new direction for the programme.

'Without going into specifics at this stage, but for example, if an undercover investigation into a Republican sympathizer was suddenly compromised, what would you expect the outcome to be?'

Christine hadn't expected a question, so she considered it carefully before she answered. She knew the IRA had given up the armed struggle but she also knew others in the Republican camp had not. 'I'm guessing, even during this new détente, that a compromised undercover officer would be in grave, if not mortal danger.'

'Exactly. Not only were jobs going wrong at an unprecedented level, and notwithstanding that the causes of such failings were never clear, no officer, or tout, fell foul. Sure, we put measures in place afterwards, but in some of the instances the bad guys had had plenty of time for a little summary retribution before we pulled the assets out.'

Christine wasn't too sure where this now going, and said so.

'It was as if some agreement had been reached. Someone at a senior level under my command was leaking information to scupper jobs, but on the understanding that no one got hurt. There, I've said it, so I have.'

Christine watched as Bury sat back in his chair, and exhaled loudly. She gave him a moment before she replied. 'Did you voice your concerns?'

'That I did. And I was told that I was being paranoid and destructive. They virtually accused me of being a closet Unionist terrorist, said there was no place for me in the modern northern Irish police service, and if I didn't go I'd be shipped off to London on some bollocks, never to return. So I went. I'd done my time so I retired.'

'I've one question left,' Christine said, edging into it slowly.

'I know what you're going to say and no, I have no evidence of this, but by God I will. You still on board?'

This was turning into something else completely now, she couldn't believe it. 'Oh yes, Paul, am I. But we will need proof, proper proof, and we'll no doubt have to tread carefully.'

'That's an understatement, so it is,' Bury said, as he stood up and pulled the stinky overcoat on, before turning back to face her.

'I'll be in touch, but it may take a while. Give me a couple a minutes before you leave, and please say nothing of the latter part of our conversation to anyone, not your DI friend and not even your editor, until I have the proof. Just keep going as per your original story, then it'll look no different.'

'Sure, Paul.'

'Promise?'

'Promise,' Christine said.

'Good, because my life might just depend on it,' Bury said, before he turned and strode out the pub.

Christine thought Bury looked a little taller as she watched him leave.

She finished her wine in one swig. This could be huge, but she would tread carefully. Paul Bury seemed an intelligent and reasonable guy, he spoke lucidly with only a soft trace of accent, which was easy to listen to. And he was clearly no fool to have reached such a senior rank. But he could still be wrong. Years of suspicion and paranoia operating in such unprecedented circumstances such as Bury had been in would have affected the most rationale of minds. She couldn't begin to imagine the horrors he'd seen or the personal pressures he'd experienced; all of which must have had some effect. But potentially, this could be massive.

She'd keep her own counsel as promised. She then got up and headed into the main bar, which was getting busier. She needed more wine.

Chapter Fifteen

Vinnie spent most of Friday helping Harry with the mundane admin involved in getting the HOLMES system fully functional, and all the initial actions issued and everyone out. Vinnie oversaw the setting up of the house-to-house enquiry team headed by a Lancashire DS called Graham something. He'd seemed a bit surprised when Vinnie had told him to leave the depository next to the crime scene off his list of addresses to be visited. He told him it was sensitive and he'd cover that omission in his policy log. He didn't like raising flags within the enquiry team, but he wanted to keep his visit there under wraps for the moment.

After lunch, Harry asked him to come with him as he attended a pre-arranged meeting with the Lancashire chief at the force headquarters at Hutton on the outskirts of Preston. Vinnie drove the six or seven miles to the HQ and asked Harry what to expect.

'I've set up a fifteen minute meet with the chief, ostensibly for a quick update. We've got him from 2.15 pm to 2.30pm before he heads off to London for a meeting or conference or whatever,' Harry answered.

'And the real reason?'

'Reedly was bullshitting me when I spoke to him yesterday, and I want to know if the Lancashire chief is complicit, and if he's not, what's going on? You're my witness.'

'Witness to what?'

'Witness to what's said. I know we are Manchester officers, albeit on a regional unit, but the chief of Lancs has overall primacy on the whole investigation, as it's happened in his area, and also because he's still a chief constable. Make no mistake Vinnie, all the chiefs piss in a very private barrel.'

Ten minutes later they had passed the security gate at the entrance and parked in the visitors' bays at the front of the main headquarters building. Vinnie had been here many times before, but never to the top corridor. They were admitted and met by the chief inspector who acted as the chief's staff officer. He recognised the insipid groveler from previous visits, usually to collect surveillance authorities and other high-level documents that had needed a signature from the top floor.

Previously the staff officer had always taken pleasure in making Vinnie wait in reception, and then gone over the top at how lucky he was that the chief or his deputy had deigned to grant whatever authority they were after. And by the smug look on his face, he'd not changed any.

'This way gentlemen, but you'll have to be brief, the chief has a very busy schedule, and it's my job—' the staff officer started, and Vinnie couldn't help but interrupt him.

He wanted to end his sentence for him with "—to wipe his arse," but managed to restrict himself to, 'Still not got an operational role yet?'

The staff officer didn't answer, but gave Vinnie a hard look, and so did Harry a moment later as they were shown into an ante room.

Ten minutes passed before Groveler showed them into the main office. Vinnie had wondered if they'd been left there on purpose, and was starting to regret his dig at the staff officer. The chief's main office was a huge grand affair, with an enormous mahogany desk at one end and a table and six chairs in front of it. At the opposite end were four easy chairs situated around a coffee table. The chief of Lancs was an imposing man, over six feet tall and with a stocky but athletic build, short grey hair, and Vinnie reckoned he was in his late fifties. His name badge over his left breast shirt pocket bore the name CC Brian Darlington. He met them in the centre of the suite and directed them to the easy chairs.

Salutations and introductions over the chief ushered his staff officer away, which gave Vinnie an inward smile.

'I'm sorry I haven't got longer with you, I've just come off the phone from the home sec whom I'm meeting later, and I have a train to catch with a car waiting outside. The home sec will be asking me how things are progressing, so an abridged update would be handy,' the chief said.

'Early days, sir, as you know, but DI Palmer here has a lead on the getaway vehicle, which we are following up covertly at the mo. I haven't shared that with the rest of the enquiry team yet,' Harry said.

As agreed before they came in, Harry being the superintendent and SIO would do the talking. Vinnie was there just to listen unless asked a direct question.

'That'll do for now, and do keep me briefed on any significant developments, Harry, but why the cloak and dagger?'

'Not too sure what we are dealing with, just yet, sir.'

'Explain.'

Harry paused before he continued, and given his concerns Vinnie wondered how far he would go.

'Be quick,' the chief added.

'I think DCC Reedly is not telling us the whole background as to why he was targeted in the first case.'

Vinnie saw the chief's eyes narrow as his friendly face disappeared.

'You accusing your force's deputy of lying, superintendent?'

'There may well be good operational reasons why certain background elements are sensitive, sir, that's all. I'm not calling him a liar so please don't take offence. And I do hope this conversation is in confidence.'

'Rationale?'

'The press related strategy to protect Charlie's undercover status was not written by us, which would be usual, but came through your office, and displayed an element of pre-planning.'

The chief appeared to consider what Harry had said for a moment before barking for his staff officer. Vinnie enjoyed watching the Groveler rush into the office, gushing with obsequious platitudes.

'Who wrote the initial press strategy for Superintendent Delany?' the chief asked.

'It came from Mr Reedly's office in Manchester, sir.'

'And do we normally allow a neighbouring force to tell us how to do our job?'

'No sir, but with it coming from Mr Reedly, I thought—'

'No, you didn't think; you should have run it past me first, now get out.'

Vinnie absolutely loved this, and gave the Groveler his best sarcastic grin as he shuffled red-faced out of the office.

Then the chief asked Harry to repeat what he had been told to say, which he did, and included the fact that the Home Office appointed pathologist had also been given instructions, by someone, prior to his examination of Charlie's body. And although disinformation is normal in protecting sensitive elements such as the undercover status of Charlie, and the fact that he was investigating an on-going threat to Reedly, it was as if they were being led to ensure it was done properly.

'This may be no more than Reedly's office trying to ensure on-going protection for their DCC,' the chief said.

'True, sir, but when I spoke to him yesterday, I was, er I was…'

'Spit it out, I've got a train to catch.'

'Can I speak candidly, sir?'

'I wish you would; and for the record, we don't all dance around the maypole together, naked and holding hands.'

Vinnie couldn't suppress a laugh, until it was half out, but then quickly regained his composure.

'He gave me the mushroom treatment.'

Vinnie had no idea what that meant, but judging by the chief's expression, he did.

'Enough said, Harry,' the chief started, his demeanour softer. 'I'll have a proper word with Jim Reedly tomorrow when I'm back from London. But this conversation stays between us, understand?'

Vinnie and Harry both said "yes" in unison, and with that the chief showed them the door and barked at the Groveler to show them out. Vinnie didn't say anything until they were driving away, towards the city. 'What's the mushroom treatment mean?' he asked.

'Being treated like a mushroom is an old cop expression; it means to be kept in the dark and fed shit.'

This time Vinnie lost it properly and nearly crashed the car laughing. When the mirth subsided, he asked why Harry had decided to be so bold, a high risk strategy he'd have thought.

'I was a bit unsure whether we could trust the chief, as we don't know him, and because of his rank, but after we'd visited Charlie's bereft parents the other night, he told me to not hesitate if I needed anything. To which I first assumed he meant resources, but then he added that if anyone gave me the mushroom treatment, I was to tell him.'

'Ah,' Vinnie said, 'I understand why you used that phrase now.'

'Yes, I'm not normally that emboldened when taking to a senior officer, but when he'd first mentioned it I had again assumed he was talking about anyone who was reluctant to assist us. It might be a *regional* homicide unit that we are now on, but we are still Greater Manchester officers operating in Lancashire Constabulary's air space.'

'And now?'

'He's obviously a very shrewd man; it makes me wonder whether he suspected Reedly from the off.'

'Well, we are in his hands now, Harry. I do hope we've made the right decision?

'So do I Vinnie. If we both end up on the traffic department after this, we'll know why.'

Chapter Sixteen

It was dark by the time Quintel and Jason checked into a new hotel. They picked one in Leyland, south of Preston, not too far from the motorway network. Handy for getting about and they could pick up the local news in the aftermath of their work a short while earlier. That said, it would also be all over the national presses and media anyway, due to Carstair's status as a retired home secretary, but they still had local things to attend to. Jason was taking a shower so Quintel took the opportunity to update the client. He dialled the number from memory and it only rang a few times before the barking voice of the client answered.

'Yes?'

'I'm fine thanks, how are you?' Quintel said, instantly regretting his lack of professionalism.

'Don't be taking the piss. I'm not paying you to take the piss.'

'Sorry.'

'There are plenty of boys who would love a crack at this, if I didn't need unknowns.'

'Sorry, again, long day. I've got an update for you—' Quintel started to say.

'Before you say any more, it's now time we took more security measures. If you are going to tell me what I hope you are, it's going to get very serious from now on.'

'Ok, do you want me to sort out a draft folder?'

Quintel knew the that client would want added security at some stage, and as unfortunate a disruption killing Charlie had been, he was just a nobody compared to Carstair. When this had been discussed previously, Quintel had suggested setting up an email account to which only they would have the password. Thereafter messages could be left in the draft email folder, where they could never be intercepted, as they were never actually sent. He'd used this method before and as long as you used publicly owned computers such as in cyber cafes, it was fool proof and left no footprints on privately owned equipment. When he'd suggested this, the client hadn't appeared too interested. He hadn't known why.

'No, I've a better idea,' the client said.

'It's no problem, all you'll need is the password, which I'll text you in parts.'

'I'm not good with computers,' the client said, adding, 'and I struggle with these modern phones if I'm honest, technology moves too bastard fast. Look, here's what we'll do.'

The client then went on to explain to Quintel how he had already identified two public phone boxes, which he referred to as A and B. He'd text the numbers in four texts. The first and third text would be the entire number for A, and the second and fourth put together would make up B. He wanted Quintel to do the same, but was conscious that as they would be on the move, they would need to add more numbers as they went along, but as soon as they had their A and B identified, they were to send the four texts with a five minute delay between each. Then they could speak properly, and Quintel could update him.

Quintel sighed as he ended the call. Although he appreciated the client's professionalism when it came to security, it all seemed like a lot of hard work for nothing. If only he'd have let him explain the draft folder lark again, it would have been a lot easier. But he was the paying client.

'Jason, hurry up in there,' Quintel shouted at the bathroom door, 'I've got a little task for you.'

*

Vinnie had spent the rest of the afternoon sorting the incident room out with Harry, who after a canteen tea had said they both should get an early night and start again on Saturday afresh. They were going to have to work all weekend as it was, so should take advantage where they could. Harry was hoping that the Lancs chief, CC Darlington, would have some feedback for them before the weekend was through.

It had just gone dark when Vinnie arrived back at his house in Manchester, and he'd just let himself in when his mobile rang. It was Harry. He wondered if the chief had rung Reedly rather than wait to see him face to face. 'Yes, Harry,' he started.

'Where are you?'

'Just arrived home, why?'

'I need you back here, ASAP.'

'What's happened?'

'Do you remember a previous home secretary called Reggie Carstair?'

'Yeah, retired from politics altogether now, hasn't he?'

'That's him. Well, he's just retired from life now as well. Or should I say, someone has retired him.'

'Sorry?' Vinnie said, before Harry went on to explain. He'd only had a sketchy brief himself as it had only happened within the last thirty minutes or so, and spookily not far from where they had been earlier today when they'd been to see the Lancs chief. It had happened on a bypass a mile or so further on from the police headquarters. Vinnie quickly asked what it had to do with them. Surely another syndicate from the Regional Homicide Unit would be given this job?

'That's what I would have thought. But the instructions came from GMP's force control room. Initially, I thought that because we had just set up our own incident room for the murder of Charlie and the conspiracy to murder Reedly, they'd want us to babysit the start until a second team set up.'

Vinnie said the 'But?' that he could feel coming.

'But, I've been instructed to SIO both jobs – crazy – and when I questioned it, guess what I was told?'

'What?'

'The CC of Lancs, Brian Darlington, who is hot-tailing it back from London as we speak, had ordered I be given the job.'

'Surely you can refuse, I mean not only should a separate team catch this, it's going to be massive from a profile point of view, especially when the press get hold of it.'

'I was left in no doubt. Meet me at the scene, we can talk there,' Harry said, before giving Vinnie the exact location of the murder.

Chapter Seventeen

Quintel sent the texts, the third of which was the actual number for A. The first had been the STD code prefixed simply by "A is". He'd already received notice that the client was at his A, so he gave it a minute and rang the number. He listened to the elongated dial tone which surprised him. He hadn't noticed it wasn't a UK number; fortunately, he had plenty of one-pound coins with him. After two rings the call was answered.

'Right we are, we can fecking talk now without worrying about any nosy bastards listening in,' the client said.

Quintel felt a tinge of worry on hearing the words. He was all for security, and he knew that most serious villains always took care what they said on an open telephone line, or more importantly, on one which could be linked to them. But he also knew it was done out of a sort of cultural habit, rather than any real expectation that someone was actually listening in. There was a tension in the client's voice that suggested a little more than custom and good operational security. It made him wonder if the client had any grounds to suspect he was being targeted by the filth. 'Just so you know, I'm one hundred percent happy that the filth here are pissing blind. I take it you've no problems where you are?' he asked, not sure what reaction he would get.

'If I wasn't a hundred percent, I wouldn't be wasting money on you Quintel, so rest assured. And whatever filth knew me was a long time ago,' the client said.

'The fact that the client had used Quintel's name wasn't good tradecraft, but he guessed it was the client's way of saying that all was sweet. He briefly considered replying in kind, but didn't want to antagonise the man further than he needed. 'Ok, just checking, we've both got a lot to lose.'

'Not as much fecking time as I've already lost thanks to those Brit bastards, you should remember that?'

'Ok, ok, look, I've only got a few quid so I'll be quick. Number two is dead,' said Quintel, avoiding using Carstair's name. Now that the shit would be hitting the fan proper he would have to avoid using his name, even if he and the client had been face to face. The client seemed to take the hint as he replied.

'Aye, number two is a good name for the little shit. Any problems?'

'None, I should have used my man from the start. Clean as you like, apart from the claret everywhere, of course.'

'Not too clean, I hope I'd like to imagine the man suffering.'

'No opportunity with a drive-past. But my man said he saw him look at him a moment before he lost his head.'

'That'll have to do, but at least it's done. Though I'd love to be with you for the next phase – number three. Torture the shite a bit first. Let him know about all the years I've had to endure because of him and his kind.'

Quintel wasn't totally surprised by this, but knew the client knew better. He reminded him for the need to keep well out of it, and by the sound of the dialling tone, he'd already taken care of this. He was itching to ask him where he was, but didn't.

'Aye, aye, I know you're right, just thinking out loud. Not something I've been able to do much of over the years because of those bastards.'

He was off on another rant, time to go. 'Sorry, I've run out of credit, have to go, I'll update you when I have more,' Quintel said, realising that by the time he'd finished his sentence, the client had gone. 'And goodbye to you too, you ill-mannered bog-trotter,' he said as he replaced the phone in its cradle. Time to eat and down a few beers.

*

Vinnie thought he'd seen most things in the fifteen years he been in the police, but professional assassinations were thankfully quite rare. Yes, he'd seen killings carried out for wages, be it by gun or knife, but nothing quite as shocking as this. The bypass where it had occurred was about seven miles outside Preston on a rural stretch about a mile past Lancashire Constabulary headquarters. It was on a section of dual-carriageway between two roundabouts; one at the village of Walmer Bridge and the second at the village of Much Hoole. Both places having delightful old-English names conjuring up leafy images of yesteryear. Both names would not look out of place on a map of the Cotswolds. But here he was seven miles from a modern northern city which still displayed its industrial heritage, between two rural spots that would be forever tarnished.

The whole stretch between the roundabouts, of about a mile, had been closed off. Heavy duty lighting was in place where the crashed 4x4 lay on its side by the road's verge which was raised. CSIs were here in abundance, several of whom were busy erecting a sort of white canvas patio-style gazebo over it. He pulled his Volvo over onto the opposite carriageway where all the emergency vehicles were parked to preserve the actual route used by the killers. He'd just finished putting his own white suit and over-shoes on when Harry approached.

'It's a mess. Body's still in situ. They had to fax his fingerprints to the Home Office to confirm it was Carstair.'

Vinnie just nodded as he followed Harry to the crashed car. He could only see the underside of the vehicle and had to use a pair of step ladders to get enough elevation to look inside.

The driver's window was gone and the body was still suspended in the driver's seat by the seat belt. It was leaning with gravity over towards the passenger side, but Vinnie could see by the blood splattering that Carstair had clearly been shot from his driver's side by a passing vehicle. But the head was gone, clean off at the shoulders save for a couple of inches of spine that stuck up above the collar line, giving the cadaver a sort of headless mannequin appearance. Without the head it just didn't look human. Though Vinnie had conditioned himself many years ago to always strive to not see humanity in dead bodies. To try and view them as carcasses as it made them easier to deal with, but on this occasion it was different. As surreal as the corpse appeared, the spine seemed to accentuate the horror that this had indeed been a person not too long ago. He could see grey matter mixed with blood the consistency of jam porridge splattered everywhere to the body's left, further confirming his initial thoughts. He climbed back down the ladder to face Harry. 'I see what you mean.'

'He'd have felt no pain, at least,' Harry said.

'True,' Vinnie said as he composed himself. He was sure that he'd see that visage again when he didn't want to. 'Drive-by shooting, probably a shotgun looking at the spread of tissue. Point blank effectively.'

'Agreed. I've already ordered a checkpoint here as soon as the scene is re-opened, and a press release for commuters to come forward. Someone must have seen which vehicle the murderers' used, even if they don't know it.'

Vinnie nodded, noting Harry's use of the plural. There had to have been at least two involved. 'What now?' he asked, as he headed back to his motor to change his white suit. Having been so close to the body, he didn't want to risk cross-contamination with anything he might stumble across which could turn out to be offender-related.

'Just bag and seal that,' Harry said, as he started to change at the back of his vehicle from the sanctuary of the opposite carriageway.

'I know that, Harry.'

'No, I mean don't bother with a fresh suit. Darlington has arrived back from London, and is in his office waiting for us.'

Chapter Eighteen

Fifteen minutes later Harry and Vinnie were sat back on the Lancs chief's easy chairs. His staff officer, whose name Vinnie remembered was Russell Sharpe, had been sent home, albeit unwillingly.

'He's usually pulling at the leash to get off, obviously today's events are a bit more salacious,' were Darlington's opening comments.

Neither Vinnie nor Harry said anything.

Darlington joined them at the easy chairs as all three sat at right angles to the other. 'Initial thoughts?' he asked.

Harry filled him in, and Darlington nodded, before carrying on.

'I want you to oversee this Harry, and before you say anything, hear me out.'

Vinnie could see Harry's mouth open and then close more slowly, as Darlington continued.

'I'm going to appoint a Lancashire detective superintendent to run the investigation into Carstair's murder, but I want you, Harry, to take a strategic overview, even though you are the same rank, the Lancs super will report to you, and he'll be told why on a "need-to-know contract" with threat of castration. You'll allow him to run it as he would otherwise, as God knows he'll be under enough scrutiny, especially by the press, but you'll need to have a daily handle on how the investigation is progressing.'

'I'm guessing there is an operational reason, sir?' Harry asked.

'Yes, I've had two little chats with DCC Jim Reedly on the phone today.'

'How did that go?'

'Same treatment you received. He tried to mushroom me. I had to remind him that he is only a deputy chief constable, even if he is pissing in a bigger pond than me.'

Vinnie enjoyed listening to Darlington swear. Very rare to hear a chief speak like this, well for an inspector anyway, he felt like he was peering through a very private window which would be normally shuttered to the likes of him.

'Did he open up?' Harry asked.

'No, he didn't. But he forgets I've known him over a number of years. We did our Senior Command Course together when we were both superintendents. I remember getting pissed with him one evening when he was bragging about some secret work he'd done for the home secretary's office some years earlier.'

'I'm guessing that was for Carstair,' Vinnie said, speaking for the first time.

'Indeed, though he never elucidated as to exactly what. I got the impression he was trying to say that he's done several different types of things on and off over the years. I took no notice at the time, as it wasn't unusual for senior officers to do various reports on things for the home sec from a strategic point of view, I just wrote it off as a braggart trying to make more of it at the time.'

'Bigging himself up?' Harry asked.

'It happens at all ranks, as you two no doubt know. Just because a bull-shitter reaches the chief level ranks doesn't mean they stop being a bull-shitter. But when Carstair was killed, I thought it too much of a coincidence.'

'A man after my own heart, sir, if you don't mind me saying so?' Vinnie said, continuing, 'I don't believe in fairies or coincidences.'

Vinnie wasn't sure whether his remark would be deemed as levity but he need not have worried, as Darlington laughed out loud.

'Exactly,' he said, adding, 'you've got a good deputy here, Harry.'

'I hope so,' Harry said, and all three grinned.

Darlington then swore them all to secrecy before he continued; Vinnie could tell that as open as he was being with them, it still didn't come easy talking negatively about a fellow senior officer, albeit from a different force.

'My first chat with Reedly was on my way to London, and I'd decided to have a face to face with him on my return. That was before poor Mr Carstair was killed. My second chat was about an hour ago, he'd seen something on regional TV in Manchester, God knows how they picked it up so quickly. It was Christine Jones who reported it – should have been a cop, that one. Do you know her?'

Vinnie and Harry both nodded, expressionless.

'Anyway, let me tell you, Reedly sounds a worried man. Say's he might have one or two pointers to help us, jobs he's worked on in the past. He made no connection to Carstair other than to say he'd seen the news and to ask what had happened. It was my turn to stonewall him. I'm going to keep some space from Reedly now, and I have already recorded all my dealings with him. I intend to keep a dignified distance, just in case you turn anything up on him that's dirty, Vinnie,' Darlington said, looking at Vinnie and using his first name for the first time.

'Me, sir?

'Yes, Harry's told me he's had you under the radar so to speak, and I want you to carry on that way. You will report to Harry, who apart from having the investigation of Charlie's murder and the conspiracy to murder Reedly to SIO, will also have the overview role into the investigation of Carstair's killing as I've said, just in case they are, as we suspect, linked.'

'No problem sir, but what about resources?'

'None official, Vinnie, but use whatever you and Harry agree on. But your first task is tomorrow. I want you to drop in unannounced on Reedly, who is currently on gardening leave at an address in Manchester. So if that's all for now?'

Vinnie and Harry both nodded and all three stood up in unison.

Ten minutes later Vinnie pulled his Volvo over to drop Harry back at his motor, and turned to face him before he got out. 'What do you reckon to all that?'

'I think he suspects Reedly of something, so he's playing it safe, but I think we can trust Darlington.'

'Agreed.'

Vinnie bade Harry goodnight and said he'd make contact with him tomorrow, and Harry left. Vinnie was just about to drive off when he remembered he still had his phone set to silent-running from the meeting with Darlington. As he turned the ringer back on it immediately rang, and the screen said, "Christine Calling". He took the call.

'Vinnie, you're harder to track down than my cameraman.'

He apologised and explained before she went on to mention the killing of Carstair.

'You're not involved in the investigation of that as well, are you?'

'Sort of.'

'Sort of?'

'Yeah, look, I might need your help again. I'll be back in Manchester tomorrow, can I give you a bell to meet up, after I've seen someone?'

'Sure, how could I refuse?'

Vinnie smiled as he finished the call, and set off for home.

Chapter Nineteen

As it was Sunday, Christine allowed herself a later start and didn't arrive at Salford Quays until gone ten. The media city that existed there now was second to none. A huge modern expanse of various film and TV offices and studios, which had helped see in a rise in northern generated material. In TV drama alone there was emerging what was being called "Northern Noir" and many authors were writing thrillers to feed this growing market. TV documentaries were generally more cosmopolitan but her current exposé had elements of both. Life in Northern Ireland post the peace agreement and the official ending of the armed struggle would have both national, regional, and hopefully international interest, or so her producers hoped.

They had made her one promise though, one she hoped they would keep; if the investigation failed to deliver, they wouldn't throw what they had together to make a programme come-what-may, as was often the case. "Non-programmes" she termed such diatribe, and she'd seen too many good reporters and broadcasters lose standing by fronting crocks of shit. But after her little chat with Paul Bury, she was confident they would end up with far more that they had hoped to find when they set off.

Reluctantly, she'd provided emergency cover for the breaking news that was Carstair's death the evening before, but her boss had agreed to take her off the air when she claimed it might spook her new contact. The less noticeable she remained, the safer he would feel. Not that she'd had much of a problem hitherto being recognised off-camera, which always surprised her, but for now she was glad. There were plenty of colleagues with fragile egos who were bothered by such lack of recognition, but she was not one. She'd always said that her job was to report the news, not to be it.

The office was mainly empty and she didn't want to hang around long after speaking to her editor on the phone to agree her strategy going forward. Next she briefed the reporter who would be taking over from her in covering all the events in Preston, and then she had some groceries to collect before waiting to tie-up with Vinnie. She hoped it would be over lunch. If she'd not heard from him by twelve, she'd give him a bell, and a hint.

She was just about to walk out the office when she heard her text alert tone go off, She thought it was Vinnie, but when she looked she saw that it had come from a number which wasn't in her phone's memory. It was a 0161 prefix though – Manchester. She read the message to herself, "Same place as the other night. Noon, regards from the smelly coat man". Paul Bury. There goes her possible lunch date with Vinnie, but it sounded worth it.

*

Christine went home via her local supermarket as planned and changed into jeans and a T shirt, which was not what she'd planned. She'd had in mind a nice flowery summer dress and a thin cardigan to cover her shoulders. It was a lovely sunny day, but still early spring. That outfit would keep. She decided not to head off too early this time, so arrived at the pub at five to twelve. She half expected Bury to be there ahead of her, but he wasn't. The whole dynamic of the pub had changed from the other evening, full of Sunday lunchtime drinkers, and the front snug was half-full she noticed as she passed. She approached the main bar and was about to order when her phone text alert went off. "Beer garden. I've got you one in" the message read. She instinctively looked towards the rear of the pub and saw that a fire door which had been closed the other day was now propped open. She walked through it into what was not much more than a large back yard, with a smokers' corner off to one side with a few tables and chairs opposite. Paul Bury was sat at the end one, in the corner with his back to the adjoining six-foot brick walls, giving him a panoramic view.

Christine sat opposite him and thanked him for the drink, before taking a sip from the large glass of chilled Chardonnay. 'You are observant,' she said as she took a second sip.

'Force of habit,' he replied.

'Now you've retired don't you switch off a bit?'

'I've been to too many funerals of those who did.'

Now she was starting to wonder what exactly he had been up to during the troubles that he still felt the need for such vigilance. 'Well at least you've left the coat behind.'

'Gave it back to the same tramp and you suppose what he said?'

She shook her head.

'*I can only give you twenty pounds back.* And folks say humanity is dead.'

'What did you do?'

'Gave him another thirty, so I did.'

'Your humanity is certainly not dead. Anyway, Paul, your text sounded urgent.'

'It is. I may have some proof soon. I can't name names just yet but the one I suspect of being at the top is over here in the UK at the moment. He's on business and is travelling all over the country, during which he will be giving press conferences from time to time.'

'He sounds important.'

'He is, but not as much as he thinks he is.'

'And you were thinking what, exactly?' Christine asked, though she thought she knew what was coming.

'How would you fancy ambushing him at one of his press conferences?'

'Wow, you don't want a gal to do much, do you? This could be career suicide.'

'I thought you said you were in the other night? Remember, I'm the one taking the chances.'

'I know, Paul, trust me I know, and I'm in alright.'

'I can feel a but coming.'

'But, it would depend of the strength of what you would have me ambush him with, the strength of its provenance in particular, and of course, who exactly it is?'

'The last bit will have to wait, but it could be a great opportunity. And I wouldn't ask you to do something I couldn't back up.'

'Would this fit into the programme, or be an aside?' she asked.

'Oh, it's definitely on track.'

'I would need to get approval from my editor and the programme's exec, and I wouldn't get that without answers to the questions.'

'Fair enough,' Bury said, taking a gulp of his pint of Guinness, before continuing, 'So long as you are up for it in principle, with whatever you need to have in place ready, I'll have the answers, and if I don't, then we abort.'

'Sounds like a fair compromise, Paul, but what's the rush?'

'It's just that when this guy is on home soil, as in back in the Province, you wouldn't get a fart between him and his cronies, and press conferences are rare, but while he is here he will have limited security with him, of which, being that you're press, you'll be allowed past anyway.'

Christine took another gulp of wine, as she considered what Paul was saying. Her imagination was going into hyperspace."Who was the man? Was he a noted business man? Or was he a current police chief?" She pondered on the latter; it would hardly endear her relationship with the local plod if he was a police chief, but if it was to do with corruption and with positive discrimination against non-Catholic officers, what a coup. "It's definitely on track," he'd said.

'Trust me, Christine,' Paul said next, adding, 'it'll be a scoop.'

She wished he hadn't used that word, but she was in.

Chapter Twenty

This wasn't how he liked to spend his Sunday mornings, but once the work was over Quintel planned to disappear somewhere warm and not work again. That said, this current job would be very good on his CV. He had renewed faith in Jason's abilities and he could see other high profile, and high paying jobs, coming his way. At least he'd be able to pick and choose. After all, you couldn't just go onto the Dark Web and search for assassins; well, you could, but you were increasingly likely to attract a cop if you did.

He shouldn't complain though, he'd just finished a late full English breakfast, whereas Jason had been out since early on. In fact, he'd awoken Quintel on his way out, should have got separate rooms. He was about to head back to his when his phone rang. It was Jason. He noted the time was noon as he took the call. 'Any problems?'

'No, I've got the perfect place,' Jason said, before giving Quintel the local address and instructions from where he should walk to after a short cab ride.

'I sort of meant with the package?' Quintel said.

'None.'

Quintel ended the call, and rang down to reception to arrange a taxi.

Twenty minutes later, he'd been dropped off at the edge of a local rundown housing estate on the outskirts of Leyland, which was a small industrial-come-market town a few miles south of Preston, but the whole area just seemed to be one big urban expanse to Quintel, with nothing to discern where Preston the city ended, and the surrounding towns began.

He checked the instructions he'd written down before ripping them up and pushing the paper down the nearest grid. After a hundred metres he turned down a wide rear entry which led to a large concreted area big enough for vehicles to enter and turn around. To one side were a row of seven or eight disused garages, with a field behind. All the doors were either missing or rusted and broken open showing that the contents were nothing but rubbish. Two had discarded sofas in, and one had a grim looking stain-covered mattress in it. The last one was the only one which still had a door on it, or a pair of doors to be exact, old wooden ones with paint peeling from them, but intact nonetheless.

Quintel noted grass growing in front of the garage through the cracked concrete; no vehicles had been round here for a long time. He knocked three times on one of the doors and then waited before doing it again.

Seconds later, one of the doors opened a couple of inches and Quintel could see Jason's face. He grinned, before opening the door wider so that he could quickly enter. 'How did you find this place?'

'An old mate of mine used to use it to store stuff, he just wasn't sure if the padlock would still be on it, or if it was, whether the key would still be where he'd left it.'

'And was it?' Quintel asked, as Jason quickly closed the door.

'No probs at all, took me a couple of minutes to loosen the lock, but its free now, so at least we can secure the place and come and go as we please.'

'Excellent.'

'There's even an old paraffin lamp, as you can see, that still works.'

As Quintel let his eyes adjust from the changing from daylight to paraffin light, he looked into the darker recesses at the rear of the windowless garage, and saw an old kitchen chair propped up by the rear wall. Sat on it bound and gagged was their guest - his uncovered eyes bright with fear in the wavering light.

*

It took Vinnie ages to park his Volvo anywhere near the address, which was a resident's only parking place. Even on a Sunday the centre of Manchester was a nightmare. He eventually gave up and parked it where he could, and put the two-penny coin on his dashboard again, hoping for the best. He hadn't seen a parking attendant but he knew they would be here somewhere.

The flat was modern and looked spacious from outside, situated in one of these new, urban trendy locations. It had obviously once been an old mill or factory of some kind, with exposed rustic brickwork to give it that new but old look. There were four floors and number twenty-one was on the top. He banged on the door three or four times but received no response. He checked his watch, 12.15; he could be out for lunch. Vinnie then realised he was getting peckish himself. He tried again, and this time he heard noises from within.

Jim Reedly looked quite shocked when he opened the door to see Vinnie stood there.

'Inspector, I thought I told Delany—' Reedly started.

'It's detective inspector, but you can call me Vinnie. And I know what you told Harry Delany, which is why I'm here at Brian Darlington's behest.'

'That's Chief Constable Brian Darlington to you,' Reedly said.

Vinnie knew this wasn't the best start to the conversation, but he hadn't expected Reedly to be gushing in hospitality regardless, and Darlington had given him backing to be as however he saw fit. It wasn't every day one got to be rude to a deputy chief constable. He walked into the flat uninvited, and turned to face a shocked Reedly and said, 'This way to the lounge, is it?' pointing at the only interior doorway.

In the front room Vinnie chose a red leather armchair and sat down opposite a two-seater settee of the same suite. Reedly sat on it and turned to face him, and was unexpectedly quiet. Vinnie had assumed he'd explode. But after a brief stand-off he spoke.

'I am still your DCC; even if you are on this regional unit – which, make no mistake about – you can be recalled from.'

That's better, Vinnie thought before speaking next. He ignored Reedly's comment, 'Look Mr Reedly, it's abundantly clear that you have not told the truth. If not telling us the truth has in any way led to, or been a contributing factor in either Charlie's death or that of your old mate Reggie Carstair, then Laurel leaves and pips or no laurel leaves and pips, I'll shove your rank up your arse, just before I arrest you and throw you in a cell.' That should do it, he thought, as he sat back into the comfy chair. He hoped the "your mate" bit might jar Reedly.

Vinnie kept his expression plain as he waited. Reedly looked at him with a mixture of shock and horror. This was replaced with a regained composure as he felt Reedly assessing what had really happened. The deadlock extended into an uncomfortable standoff. But years of doing interviews with criminals had taught him never to be dragged into the void. Let the other person speak first. Reedly did.

'How much do you know, or should I say, how much do you think you know?'

Clever; Reedly was trying to illicit information from Vinnie now, rate what he had, so he knew how much to give. 'Enough to suspect you of being in the wrong uniform.'

'What's that supposed to mean?'

'Perhaps yours should have "Inmate of Her Majesty's Prison Service" written on it.'

Now Reedly did explode. Vinnie just sat there and let him rant, not so much about his impertinence but the suggestion that Reedly was bent. When he eventually calmed a little and Vinnie had refused several orders to leave, Vinnie held his courage until Reedly had fallen fully silent.

'We need to know why you and Carstair were targeted. We need to know who you upset when you worked for Carstair. I'm sorry for accusing you of corruption, but I had to get a steer on you, had to open you up, sir,' Vinnie said, trying to kiss and make up a little. 'We don't know who else is on this hit list.'

'I can assure you Palmer, I am not bent, and in any other circumstances I would have your badge for the way you've just spoken to me, just wait until I speak to Darlington.'

'He won't take you calls, sir. Try if you don't believe me. I'm it, and I'm not officially on "it".'

Reedly sat in obvious contemplation for what seemed like an age before he next spoke.

'I've worked on several top secret initiatives as a senior officer, but if the threat is linked to Carstair, then we are going back to the nineties or into the early zeros.'

'Can you be any more specific?'

'I can't, but now I know Carstair is dead, I can focus my thoughts a little.'

Vinnie wasn't sure whether Reedly was becoming intentionally vague again with some renewed composure, but at least the strategy seemed to be working. Before he could ask, Reedly carried on.

'Look, I'm not messing you about now, I genuinely don't know, but I will be doing my damnedest to find out. I had just hoped you'd find this Quintel and the other one before now.'

Vinnie decided he'd pushed his luck enough for now; at least he'd been able to cut through Reedly's default bullshit position, and apparently had him onside now, so he apologised for his direct approach and wrote down his mobile number for Reedly before getting up to leave.

'How wide is this? Reedly asked, as he followed Vinnie towards the front door.

'Just Darlington, Harry and me.'

'Ok, I can live with that,' Reedly said, before opening the door for Vinnie.

Vinnie blew out a huge sigh of relief as he walked down the stairs. His approach had been high-risk but seemed to have worked, though he'd reserve judgement on Reedly's culpability until he actually knew why, and who, was behind all of it.

He left the front of the building more upbeat than he'd approached it. He'd been bricking himself if he was honest, but his renewed enthusiasm disappeared as he reached the Volvo and saw the parking violation envelope stuck under the windscreen wiper.

Chapter Twenty-One

'Has he said much? Quintel asked.

'Not a lot apart from the expected denials, though I've not had too long with him.'

Quintel could hear the man making muffled noises from behind the gaffer tape across his mouth, and looked at him as Jason gave him a severe backhand which nearly knocked him to the floor.

'Shut up until you are spoken to,' Jason said.

Quintel told Jason to remove the tape from his mouth, which he did in one fluid movement. The man stifled any exclamation of pain into a sort of squeak. 'Good, now if you make any more noise, other than to answer our questions, then you will feel pain, and trust me, Jason is an expert. If you lie to us, you will feel pain, and believe me, pain when you are gagged is worse. I've often wondered why, but it is. The act of being able to let out a scream somehow reduces the agony, a little anyway. Do you understand?

If the man looked terrified before, he appeared near petrified now as he stuttered an answer.

'Yes, yes, sir.'

'First question, Dempster; why did you blow us out to the filth?'

'I promise I never did that, I promise sir, I wouldn't,' Dempster answered.

'Gag,' Quintel ordered, and enjoyed seeing Dempster's eyes register even greater fear, as Jason re-attached fresh gaffer tape. 'Left ear,' he said.

He watched as Jason then took a firm hold of Dempster's left ear and in one mighty downward action, he ripped the top half of Dempster's ear clean off his head. Dempster let out a stifled scream, which sounded as if he was under water, as blood poured from the wound down his cheek. Quintel waited a couple of minutes for Dempster to calm a little before telling Jason to remove the tape, which he did after throwing the severed cartilage in Dempster's lap.

'I believe this is yours, and I suggest you keep your ears out for the next question,' Jason said.

'I would add that you need to be all ears, but you've only got one left,' Quintel said, joining in Jason's attempt at black humour.

'Honest, I'm telling you the truth,' Dempster gasped. 'I'm no hero, I can't stand pain, I'm telling you the truth. It must be either Charlie who went to the filth, or he told someone else who did.'

'How long have you known him?' Quintel asked.

''bout a year, maybe longer. He started coming into our boozer, *The Fox and Shovel* way back. He's always in there.'

'How do you know he's to be trusted?' Quintel asked.

'Well, he was always telling tales about the jobs he'd done, and he often brought dodgy gear in to sell. Don't take my word, ask anyone in the Shovel.'

Quintel didn't answer but looked at Jason, who shrugged his shoulders.

'Said he'd done time for murder in Birmingham, but didn't get lifed-up as he got it reduced to manslaughter on appeal. Said he only did six for it.'

Quintel beckoned Jason to follow him to the door of the garage, where he spoke quietly, 'That the same script Charlie gave you?'

'Yeah,' Jason said, 'I even rang a mate in the Midlands who made some calls and Charlie was known down there as a bit of a handful, but on reflection my mate didn't know of anyone who'd actually worked with him.'

'What about anyone who'd served time with him?'

Jason shook his head, before adding, 'But that's not too easy sometimes; as a Cat A prisoner he'd have been shipped from nick to nick.'

Quintel knew this would have been true at the start of Charlie's sentence, but at some stage towards the end of his time he would have been downgraded, and more likely to have been left in the same jail, unless he'd kicked off or something. He could see a look in Jason's eyes, a sort of apology, but he didn't blame Jason. It was as much his fault for trusting an outsider.

'I reckon Charlie was either a cop or a snout. Or perhaps not, but the filth caught wind and gripped him, giving him only one way out.'

'Hence the mock execution,' Quintel said.

'What about Dumpster here?'

'I'm tending to believe him, what about you?'

'Yeah, I agree. Do we need him again?' Jason said.

'Might do, but can we trust him?'

'I think he's properly shit scared now, but I can knock a couple of teeth out if you want me to, to reinforce things,' Jason offered.

Quintel considered things. They couldn't afford to make another mistake, but Dempster had his uses. It was a case of weighing the uses up against the drama that might follow if they offed him. He walked back over to the end of the garage. 'Ok, let's say we believe you, that it was all down to Charlie, though we can't really ask him now, can we?'

'Honest, Boss, I'm not shitting you, and I'll do any other stuff you need me to do. I've not let you down before, have I?' Dempster said, aiming his last remark at Jason, who was now stood next to Quintel.

'Ok, but if you breathe a word about this to anyone, or any of our business dealings with you for that matter; it'll be more than your other ear that you'll lose,' Quintel said.

Dempster nodded enthusiastically, and Quintel nodded for Jason to follow him outside. Once in the fresh air, he told Jason to clean Dempster up and drop him off with a bung, then to set fire to the garage, just in case, and see him back at the hotel. It was a lovely spring day, so he'd enjoy a walk into the town centre, where he'd grab a cab. Jason nodded and Quintel set off without turning around.

*

Vinnie had rung Harry first to update him on his chat with Reedly, and though Vinnie hadn't known Harry for too long, he really liked the guy, and when he roared with laughter on hearing of Vinnie's direct approach, he made himself even more endearing. Harry told him to stay on Reedly, as he was sure he would "remember more" at some stage. But the fact that he'd not thrown Vinnie out and had not reached straight for the phone to make a complaint, suggested that they were on the right track. Their suspicions seemed to be right, but just how right, only time would tell.

Secondly, he'd rang Christine, and they'd met at four at the same pub they'd had a nightcap in. They'd both just finished a late lunch, or early tea, when they sat back and started to chat.

'So, what was your appointment then?' Christine asked.

Vinnie brought her up to speed and enjoyed it when she rocked with laughter; he enjoyed her approval even more than Harry's.

'And you're still in a job? Amazing.'

'Not a hundred percent sure on him yet?'

'What, you mean corrupt?'

'Could be. Until he fully opens up, or "remembers" why someone is trying to kill him, I'll keep an open mind.'

'I've worked with many editors over the years that I'd love to have spoken to like that. TV editors are a different breed from other media editorial. Don't ask me why.'

'Anyway, what have you been up to?' Vinnie asked.

'Out meeting a source, regarding the exposé I'm working on.'

'You sound like a cop.'

'I'm starting to feel like one. I guess there are a lot of similarities between investigative journalism and detective work.'

'Can't you give me a hint about what you're doing? It sounds intriguing.'

'Ok, but only a taste. I'm looking at things in Northern Ireland since the peace process, in particular how an advancement of Catholics into prominent public positions might perversely be creating a reverse discrimination against the Protestant majority.'

'That sounds like one documentary I'd like to watch. But isn't such an in-depth look fraught with danger?'

'There are still tensions on both sides, and it is difficult trying to navigate through it while ensuring impartiality.'

'I bet it is.'

'Whenever I speak to someone of one particular view or religious persuasion, they automatically assume I am either on their side, or against them.'

'Tricky. What has your "source" told you today?'

'Let's just say he's very high profile, and has certainly added ink to my pen.'

'Come on, Christine, you know all my secrets; give. I promise I won't tell.'

Vinnie could see Christine wrestling with her decision, before finally speaking.

'Ok Vinnie Palmer, I know I can trust you, and I might need your help at some stage. I'll leave any names and exact positions of those in authority out of it for now, but it'll give you a good overview nonetheless. But you'll need to fill that empty wine glass first.'

'On it,' Vinnie shouted as he grabbed the glass and his own and headed to the bar.

Chapter Twenty-Two

'Why has he got to work as a bastard milkman?' Quintel muttered, looking at his watch.

'Not sure, Boss, but at least it'll be quiet,' Jason replied.

'True, but are you sure this is the best spot?'

'Not really, but I thought if we followed him from a safe distance, we could map his route, and then come back and pick a good place.'

'Well, at least we won't lose him,' Quintel said, before Jason went into painstaking detail to explain how it was much harder following a slow-moving target than a faster one. Greater risk of being noticed. He realised this; he didn't need to be surveillance trained to work it out. He brought the lesson to an end. 'Yeah, yeah, look it won't be the end of the world if he does clock us; we'll just do one.'

'And then what, Boss?'

'Then we just pick another one, Milky's wife, or another family member, it's all the same to me.'

'Look,' Jason said, pointing ahead.

Quintel looked at his watch, 2.30 am; he didn't think he'd ever started a week so early. He looked at where Jason was pointing. He could see the milk float reversing out the driveway onto the street. They were parked thirty metres away in the shadows. At least it wasn't one of those electric vehicles - even Jason with all his skills might struggle then. It was a converted Ford Transit flat-back, and although it had a diesel engine, it would still be travelling slowly, well once it had started it's deliveries it would. Initially, Jason had suggested they follow the vehicle from the dairy after it had collected its load, as the best opportunities would no doubt be while it was stop-starting on its round. And although this would probably be so, Quintel wanted to follow the truck from the off, get the whole picture.

It took only about ten minutes to the dairy, which was a farm on the eastern outskirts of Preston. Quintel knew that doorstep deliveries were almost a thing of the past, but this place looked busy, so they left the flat-back to run in and pulled off it a few hundred metres short. They then plotted up on the same road they had followed it in on hoping it would return the same way, people were usually creatures of habit, unless they had reason to be careful, and this milky looked anything other than a criminal mastermind. 'Did you text Dempster this morning before we left?' Quintel asked as they waited.

'Yeah, and he responded pretty quickly, given the time. I told him to get to the hotel this morning and pay our tab in cash. Told him to stand it out of the bung I gave him yesterday when I dropped him off.'

'How much did you give him?'

'A grand wages and a grand for his ear.'

'Fair enough. We can send him a bonus when the whole job's over, keep him sweet, after all, we'll be rolling in the stuff.'

Fifteen minutes passed where neither spoke, before the fully crated-up vehicle they had followed passed them. They were set back from the road, but effectively on its return route. Quintel and Jason had now changed seats, and although one or two possibilities had become apparent on the way to the dairy, Quintel knew Jason would be right about there being more once Milky was on his round. He also knew that they had the right man, as his name was written on the Transit's doors, followed by the words 'Home Dairy Deliveries'. As a target, Milky would do nicely.

'Is it still just a dry run today, Boss?' Jason asked.

'Probably for the best. Let's just identify possible locations for use, but I've got it with me, just in case. I'll let you know if it changes. But for now, we'll just follow,' and with that, Quintel pulled out of the turnoff and started to tail the van from a safe distance.

'Do you think he'll give us what we need, Boss?' Jason asked.

'Like I say, either him or a member of his family will do,' Quintel answered, as he pulled over and killed the lights. Up ahead he could see the brake lights come back on the pick-up as it pulled over. From the shadows, he could see Milky jump out and carry two bottles of milk to an old stone cottage on the opposite side of the road. The lane they were now on had meandered from the main road, and he suspected it would reconnect to the A road further on. Milky had by-passed this on his way to the dairy. It was a quiet, sleepy turn-off, maybe a possibility? On their side of the lane Quintel could make out a long, high wall from where the pick-up had stopped. Its exhaust spooled through the glow of the vehicle's rear lights, giving the place an eerie feel that was quite appropriate.

Milky walked back to his vehicle but didn't get in. He put two empties into a crate, but then pulled out two more bottles of milk. Quintel couldn't see any other houses, and as he looked around, Jason spoke.

'Behind the pickup, Boss, there's a break in the wall, it must be a driveway.'

And as Quintel watched he could see that Jason was right. Milky walked 'through' the wall and was gone. Leaving their car lights off, Quintel drove off and a moment later passed the pick-up, but he glanced through the opening in the wall first, where he could see Milky walking half way down a long private road towards a converted barn. Perfect. He pulled over and, using as few revs as possible, he reversed the car until they were right in front of the pick-up.

Turning to face Jason he said, 'This will be a perfect spot.'

'I agree Boss, but shouldn't we do one before he comes back?'

'Fuck it. Let's do it here. It's pitch black, the only other house is that cottage opposite and that's facing at right angles to the road, just the gable end towards us, it's ideal.'

'I know Boss, but—'

'I mean do it here, and now,' Quintel said, as he reached for the glove box.

'I told you I had it with me,' he said as he pulled the large stun gun out and handed it to Jason, who took it and smiled as he turned it around in his hand.

'I've never seen one this big before,' Jason said as he orientated it in his hand.

'Chinese made, not strictly for human use,' Quintel said, and they both laughed. 'You know exactly what to do, Jason?'

'Sure do,' he replied as he slowly got out of the car and walked towards the idling pick-up truck.

Quintel smiled to himself as he watched Jason in his door mirror as his shadow hugged the wall close to the entrance. The sound of their car engine was masked by the noisy rumble of the pick-up's diesel note. Milky was in for a surprise.

Chapter Twenty-Three

It was 10.30 before Vinnie arrived back on the estate in the Ribbleton area of Preston. The traffic from Manchester hadn't been good, though to be fair; most of it had been going the other way. He'd rung Harry en route and neither had anything to add since they'd last spoke. Other than the fact that the post mortem examination had been completed on Charlie and he'd definitely died from catastrophic blood loss as a result of his neck wounds, as opposed to from the fire itself, apparently there was no evidence of smoke in his lungs, not that they'd expected the result to be any different. Harry was apparently hoping to get Carstair's body moved sometime today, just as soon as the forensic scientists had finished examining the inside of the car – not that there would be any doubt about his cause of death. Vinnie told Harry where he was going, and that he'd ring him again later.

Vinnie drove onto the estate and recognised it, as the houses were all painted the same putrid colours of dirty cream and lime green – there must have been a special offer on where the council bought their paint. He pulled up short of the address, and walked to the front door. There were no obvious signs of life, but it was hard to tell as all the front windows had dirty net curtains across them. He banged on the door like a policeman and waited. No answer. Standard response. He banged again, louder. No reply. He knew that if he was in then eventually his annoyance would bring him to the door. Then he had an idea. He bent down to the letter box which was half-way down the door and opened it. The offensive waft of stale air made him cough, before he shouted through the opening. 'If I keep banging like this, the whole street will know it's the filth at your door.' He then stood up and waited. Two minutes later the door opened and Dempster was stood there, still with that AC/DC T shirt on, but with added dark stains over his left shoulder. Plus, he had a bandage around his forehead and a wider one going from under his chin around the top of his head. He looked as if someone had started the process of mummifying him but had taken a break.

'For fucks sake, keep your voice down and get in before any of those grassing bastards I call neighbours clock you.'

It had worked, and Vinnie quickly complied as Dempster closed the door behind him. He noticed something else about Dempster too, apart from his distinctive aroma. Terror. In his eyes, on his face, and in his scent. 'What the hell happened to you?'

'Look, your other lot said they had a duty of care to me when they signed me up.'

Vinnie knew that he was referring to his handlers when they had recruited him to introduce Charlie to Quintel and Jason.

'Yes, why?'

'Well, why is it then that every time I try their number it's switched off.'

'Ah,' Vinnie said. He knew that as soon as the handlers had finished working with Dempster, and he'd done his bit introducing Charlie to the undercover bloke, then they would break contact with him for safety's sake. He tried to explain this to Dempster, in principal of course, as he wasn't supposed to know that Dempster had been an intelligence source.

'Fat lot of good they were to me then.'

'I'm guessing by your dressings, all's not well.'

'You got that fucking right. Jason and his boss paid me a little visit.'

'What, here?' Vinnie said as he instinctively looked around. Not sure what he was really expecting to see, but if they'd been here then there might be forensic opportunities.

'No, not here. Jason rang me to meet him before I was taken somewhere else.'

'Where?'

'I'm not telling you. It took all I had to satisfy them that I'm not a snout. I managed to put it all on Charlie's shoulders, but it cost me an ear to convince them.'

Vinnie felt sorry for Dempster; he hadn't deserved any of this. 'Why don't you make a formal complaint?'

'Are you fucking mad? Look, no offence, but just tell those other twats to pay me what I'm owed and then we can go our separate ways. You catch and convict those two bastards and I'll think about making a complaint, not that it'll make any difference if they've both been lifed-up for murder, but just so I can have a go at the CICA.'

Vinnie knew he was talking about the Criminal Injuries Compensation Authority; Dempster was truly driven by greed, but then again, so were most informants. 'Just tell me where they are.'

'Can't, they checked out of their hotel earlier on. I had to settle the bill for them.'

'Which hotel?'

'Not saying, it's too dangerous, but it's local.'

Vinnie then tried to reassure Dempster that if he told him it would be off the record, he wouldn't just go straight there, he'd visit a couple first, but he was having none of it. He said they'd suspect him and he couldn't take the risk. Vinnie didn't blame him. 'What if we have every major hotel in the Preston area spoken to with their descriptions?'

Dempster didn't answer.

Vinnie continued, 'It would just look like a blanket enquiry in an effort to establish whether our murder suspects had been staying in a local hotel. Nothing to do with you, then.'

'Good luck, but I'm too scared that if I tell you, you'll just go there first. I can't take that chance.'

'I understand,' Vinnie said, and he did. He went on to reassure Dempster that if they found the correct hotel and he appeared on any CCTV footage paying their bill, that the CCTV and information would be kept out of the evidence chain.

'What, you mean you'll bin it?'

'No, I'm not bent, we'll just show it to the trial judge in private and he'll order it be kept secret to protect you, trust me this is not bullshit.'

'I do, but you'll have to find the hotel the hard way, now if we're done here, do me a favour and leave via the back alley.'

Vinnie agreed and told Dempster to get his ear looked at before it became infected. As soon as he was back in his motor he gave Harry a bell with the update. Harry said he'd get the house-to-house team's DS on it straight away. They could narrow it down on the phone first and only visit those premises that had had two males checking out earlier today, there shouldn't be too many to then follow up with a visit. Vinnie agreed but asked Harry to pass any possible results to him, that way he could ensure Dempster was kept out of it and therefore safe.

Chapter Twenty-Four

Quintel was pleased the unexpected opportunity had presented itself. After they were done, they drove straight to Manchester before the morning traffic arrived, and dumped their motor at a city centre drop-off park for the vehicle's hire company. They then strolled onto the concourse of Piccadilly railway station and had an early breakfast at one of the many twenty-four hour food outlets. It was 5.30 am by the time they sat down to eat, and the vast concourse was already starting to get busy.

He hadn't told Jason the significance of Milky, just that it was necessary to further their aims. And professional to the end, he hadn't asked other than to hope that what he'd done would obtain what Quintel needed. He was sure it would. Over breakfast in a quiet corner he had filled Jason in. He could see he'd been impressed.

They grabbed the morning's newspapers and more coffee to while away the clock until it was eight, when he sent Jason off to a different national franchise to get a new set of wheels. He'd have to use his own details now, but as no one knew they were in Manchester, that shouldn't present any problems. They'd just keep hiring different cars from different firms, all with national coverage dropping them off in different places every few days until the job was over. That was the thing about leaving footprints; as long as they weren't connected, who could ever place them together. Too many villains were lazy, and that was often their downfall.

While Jason was sorting the car out, he'd speak to the client. He'd use one of the many public phone boxes in and around the railway station, but ensured he found one with no apparent CCTV coverage. He sent two texts to the client; the first said "C - 0161" and the second contained the rest of the number.

He got a text back saying "Give me 10 mins to my A". After nine minutes he was about to pick up the phone to ring the client's A when the public phone rang, making him jump. He answered it, and it was the client.

'I hope you've got some more good news for me? You've just interrupted my Monday morning fun, so you have.'

Too much information, Quintel thought, but he was sure the client's inflatable friend would wait. 'Ah right, look I've had a diversion to attend to—' But before he could explain further the client started on one of his rants. Quintel cut back in, 'If you'd fucking let me finish.'

Silence, followed by the client, who was calmer now. 'This had better be fucking worth your cheek, go on.'

Quintel did. He explained his other business that morning, its relevance and the significance of what he'd planned next.

'I fooking love it. It reminds me of the old days; before half my life was robbed from me by those Brit bastards, that is. But where will you get the kit from, or the knowhow?'

Quintel hadn't wanted to tell the client that Jason was ex-British Army; he thought it might cause cultural difficulties, so he said he'd served in the French Foreign Legion, and had seen active service in Africa protecting French interests. He seemed to buy it.

'So he can get his hand on grenades, still?'

'He says so, which will be a lot easier than homemade stuff,' Quintel said.

'We could have done with him back in the day, and maybe we can still use him come the tomorrow,' the client said.

Quintel didn't say *up the revolution*, but closed by adding he'd bell him again in a couple of days.

'Just before you go, I may need you to fit an extra target in, say for ten large?' the client said.

Quintel hadn't expected this; the business plan was working already.

'It'll be a piece of piss, no bother, I promise – if at all,' the client said.

'Unrelated?'

'Yes, there's talk of someone sticking their nose into our business, which isn't that rare, but if it's true then they are over on the mainland, so you may as well have it.'

'No problems, just let me know,' Quintel said, before they ended their call.

He smiled as he walked away, at least now he knew where the client was, though it would have been easy enough to trace from the telephone number. Not that it really mattered, but it was nice to know. Now, he'd head back to the concourse and wait for Jason. They had a busy couple of days ahead of them, and it was time to use his contacts to get hold of the hardware, and then explain to Jason exactly what he wanted him to do with it.

Chapter Twenty-Five

Vinnie spent the rest of Monday chasing dead ends fed from the DS running the house-to-house team – via Harry. Eventually he landed on the correct hotel around teatime. It was part of a national chain in Leyland, close to the motorway network. The uninterested youth on reception had been on duty all day, and had been there when Quintel and Jason arrived, though they hadn't booked in under those names. Regardless of the lack of information the receptionist was able to provide, Vinnie was sure it was the right hotel. He showed the youth a photo of Dempster and he confirmed that he was the one who'd paid the bill. He hadn't realised that they'd left before then. He showed Vinnie a copy of the CCTV at reception when they first arrived, but both had been wearing baseball caps pulled down to obscure their faces. No court of law would allow a positive identification from this partial view, but Vinnie was certain it was them. The youth gave him copies of all the CCTV covering the relevant times, for what that was worth, but someone would have to check them over, they may be on record at an unguarded moment. Not that it would lead them any closer to them.

What Vinnie did find interesting was that both baseball caps had a "Kiss Me Quick" logo. They'd obviously been to Blackpool at some stage – another line of enquiry for someone else to follow; but where would you start there? He knew Blackpool had hundreds of hotels, motels and guest houses.

He put a pair of overshoes and surgical gloves on to search the room while he waited for CSI to arrive. The place looked clean, the bin was empty, and the bed had already been stripped. When Vinnie asked the youth about this, he said the maid service hadn't been in the room yet. A further search located blankets and pillows in a wardrobe, but the sheets and pillow covers were missing.

As he waited for CSI, Vinnie grabbed a local evening paper from reception. The headline was about some poor milkman who'd been found dead on his round that morning. He didn't realise doorstep deliveries still existed. He read on to discover that the unfortunate bloke had apparently had a suspected heart attack and had been found in the early hours by a passing police patrol that came across his idling but unoccupied milk float. A quote from his wife blamed the stress caused by the commercial pressures facing dairymen unable to compete with the big supermarket chains buying their milk direct from farmers at ridiculously low prices. Who'd have thought being a milkman could be stressful, but his wife made a valid point.

Thirty minutes later a CSI from Preston arrived, and as Vinnie suspected, the forensic search was a waste of time. According to the CSI – Derek, he said his name was - all the surfaces had been wiped down with what he assumed was bleach. Vinnie thanked him for his time and dropped the newspaper back at reception as they both left. He'd ring Harry before heading back to Manchester. He remembered he'd need to call in at his local Spar to pick up some fresh milk, and he felt a twinge of guilt remembering the poor milkman – Mark something-or-other – the article had named him as.

*

Christine had spent most of Monday going through some of her earlier narrative on her Northern Ireland piece. As with her last major work, which she'd done after Vinnie and she had caught up with the deranged killer Daniel Moxley – virtually all the scenes had to be shot as reconstructions.

She'd had a meeting with her editor and the programme's producer to run Paul Bury's request past them. She'd faced a mixed response. The editor was worried that Bury might be using them for his own political agenda. She knew and accepted this, but argued that as long as what he was bringing to them fit in with the programme's objectives, and that they managed Bury with that in mind, it could be gold.

The producer – Sally Ainsworth, a veteran of making such programmes, was clearly up for it, but with concerns.

'We have to be careful. Investigative reporting has ended up in the dock, literally in some cases, so we do need to tread carefully, but in principle it sounds good,' Sally said, turning to face Christine's Editor – June Jackson – who looked less than convinced.

'We need to know who we're dealing with first, Christine. Don't forget it's my job to rein you in when needed,' June said.

Christine knew June was in a difficult position sometimes, but she was offended by her remark. 'Hang on June, have I ever gone off on one and left you exposed? I'm not some over-excited intern fresh from Journalism school.'

'I was talking generically,' June said, with the same stormy countenance.

'Well, that aside then, don't forget we have total control on what we use. If in the end what Bury brings is too high risk, then we can still bin it,' Christine said.

'Not if we have already ambushed some public figure in front of the rest of the media on some politically driven crock of shit.'

'Now hang on a min—' Christine started, before Sally cut in.

'Ladies, please. No decisions have yet been made, but let me remind you that the British media is not the envy of the civilised world because we aren't prepared to grasp the odd nettle, even if it is dripping in piss.'

Christine couldn't help but grin, and noticed that June's expression had cracked as well.

'Step at a time is all I'm saying,' June said. 'We are also envied for our fairness of reporting; remember our reputation opens doors for us where others are barred.'

'Accepted,' Sally said, adding, 'and as you point out June, we need to find out whom first, and then take it from there.'

Christine and June both nodded before Sally bade them goodbye. After she had left the office, her editor spoke. 'I'm on your side, Christine, just watching yours and the company's backs, that's all.'

Christine noticed a full smile now creeping across June's face, and her own temper softened. 'I know, June.'

'Couldn't you get your police friend Vinnie to check Bury out, discretely? Seeing as he's now retired, Vinnie may be able to give us a steer on him without leaving any footprints?'

Christine was pleasantly surprised by June's suggestion, and said she'd speak to him.

'After all, they brought us into their trust on that Moxley thing, perhaps it's time we did the same. Or I could speak to his boss, Harry whatever-his-name-is?'

'Delany, but thanks, let me try Vinnie first.'

Back at her desk, Christine checked the wall clock. It was gone six, and she decided she'd give Vinnie a call before she headed off home. She dialled the number which rang out to voicemail. "Hi DI Vinnie

Palmer here..." After the beep she said hi and told Vinnie about their chat and what she was doing. She asked if he could do some very sensitive digging at her editor's request. 'Wonders abound,' she said, and added, 'she must have got lucky last night.' She then left Bury's details and asked him to call her when he got chance.

Ninety minutes later, Christine was curled up on her leather two-seater, fed and with her first glass of wine in hand; she was preparing to catch up on the soaps. She had started to try and limit her wine intake of late, not that it was out of control or anything like that, but just a health kick. She needed to start jogging again now the days were getting longer, but she'd consider that more another day. For now, not having a glass of wine until after she'd eaten – at home anyway – would have to do.

Then her mobile rang; she hoped it was Vinnie, and sighed when it was not. It came up number withheld, and she could never resist those.

Chapter Twenty-Six

Jason's contact lived in Birmingham, so even though he'd just hired a new car, Quintel suggested they leave it parked up and grab the train to Birmingham New Street. Apart from being a lot quicker, it would also be much safer.

'The last thing we want is to get stopped by the filth with a boot full of toys. I mean, when was the last time you ever heard of a random stop and search on a train?'

'Not unless it was full of football supporters, Boss. Fair point.'

'We could get a cab all the way back, taxis' never get pulled either, but the train should be ok, and cheaper. How much will the toys cost?'

'Two-fifty for each grenade, and the same for the extra ammo for our guns, though I'm hoping to swap the sawn-off for a second handgun.'

'What, you've got it with you?'

'Yeah, in the holdall with the clothes. I just thought...,'

'Ok, just so I know to leg it if you do get a tug on the way down. But seriously, it makes sense to move it on anyway. And are you sure the grenades can't be traced?'

'Other than back to the British Army, yeah.'

Quintel and Jason both laughed in unison. 'Fuck me, I thought they were supposed to be keeping us all safe,' Quintel said, before laughing again. He knew Jason had served in the Signals which was where he'd learnt all his surveillance skills, but wasn't too sure about all his other operational experience. 'You sure you know how to lob those things?'

'Trust me. And we'll only need one; we can keep the second one for something else, if you want.'

'Fine, so long as you get the bastard. I want to see his bollocks flying through the air.'

The rest of the trip to Birmingham passed without a hitch. The supplier they met was a world away from the dickhead they'd bought their original guns from in Blackpool. He was clearly an ex-squaddie and Quintel kept quiet and left Jason to give it the 'old veterans' banter. He swapped the sawn-off no problems, and when he asked if it had been used, Jason told him it had. That didn't seem to bother the supplier, who said he'd add a few striation marks to the barrel and firing pins so if it ever did fall into the wrong hands – as in the police – it wouldn't match any recovered ammunition. Jason said he'd already disposed of the empty cartridges, but his mate said he'd do it nonetheless. He was clearly a professional.

Quintel's interest kicked in when the supplier produced the 'Frags' as he called them from a box. He'd never seen grenades before and expected them to be segmented, like the ones you see on the telly in war films and suchlike, but these ones were round, smooth, and painted black with yellow writing on. They were also smaller than Quintel would have expected.

Jason called them an L.A. – something or other, and said they had a three to four second fuse delay. That would do nicely. Business over, and Jason put the new handgun, a further Glock, and the ammo and grenades into his holdall, and Quintel sat away from him on the return train journey. Once back in Manchester, they grabbed a KFC before picking up the motor and heading to their next destination - Blackley cemetery.

Quintel had taken a call whilst they ate, giving them details of the funeral, which according to the obituary notice would take place at Blackley cemetery the following day. Quintel had a network of people in most parts of the country which could really come in handy sometimes. He insisted each maintain a local post office box to where he could post the odd bung in the form of a retainer or wages. Jason researched the cemetery on his phone and said it was a large municipal multi-faith graveyard situated over rolling landscape in north Manchester. The timing was perfect; they could sort this part of the plan out before moving on to the rest of the business. He'd briefed the client earlier on what he had planned, and he said that he was happy about the diversion. If it went to plan, it would be a shortcut.

They arrived at the cemetery just after seven. Quintel was surprised by the size of the place, which was apparently split into several different burial grounds. The perimeter road seemed to go on for ever, encircling what had once been a golf course, and judging by its size and the established woodland around it, he could easily imagine this. He'd always thought that golf was a game for people dead in spirit, he reminded himself with a grin. Jason said they could risk one drive into the carparks, as it would only be on subsequent occasions that anyone might take any notice. But in any event the place was due to close at dusk, and as it would be dark in less than an hour, they'd only be able to visit it once before the close of play. One visit should be all they'd need. As it was, the place was quiet and even though he thought Jason was being over-cautious, there would be no need to argue.

They parked up and set off on foot to find the Jewish sector of the cemetery. Quintel was carrying a bunch of petrol station-bought flowers that they'd picked up en route. It didn't take long before they found what they were looking for. Jason paid particular attention to a line of established trees in the foreground, and as they wandered back along one of the many paths, Quintel threw the flowers at one of the graves. 'What about pinch points?'

'I've spotted a couple, not least on the entrance to the site,' Jason answered, adding, 'but I wouldn't mind a look at those trees from behind. I'll drive out and park up on the perimeter and have a quick look.'

'I'll wait in the motor then,' Quintel said.

They returned to the car and Jason drove out of the carparks and stopped on the perimeter road, close to where an elevated ridge supported a group of mature trees. Quintel put the car radio on and waited.

Thirty minutes later, Jason returned to the vehicle. 'Any good?' he asked as Jason closed the driver's door.

'Perfect. We get a great elevated view, and it's relatively close to the road, so all good news.'

'So we can leave the car here, get the view we need, and be off in ragtime?'

'Absolutely.'

'Brilliant, let's go and find a local hotel for the night.'

Chapter Twenty-Seven

Christine checked the time on the dashboard clock as she pulled up outside the same pub. It had just gone eight and dusk was turning into nightfall. She glanced through the bay window into the pub's front snug, half expecting to see Bury sat in there waiting for her, but the room looked empty. Then she heard the passenger door being opened. 'Bloody hell,' she exclaimed before she realised that it was Bury.

'Sorry, I didn't mean to startle you,' he said as he closed the car door.

'Where did you come from?'

'Been stood in the shadows, until I saw you pull up.'

'Well, give me a bit of warning next time; you nearly gave me a heart attack.'

'Sorry, again.'

'Ok, Paul, what's so urgent you need to separate a girl from her Prosecco?'

'The main man, the one I told you about. He's meeting some local Republican cronies in an Irish bar in the northern quarter of the city.'

'You've got good intel.'

'We never ask about such matters but, yes, he'll be there for a couple of hours.'

'So do I finally get to find out who your nemesis is?'

'You do.'

'That'll please my editor.'

'Glad to hear it.'

'I hope you aren't expecting me to ambush him tonight?'

'No, I need more proof yet, but if I'm right, the bastard is playing both ways.'

Christine asked Paul what he meant, and he told her that the guy was Catholic, and in a senior position in Northern Ireland; on the face of it he was all for the new power sharing assembly helping to unite both Unionists and Republicans in a common goal. There was even talk of him being nominated for an award. But if Paul was correct, he was at the heart of all that was corrupt inside NIUCS – Northern Irish United Crime Squad. According to Paul he was due to meet local Irish Republicans for a social gathering in an Irish boozer called *The Blarney Stone*. She knew the place. A typical commercial Irish pub full of TV screens with every possible sport being shown at the same time.

'As I recall, it's a bit of a man's pub - won't I look out of place in there?'

'I just thought you'd like a look at the man close up, and witness who he's meeting.'

'How do you mean?'

'He knows me, so I can't get too close, it'll spook him, but the guys he's meeting are all from over here, so they won't know me, but trust me, they will be bad boys. Surely it would help your story to put him together with undesirables?'

'It might if I knew who we were talking about?'

She watched Paul take a deep breath before he said, 'Mathew McConachy.'

'As in the First Minister in charge of the Northern Irish Assembly?'

'Aye, that's him.'

That would be a scoop, Christine thought - the effective leader of the regional government in the Province who was currently the darling of Westminster. She understood why Paul seemed so jumpy. He showed her a photo of McConachy on his smart phone, and she instantly recognised him, but it didn't do any harm to refresh her memory. Then she asked Paul exactly what he had in mind.

He suggested that she simply locate where McConachy was in the pub, note who he was with, and try to get a photo if possible, perhaps by taking a selfie or something, then he would be able to ID who McConachy had met. If she got in close enough she might be able to hear some of their conversations. He'd stay outside in the car and try to clock them as well; as they came and went.

It was all starting to sound a bit like a surveillance operation to Christine, and she wished Vinnie was with her. She suggested bringing Vinnie into it so he could go in the pub with her, make it all easier.

'No offence, but I don't want to trust anyone else just yet, these men have contacts all over the place.'

She tried to argue Vinnie's position but Paul was having none of it. She asked him if he had any idea who McConachy was meeting, but Paul said he didn't.

'Look, just give it twenty minutes, like you've been stood up, enough at least to put McConachy together with men he would no doubt not want to be publically seen with. He's not really known this side of the water, he'll feel safe.'

Truth was she'd been in as soon as she realised who was involved. She drove the short distance to *The Blarney Stone* and parked up on the road outside, opposite the main door. The time now was 8.45 pm and according to Paul, the meeting was due from 9 pm. She took a deep breath and left Paul in the car as she walked confidently to the main entrance to the pub. It was a large two-storey building with its front aspect painted white, with large brass lamps sticking out over bay windows.

The main room had a long bar at one side facing a brick wall with several flat screen TVs on. Off to the right under the two ground floor bay windows were alcoves with table and chairs. The place was quiet, as after all it was a Monday evening and as far as she was aware, there were no major sporting events on that night. Indeed, the TV screens seemed to be playing replays from the weekend's football action, and all had the volume turned down low. Two guys who were sat at the bar on stools glanced up momentarily as her stilettoes clicked against the hardwood floor.

She bought a wine and lemonade and noticed a group of four men in their forties or fifties sat around an oblong dark wood table in the first alcove nearest the door. They all glanced at her when she'd first entered, and she reckoned they must be the group. She picked a table under the TV screens to sit down at, and chose a seat that put her at forty-five degrees to the bunch. She could see them without being in their faces, and could pretend to take a selfie but actually catch them by taking an outward facing shot. If anyone asked her what she was doing, which she thought highly unlikely, she'd claim she was taking a photo to show her date what he was missing by standing her up.

As she sat down, one of the men, a short stocky man with thick black hair wearing jeans and a dark blue T shirt, shouted across at her.

'Come sit with us why don't you? And let a man buy a lady a drink,' he said with a friendly smile on his face.

'I might just do that, if my date doesn't show. This is the second pub he's sent me too, I'm not going to a third.'

The man laughed and said his offer remained open, before turning back to his mates, who were huddled forward in conversation. By the accent Christine reckoned they were from north of the Irish border, Belfast accents. Not that she was an expert but the Belfast accent was guttural and a little harsher in tone than the rounded vowels of say, a Dubliner by way of contrast. She wrote a quick text to update Paul and as she pressed send, a huge man in his fifties who looked like he'd come straight from a building site or the docks came rushing in and went straight over to the first alcove. He stood over the group of men. The dark blue T Shirt Man looked surprised to see the new arrival, as did the rest of them.

'What the fuck are you doing here?' T Shirt Man said, adding, 'If The Man walks in and sees you, he'll know. Haven't you forgotten?'

'The bastard's not coming.'

'Don't be saying that; how many chances are we likely to get to have the opportunity to get this close to him?'

'It's true, he must have sussed it or been tipped off. Realised it was foe and not his new Brit-loving bedfellows waiting to greet him.'

The T shirt man then stood up and backhanded the big man hard across his face. The size difference was huge, it almost looked comical, but the big man didn't flinch, nor did he react.

'Watch what you're saying out loud,' T shirt man said, followed by turning to look around the room. The two guys by the bar were watching one of the TVs, Christine noticed, and the barman had his back to the group washing glasses. Christine suddenly felt very uncomfortable, especially when the big man joined in this knee-jerk recce and his gaze seemed to rest on her. As did T shirt man's look; this time without the smile. She'd no idea exactly what had just happened, but guessed McConachy wouldn't be making an appearance; it was time to go.

She left her drink and hurriedly rushed out of the pub without looking at the group of men, though she was sure she could feel five pairs of eyes tracking her every move. The moment she was out in the fresh air, she felt a relief run through her and as she hurried across the road to her car, she noticed the headlights switch on, as did the engine. Paul was in the driver's seat now so she quickly jumped into the passenger seat and said, 'Just get me out of here.'

Paul didn't speak; he just pulled out into the traffic and drove. She sighed and risked a backwards glance at the pub disappearing in the background. She could see the big Irishman stood outside the front of the pub with T shirt next to him; both seemed to be staring at her.

'Are you ok?' Paul asked.

'No, I'm not. It was a set up.'

'What do you mean?'

'There definitely was a reception committee in there, but they weren't there to shake McConachy's hand,' Christine said, before repeating what she'd heard. She went on to explain how Dark Blue T Shirt had originally engaged her and how the big man and he had later looked at her. Paul tried to reassure her that if his intel was wrong and they were foe, then there would be no reason for the men to suspect her of anything, they would just be in challenging mode. The two guys on bar stools watching TV would no doubt be spoken to next.

Christine wasn't so sure.

'Look. I'm really sorry about this,' Paul said as he pulled over. 'I'll not put you in that position again, I promise.'

He'd got that bit right. Then he said he'd jump a cab and leave her in peace until he had all the proof they'd need. He apologised again and got out straight into the path of an approaching black cab with its yellow For Hire sign lit. She slid across onto the driving seat as Paul jumped into the cab and was gone. Christine took a moment to catch her breath. It had been ten years since she'd given up smoking but a sudden desire for nicotine rushed over her. She ignored it as it was replaced with a need for a very large glass of wine. Now, that was something she could have. She'd also ring Vinnie as soon as she got in and ask for his help. She was starting to feel unsure about Paul Bury.

Chapter Twenty-Eight

Jason suggested that Quintel wait in the car whilst he took up a vantage point. He said it would be quicker to exit, and Jason knew exactly where to go after his earlier recce. Quintel could see the validity in his suggestion, but was having none of it. He wanted to see, and in any event there would be time enough to get going. Their car was parked on the perimeter road nowhere near the actual entrance. He glanced at his watch; 1.30 pm. People would be starting to arrive soon for the service, which was due to start at two. It would probably be another hour before the mourners were graveside, but it would soon pass. He was looking forward to seeing their subject in the flesh again.

The weather had turned since lunch, and the intermittent rain would make it less comfortable, though it did add to the aura of the place. Discussion over, he followed Jason away from their hire car and through a break in the hedge down a narrow unmade path behind a coppice of established trees. The way rose steadily and by the time it levelled out, he could tell that they would have a decent elevation looking down onto the gravesides. Where the track levelled, Jason turned right and started through the trees, which were mainly silver birch set one to two metres apart. He came to halt behind Jason as he squatted down a couple trees from a steep grassy hill that led down into the cemetery. Quintel noticed that, although still high, the sun was behind them now and would be in the faces of those below – if it ever came out again - Jason had chosen well.

He crouched down next to his man and made himself as comfortable as he could. Looking down to the many rows of graves, some freshly laid, some not, he noticed that there was only one which was open and freshly dug, with earth stacked up beside it. It also had what looked like astro-turf around the hole, ready for the mourners to get in close without soiling their shoes. He knew it was the right one. 1.45 pm; it wouldn't be too long to wait now. He watched as Jason unpacked his rucksack, first handing him a small pair of field glasses. He practiced with them for a few minutes whilst Jason sorted himself out.

'I'll be happier once he's in the ground,' Quintel said.

'Pity they're not cremating him,' Jason added.

'It's against the Jewish faith, apparently.'

'No matter, once he's buried, he's buried.'

'Very profound, but I know what you mean. Anyway, our local contact has said there are no problems. And the funeral is not what we've come to see,' Quintel said.

'Once we've watched the burial, I suggest we move back towards the road, to get a better view,' Jason said.

'Why's that?'

Jason explained that the path through the cemetery neared the embankment further along; it came within ten metres, which would be easier for them, plus it'd give them a head-start back to the motor.

'Fair enough, plus it'll separate things from the other bastard a bit; at least physically.'

Thirty minutes later, the funeral party arrived at the graveside, and Quintel could see that their main interest was one of the pallbearers. There were six and he was one of the rear two. Quintel watched the proceedings through his binos and felt relief as the coffin was eventually lowered into the ground. The stiff had done its job. He looked at Jason as he packed up his bag and saw his hand-signal that it was time to leave. Slowly and quietly they backed up into the trees and then he followed Jason to the next vantage point. As they settled in Quintel could see the advantages; not only were they a lot nearer the path, but the embankment was steeper here, giving them a more elevated position. Then he had a thought. 'What if they about-turned and head back the way they'd come?'

'If you look, there are little blue signs signifying that the path is one-way. I guess it stops any chance of folk walking into the incoming stiffs,' Jason said.

Quintel relaxed and settled himself, and then looked through the binos. He could make out the entourage by the graveside. 'I can still see them; I'll give you a shout once they move.'

'Cheers, Boss; it'll be easier with you spotting for me, but I'll be ready.'

Five minutes later and the party were on the move, and a further three minutes after that and the group of about thirty people were slowly meandering their way towards their position. The path narrowed as they neared, forcing the mourners into single-file. Perfect. 'They're getting close. Ready?'

'Ready, just a little nearer.'

Quintel could hear Jason's movements but didn't look; he kept his eyes on the target. He was about midway in the group, with a break of about five or six feet between him and the rest of the party, front and back. Even the mourners don't like him, Quintel thought, as he watched the front of the line start to pass their location.

Then he heard a metallic click coming from Jason's position.

Quintel watched as the small metal object looped through the air. He could hear Jason packing his stuff away, but Quintel couldn't take his eyes off the event. Their target was still in the narrow part of the path, still with several feet of space before and after him. As the grenade passed the half-way mark, their target looked up. There was no noise, but perhaps his peripheral vision had picked up on the movement. He seemed to look puzzled as he viewed the advancing object, now three-quarters of its way towards him.

Then Quintel saw the recognition flash across their target's eyes; a horror-struck expression replaced his quizzical visage. The man started to run whilst he bellowed out a warning, which Quintel was sure wouldn't be understood by the others until it was too late. 'Get down, Boss,' he heard Jason say, but ignored him. He was mesmerised by what he was seeing. But he couldn't quite understand why their target was running towards the advancing object, rather than away from it. In fact, he passed under it as he headed towards the embankment. If he'd been playing cricket or baseball, he could have caught it.

Then he felt a hand drag him harshly backwards, away from the edge of the trees and the view. Jason then threw Quintel onto the ground and landed on top of him as the explosion roared overhead. A second later and there was absolute stillness, but for a cacophony of sound caused by hundreds of birds lifting off from the treetops.

Two seconds later, and the bird noise was drowned out by unmelodious screaming with an intensity Quintel hadn't heard before. It was hard to discern whether it was exclaiming pain or terror; probably a mix of the two. As he listening in this instance he realised he was being dragged backwards again.

'Come on, Boss, time to get out of here,' Jason said.

On hearing Jason speak, he broke his reverie-like state and realised that his ears were ringing, too. He turned to see Jason ahead of him, running down the track towards the road. Quintel would have dearly loved to go back and take a look at the utter carnage they had no doubt caused, but knew it was not a risk worth taking. For all he knew someone might already be scaling the steep embankment, though he doubted it.

They arrived at the car together and Jason drove. Moments later they were well away from the area where they had entered the grounds. 'That was fucking amazing,' Quintel said.

'You're lucky you didn't get your head blown off,' Jason said.

Quintel looked at the fresh mud down his front, before replying, 'Yeah, I owe you, I was just stuck in the moment.'

'I know, it does that the first time you use one of those little rascals,' Jason said.

'One will have done the trick, wouldn't it?'

'To be honest, Boss, it would have been too risky throwing a second one; we'd have been exposed. People's natural reaction is to look towards where the threat is coming from, rather than to hit the deck, as daft as it sounds. Pros hit the deck, whilst evaluating the threat. But I can't see any way our man could have survived that. Had it been any closer the fucking thing would have bounced off his head.'

Chapter Twenty-Nine

'Sorry I couldn't chat when you rang, or make it around here last night, I was in conference with a barrister and his legal team over an old job that's at court at the moment,' Vinnie said.

'No problems I hope?' Christine asked.

'No, they just needed a further statement from me to nullify some bollocks the defence were coming up with. I've only just finished it,' Vinnie said, looking at his watch. It was gone three, most of Tuesday already over. 'Is everything alright?' he asked. 'You seem deep in thought.'

'Well, I had quite an evening,' Christine said as she placed a mug of coffee down on the occasional table and sat opposite Vinnie.

'By the way it's a great place you've got here,' Vinnie said, hoping to elicit a smile, but none was forthcoming. Then Christine told him everything, including what had happened the night before.

'That sounds well iffy. You think it was a set-up?'

'Undoubtedly, if this McConachy had expected a welcoming committee from fellow Republican sympathisers, then he was in for a shock.'

Though Vinnie didn't know much about Mathew McConachy, the fact that he was the First Minister of the Northern Ireland regional assembly was massive.

'Well, if it was McConachy who was due to attend, he was obviously warned off.'

'Obviously, but why do you say if?'

'I was just thinking that as he didn't show, you only have Bury's word that it was McConachy who was supposed to attend.'

'True,' Christine said, before adding, 'so are you wondering about Bury, or whoever is supplying him with intelligence?'

'Either could be flawed, but if it is all about McConachy, and if he is still an active Republican feeding titbits to paramilitaries, then you'll need to tread carefully, Christine. I mean, how much do you trust Bury?'

'He seems on the level, and he is clearly under a great deal of pressure and doesn't appear comfortable or over-eager in what he says. In fact, it took many conversations of reassurance over the phone before he agreed to meet me. Unless you're about to tell me different? I'm guessing you got my voicemail message?'

'I did,' Vinnie said, 'and I have made some very discrete enquiries this morning before coming here. As far as I can find out without scratching too deep and causing an alert, he was a very well-respected senior officer, with an impartial agenda.'

'That's the way I had read him. In all my enquiries into this story, people I have spoken to were mostly Catholic and Republican, or Protestant and loyal to the UK crown. Bury admits he is a Protestant but points out that his wife is Catholic.'

Vinnie had an old mate who had done some undercover work in Belfast years earlier as the troubles were coming to an end. Long since retired and living abroad. As he had told Vinnie at his leaving do, he'd been an undercover operative for twenty years and was running out of places to live in the UK where he felt safe. Vinnie didn't mention Jimmy to Christine, there was no need, he might have nothing to add, but if anyone would have an inside view on Bury, it would be him. He'd left him a message to ring but without saying why. 'I'm just waiting for one call back, but Bury on the surface looks genuine enough,' he said. Then added, 'But I'm worried about you putting yourself in any danger, like last night. Even though they probably looked twice at everyone in the pub, not just you.'

'That's what Paul said.'

'There you go, then.' Vinnie's mobile vibrated to life on the table. He picked it up hoping it would be Jimmy, but saw it was Harry. He mouthed the word "Harry" at Christine before answering it.

'You still in Manchester?' Harry started.

'Yes, why?'

'Because some sicko has just thrown a hand grenade at a funeral in Blackley.'

Vinnie had seen many things in his job, but this was a new low. 'Who in God's name would do such a thing?'

'I'll give you a guess in a minute,' Harry said, before he went on to tell Vinnie of the brief circumstances as he had them. Amazingly, no dead yet, but seven were injured; two of which were serious, and one of which was critical. It appeared that the grenade had been aimed at one individual who was partially separated from the other mourners at that moment.

'I'm guessing the target is the critically injured, then?' Vinnie said.

'Amazingly, no.'

'Well, one of the serious, then?'

'Amazingly, no,' Harry repeated, before going on to explain that the target must have seen the grenade coming as he shouted a warning, before diving underneath it.

'Why underneath?'

'There was a steep embankment from where the bombers struck; but where it flattened out on to the ground there was a drainage ditch. The target had the presence of mind to dive into it and missed most of the blast. He does have some lacerations to his arse, which must have been sticking up, but he'll live.'

'Ok Harry, it's guess time. You said Bombers with a plural, but before I try, who was the intended victim?'

'Jim Reedly.'

Vinnie hadn't seen that coming. 'No need to guess now. But where did those two get a grenade, and how did they know Reedly would be there?'

'Questions I'm hoping a further chat with Reedly might help answer.'

'Where is he?'

'North Manchester General Hospital, under armed guard. Incidentally, Vinnie, I think it's time you called into a local armoury and re-equipped yourself for defensive purposes. I'll get the relevant authorities signed by Darlington, to keep it secret.'

'Ok Harry, if you text me when Darlington's signed and informed the Greater Manchester Police, I'll call in at one of the city centre nicks and collect a handgun and a clip of ammo. Then I'll go and pay Reedly a visit. But why use a hand grenade? We know they have guns.'

'Been wondering the same; perhaps it's to do with the topography at the cemetery? As you know handguns are only effective close up, but if they could get hold of a bloody hand grenade you'd have thought a rifle would have been easy enough to source.'

'Unless they wanted to make a show of it?

'I'll be able to sus it more when I get there.' Harry said, before adding, 'Any questions before I get going?'

'Just one, Harry, whose funeral was it?'

'Some bloke called Devers; apparently he was Reedly's brother-in-law.'

'He shouldn't have attended without protection.'

'I'm guessing he didn't want to turn a sombre occasion in to a spectacle just because he was going,' Harry said.

Vinnie could understand that on reflection, but still couldn't work out how the bad guys could have known. 'Fair enough I suppose,' Vinnie conceded, before adding, 'But who exactly was this Devers bloke, anyway?'

'I've only got the scantest of details yet, Vinnie, all I know for now is that he died of a heart attack within the last two days whilst going about his business.'

'What was his business?'

'Nothing significant; he was just a milkman from Preston.'

Chapter Thirty

'How are you feeling?' Vinnie asked, as he entered the private room on the first floor of the North Manchester General Hospital. The armed police constable, who had checked his warrant card before letting him in, popped his head back around the door.

'The doc say's you've got five minutes, sir, Mr Reedly's been through a lot.'

Vinnie nodded at the constable before turning back to face Reedly, who was on his side with several pillows supporting his back, his bed up against a wall.

'I've felt better Palmer, but I'm ok.'

'Please call me Vinnie.'

'Ok, it's Jim, too.'

Vinnie noticed a distinct difference in Reedly, since they'd last spoke. 'Ok Jim, we are on the same side.'

'I know.'

'I understand your reactions probably saved some of the group from certain death, including yourself.'

'I just wish I'd kept my arse below ground level.'

'How bad are your injuries?'

'I'll probably need some restoration work doing on my right buttock, which is a mess; but as I said, I'm ok, I'm alive.'

In any other circumstances Vinnie would have allowed himself a smile at Reedly's injuries, but he knew now was not the moment. 'I was hoping you might have had time to think?'

'It can only have been the same two. But how did they know where I'd be?'

'I was hoping you could help with that one.'

'Look, I told no one I was attending. I even told my sister that I couldn't make it. I just turned up.'

Vinnie thought for a moment before speaking. 'Why was Devers buried so quickly?

'He was Jewish; it's part of their faith apparently, to have the burial as soon as possible and usually within twenty-four hours. I wondered if it was terrorist related.'

'I'm sure the investigation team will be looking at all possibilities. But what did he die of?'

'Heart attack apparently, which surprised us all, he was always so fit.'

'And you told absolutely no one you were attending?'

'No one.'

'What if Quintel and his mate learned of Devers' death and turned up hoping, but not knowing, that you'd be there?'

'It's possible, I guess, but they'd have done well to find out that he was my brother-in-law.'

This was true, Vinnie thought, then he remembered how well connected Quintel was with local petty crimes. Was it Dempster? Then another thought hit him.

'Jesus. What if it wasn't a heart attack? What if the attack on Devers was a pre-curser to getting at you? We'll need to consider a full re-examination of Devers by a home office pathologist.' Vinnie knew that if no foul play had been suspected, and the circumstances of Devers' death pointed to a heart attack, then the post mortem operation would have been very limited. The doctor would have gone straight to the heart and probably nowhere else. A home office pathologist, however, as were used in all homicides, would have examined every inch of his body, and looked beyond the obvious.

'You're not suggesting what I think you are, are you?'

Vinnie nodded, and Reedly groaned. Both of them sat in quiet contemplation before Reedly broke the silence.

'If these two twats are that serious, then I may have an idea as to motive.'

Vinnie pulled a notebook and pen from his pocket before asking Reedly to carry on.

'I did some work for Carstair when he was the secretary of state for Northern Ireland back in the mid to late nineties. I was a DI, like you, but was seconded to the Royal Ulster Constabulary, with a remit to look at all killings by the security forces, to see which ones could be written off as "justifiable homicides". I was supposed to give the issue an air of independence, but in truth the powers that be just didn't want to see police or army being erroneously put on trial for murder in order to satisfy certain sections, only to be later acquitted because their actions had actually been lawful.'

Vinnie took a second to absorb what he was being told.

'Look, this is all highly classified, so it stops with you, Delany and Darlington, ok?'

'Of course,' Vinnie answered, not sure whether he'd be able to keep that promise.

Reedly looked reassured, and carried on. 'We had some highly classified cases to inspect back then, and that didn't make me very popular with the Provos – Irish Republican Army. As to exactly who are behind these attacks and why now, after all these years, I honestly don't know. But if Quintel is who I now think he is, you need to be very careful, Vinnie.'

'Why didn't you tell us this before?'

'It was only really after Carstair copped it that I started to put it together. But if Quintel is working for some disgruntled Provo, then he'll be a very dangerous man.'

'Are you telling me that it was your job to make killings committed by the police or army into justifiable homicides, even if they were murders?' Vinnie asked.

'Don't you dare insult my integrity. Even though it was war in all but name, the good guys had to play by Queensbury rules. A squaddie, or Special Branch man, would shoot a terrorist who was on his way to bomb the shit out of a shopping centre or wherever, and the tossers in Whitehall wanted to put the squaddie or whoever on-fucking-trial. I wasn't there to cover things up, but to stop politically motivated false accusations.'

Vinnie knew he'd touched a nerve, but had had to ask the question. Whether he was convinced by the answer, he wasn't sure. But that would no doubt be an issue for others to consider when this was all over. On the one hand, Reedly seemed to over-defend himself; but then he had opened up about it willingly. Even if a serious threat to his life was the incentive. 'Look, I didn't mean to insult you, but regardless of how honourably you did do your job, I'm guessing you were in "a lose-lose situation".'

'You can say that again. The killings of the pro-Unionist terrorists were a lot less in number, but that was only because they were a lot smaller in number than the IRA - who conversely made far more attacks so lost a greater number of their members to intervention by the security forces. But I did my job as honestly as I could, and without fear of intimidation.'

'But I'm guessing the IRA in particular didn't see it that way.'

'You could say that.'

Vinnie knew it must have been a hell of job getting any terrorist to trial over there during the troubles. He remembered reading about the Diplock courts that had been brought in at the time, where the usual jury trial system had been suspended and replaced with a single judge. It had proved impossible to get an impartial jury due to the sectarian religious divides, so a report to government by Lord Diplock had recommended that trial by jury be abolished in terrorism cases. The courts had since returned to the normal jury system now, but certain cases could still be heard without a jury in exceptional circumstances. 'I'm guessing the Diplock courts would have been used for a trial involving homicide, where the defendant was a policeman or a soldier? I mean, at least then just a judge would weigh the evidence on its facts without having to rely on a biased jury.'

'No guarantees, but regardless, it was my job to prevent erroneous prosecutions from the outset, irrespective of whether any trial would have been by jury or judge alone.'

'That was some poisoned shamrock you had then. Mr Unpopular from all sides.'

'Would it answer your question if I told you that the IRA targeted me twice?'

Vinnie didn't answer, but asked, 'When did you leave?'

'They pulled me out in ninety-eight as the peace process was being negotiated between the government and the terrorists.'

'Why didn't you mention any of this when we last spoke?'

'Because I didn't want to consider it. Many years of relative peace have passed since then. There is a power sharing assembly running Northern Ireland now, staffed by both Republicans and Unionists, so any grievances about my work should be well in the past. I still don't understand why now?'

Reedly had asked a very good question, one that Vinnie couldn't even guess at.

'I mean, it still might be nothing to do with that, but when Quintel goes to these lengths, and starts lobbing grenades...,' Reedly added.

'Did you do any other sensitive work for Carstair?'

'Yes, but only the usual stuff; preparing reports on organised crime and such when he became home secretary later on. My work in Ulster was the only operational stuff.'

'Ok,' Vinnie said, adding, 'can you think of any individual case that stands out?'

'Trust me, I'm thinking as hard as I can, but there were quite a few, and after I left all the files were shredded.'

'Convenient,' Vinnie added.

'Just security. Though any that went to a coroner were obviously preserved, and will be locked away in various court vaults, but the vast majority that were not marked for investigation with a view to prosecution, were held by Carstair, who told me he'd disposed of them once the peace agreement had been signed.'

'Should he have done that?' Vinnie asked.

'Not too sure if I'm honest with you, but he was the home secretary by then.'

And we can't exactly ask him about it now, Vinnie thought. 'But why now after all these years?' he asked.

'I only wish I knew, and that's the truth,' Reedly said.

Vinnie believed him. Then the door swung open and the constable popped his head in.

'Sorry, sir, but the doc say's your time's up.'

Vinnie nodded at the cop before checking that Reedly still had his mobile number, and asked him to keep in touch before saying his goodbyes. As he made his way out of the huge hospital complex he was wondering how he was going to brief Harry with all this. It would no doubt trigger some serious head-rubbing.

Chapter Thirty-One

'I didn't really want to tell you all this over the phone, but as it's getting late, I thought you'd want to know rather than wait until the morning,' Vinnie said.

'I'd rather not have heard all this at all, but yes, thanks,' Harry replied.

'If Reedly is right, at least the motive should open up new lines of enquiry.'

'*If* he's right. But potentially, yes. That said, the need for caution and a covert approach to this is all the more necessary now. Have you collected your sidearm?'

'Yes, thanks, and two clips of ammo. I'll be in the office early in the morning, if only to beat the traffic. Is there anything you want me to do before then?'

'We'll need to consider applying to court for an exhumation of Devers' body, but I'll get the original pathologist's report faxed here first. My first task is to brief the chief constable; he will be pleased.'

'I was thinking about paying Dempster a visit. I could do that tonight if you want?' Vinnie said.

'Leave it until the morning, Vinnie, he'll more than likely be in his pit then and you may as well have an evening off while you can.'

'What about you?'

'I'll be heading back to Manchester just as soon as I've been to see Darlington.'

Vinnie didn't envy his boss on that one. If Reedly was correct, finding Quintel and his thug mate would only be the start of it. He ended the call and went into his kitchen to grab a cold beer before returning to the lounge. He relaxed into his leather recliner before musing over events. He purposely hadn't told Harry about Christine's evening with Paul Bury. What she was doing was all about life in Northern Ireland now, many years post the peace agreement of ninety-nine - or the "Good Friday Agreement" as it was known as. Although Vinnie knew that the power-sharing agreements had been made in Belfast on Good Friday in 1998 between the UK and Irish governments, it wasn't until December

1999 that they came into effect. What Reedly was suggesting was from many years before that.

Vinnie made the short visit to his fridge and back before thinking about Paul Bury. He's a man who traversed both these very different times, and it may be worth asking Christine to see if Bury could add anything that might prove helpful. He reminded himself of Reedly swearing him to secrecy, so he would have to give this one some thought first. Then his phone rang, and he couldn't believe the timing when he saw who the caller was.

*

Quintel eased himself onto an easy chair with a beer from the mini-fridge, and took the top off it as Jason joined him. 'We'll have to get us some more of those things; I mean, how much fun was that?'

'Well, we do have one left,' Jason said, before taking a sip of his drink.

'I know, but will your mate in Birmingham be able to supply us with a few more?'

'We may have to leave it a while.'

'Why?'

'Well, when he sees the news about the cemetery he'll probably not want to know us until the shit dies down. Just in case.'

Quintel could understand that - the man was a pro and wouldn't want anything connecting them in any way - for now, anyhow. He'd turned Sky News back on, but there were still no details of the casualties. 'You'd have thought by now that some fucker would have leaked the details of Reedly's death?'

'I wouldn't worry, Boss, there is no way that he could have survived the blast. Not from that distance.'

Anger flashed through Quintel as he answered. 'I'm not fucking worried, I just like things confirmed. Which is why I'm the boss. You'd be wise not to forget that, Jason.'

Jason put both hands up in surrender, and Quintel accepted his tacit apology, before adding, 'It's not you who will have to speak to that annoying Irish twat.'

Jason nodded, and Quintel's phone vibrated and danced on the table in front of him. It was a text from the annoying Irish twat. He must have been watching the news.

Twenty minutes later, Quintel had gone through the security protocols and was stood in a phone box near their city centre hotel whilst Jason kept the hire car's engine running nearby. He rang the two halves of the number for the client's "B" call box. It was answered after the first ring.

'Did you get the fucker?' the client asked.

'Awaiting confirmation, but it's academic; it was from point blank range, damn near,' Quintel said.

'I hope the fucker lived in agony for a bit first. Like the agony him and his kind made me live in; except mine lasted for twenty fucking years.'

The client was off on one, it was time to intercept. 'If only, but we had to make sure. We had one chance to get at him after last time, and you know what we had to do to make this happen.'

'I know, I know,' the client said, as his tone calmed. 'I'm just thinking out loud, is all.'

'As soon as we hear confirmation I'll let you know, then we can discuss your next instructions,' Quintel said.

'On that, there might be a slight delay. The fooker is slippery and recent events will have made him more cautious.'

Quintel had no idea what the client was saying. He didn't even know who the target was. The man had been very circumspect on the details thus far. 'Ok,' he said, 'just let us know when you want us.'

'Oh, I've a nice little job for you in the meantime,' the client added.

Quintel recalled their previous conversation, when the figure of ten grand had been mentioned. 'Is this the ten large job you mentioned earlier?' Quintel knew it would be, but this was a good way to reaffirm the additional fee without being too crass. Only once that was confirmed would he be interested in whom.

'It is, and it should be a piece of piss for you. Just someone getting in the way.'

Quintel guessed it was an informant of some kind, so knew better that to treat it as "a piece of piss". 'Over on our side of the water?' he asked.

'Been both, but on your side at the mo,' the client said, before he gave Quintel the details.

Five minutes later, Quintel had all the information he needed. He ended the call and quickly briefed Jason during the short journey back to their hotel. It was mid-evening now and Jason suggested they stay out and grab some food. Quintel was hungry but wanted to lose the motor for the night, and needed to check back in their room first.

Once back in the room, he quickly freshened up and took a leak before turning the TV news on for one last look before they headed out. "Breaking News: from the scene of the Manchester bombing" read the tickertape. He un-muted the sound as Jason emerged from the bathroom. The screen was filled by one of Sky's senior news reporters, stood outside North Manchester General Hospital. "A casualty from the cemetery bombing has sadly died," the news reporter said, adding, "and it has now been confirmed that the deceased is Jim Reedly, the deputy chief constable of Greater Manchester Police."

Chapter Thirty-Two

It was about ten-thirty and Vinnie was starting to think about his bed. He hadn't rung Christine, as he needed more time to think about whether he should approach Bury or not. He'd still not heard from Jimmy, the retired undercover officer, and the film was nearly finished. He'd seen it before anyway so he switched his TV from the online source back to the normal digital TV. Then his phone rang and he saw that it was Jimmy, at last. He muted the telly and answered the call. 'How's retirement treating you? Or is it too hot on the Costa del Sol?'

'Retirement? I wish, I've never been busier,' Jimmy said, before going on to explain that he was now freelancing for the regional government who were keen to clear out all the Brit criminals living under the radar whilst being wanted back in the UK. Apparently, only the week before he'd been able to bubble one bloke from London who'd been on the run from the Met for twenty years. He'd been given bail prior to being sentenced for a string of armed robberies on cash-in-transit vans so fled to the Spanish sun and had been there ever since - until he bumped into Jimmy.

'You undercover operatives, you just can't leave the buzz, can you?' Vinnie said, smiling.

'Easy money, and if it helps clear the turds off the beach? Win-win,' Jimmy answered.

Vinnie spent the next minute giving Jimmy a quick update as to his current situation before broaching the real reason for the contact. 'Do you remember Paul Bury?'

'I think he was a super when I knew him, he SIO-ed at least a couple of undercover jobs I did in Belfast back in the day.'

'Straight?'

'As far as I could tell. There were some over there who were as bent as a dog's hind leg, but Bury wasn't one of them. Don't get me wrong, he could be as slippery as the next, and was very good at playing the "I'm only a simple country boy at heart" bullshit, which often disarmed folk. Especially the English. Why do you ask?'

Vinnie took a deep breath and then told Jimmy. He trusted the guy and thought that if he understood the context it might illuminate his thought processes.

'I see,' Jimmy said, 'that should make for a very interesting documentary when your reporter friend has finished, but she needs to be careful, there are still some dangerous players over there.'

'Looks to me as if Bury is the one taking the risks?' Vinnie said.

'Yeah, but I'm sure he can look after himself is all I meant, your mate could find herself guilty by association.'

It was a good point Jimmy had made, especially when Vinnie remembered Christine's visit to *The Blarney Stone*. He thanked Jimmy and promised he'd make an effort to come and see him sometime soon. He was overdue a holiday and could think of nowhere nicer than a Spanish Costa at this time of year.

He ended the call and was about to turn the TV off when he saw a "Breaking News" tickertape on the bottom of the screen. He un-muted the sound and turned the channel to Sky News. He sat down as he read of Reedly's demise. He couldn't believe it, how could he die from a sore arse? But then he wondered if blood poisoning had set in, or something like that? He remembered how he'd said one side was a mess. But it must have been fast acting; he'd seemed fine only a few hours ago.

Vinnie spent the next ten minutes trying to get through to Harry Delany, but his phone seemed to be permanently engaged, which was understandable. And as it was gone eleven Vinnie gave up and left Harry a message to call back if he needed anything doing during the night. If not, Vinnie would see him early doors in the morning.

*

It had taken Vinnie a while to close his mind and allow the beer to induce sleep but it had eventually done so, and he'd awoken at five desperate for the loo and had stayed up. By 8 am he was arriving at Harry's and his temporary office in Preston, having first spent a fruitless ten minutes with Dempster on his way in. The place was buzzing with activity and Harry was already sat at his desk; he may have been there all night for all Vinnie knew. He walked in and closed the door as Harry spoke.

'How did you get on with Dempster?'

The question took Vinnie by surprise; he wouldn't have thought its answer was a priority given the news the previous evening. 'Oh, er not so good,' he stuttered at first, before adding, 'the poor guy is proper shit-scared, and who can blame him, but I believe he's had no further contact from Jason or Quintel. He wants them nicking as much as we do. Says he'll bell me straight away if anything changes. Though he did add that it had been in the local news about the milkman - Devers' - death, mainly because it was common local knowledge that he was related to Jim Reedly.'

'So any shithead on Quintel's payroll could have fed the details to him, and they just plotted up the cemetery and got lucky?' Harry said.

'Looking that way, and if it was an opportunist thing, then the circs of Devers' death could be straight?' Vinnie added.

'We'll have to think about that one, applying for an exhumation order is not a step to be taken lightly, and no judge will grant one without good cause.'

Vinnie knew all this and was getting frustrated. He was about to ask Harry about Reedly when Harry continued.

'The Army have a large barracks in Fulwood, north Preston, which is the North West headquarters to the 42nd Infantry Brigade, among others. It also has a Royal Military Police base there and an SIB – Special Investigations Branch – office within it.'

Vinnie nodded, he knew that the SIB was the Army's equivalent to the CID – their detectives.

'The local CID here have a good relationship with the SIB and often have game nights with them in the Warrant Officers' mess.'

'Game nights?' Vinnie asked.

'Don't ask; it involves such sports as beer draughts and bar-diving.'

Vinnie had seen bar-diving done, it was where a drunk would dive from a bar as far as he could reach, hoping the two rows of mates in front would catch him. Whoever dived the furthest, won. He'd seen it done many times in Rugby club bars, though he'd never been tempted to try it. But he'd never heard of "Beer Draughts", and asked Harry to explain.

'Apparently, it involves two teams of six and a giant chess board. The counters are made up of half-pints of lager and dark ale, and if you get jumped, huffed or whatever they call it, one member of the huffed team has to down that beer in one.'

'Sounds like fun,' Vinnie said.

'Anyway the locals have set up a meet for you and me to see one of the SIB's commanding officers. Now we know Jason and Quintel have access to hand-grenades for God's sake, they must have some military connections. I've already emailed the details of both of them as we know it, and the CO has promised cross-referenced checks before we arrive, so when you're ready.'

Vinnie was impressed and said, 'No probs, Harry, sounds like a good line of enquiry, but shouldn't we be discussing something else first?'

'Like what?' Harry asked as he rose from his desk.

'The death of Jim Reedly, for one?'

'Oh damn, I forgot to ring you back last night, sorry, it got late, my phone never stopped,' Harry said.

'I can imagine.'

'I've had to direct all enquiries via a prepared statement being handled by the chief's office, but that doesn't stop the local press who have my number hounding me. In fact I'm surprised your mate Christine Jones hasn't been on the blower, or has she?'

Harry had made a good point, he'd not heard from Christine, which was strange in itself, and he told Harry as such.

'We'll have to decide what to tell her when she does make contact,' Harry said.

'What do you mean?' Vinnie asked.

'Sorry again, Vinnie, I keep forgetting I've not told you yet. Come on, I'll explain en route to the barracks.'

'Explain what exactly?'

'Reedly's not dead. It's just a ruse to protect him from further attempts on his life. It was Darlington's idea, neat eh? Anyway, come on, Major Crompton is waiting for us.'

Chapter Thirty-Three

As Vinnie drove his Volvo, Harry brought him up to date. Reedly had been moved to a military hospital while his bottom recovered and would then be taken to a police safe house. It was a good plan to keep him safe, apart from the fact that the press was descending on them. Darlington had said that the ruse would only buy them so much time before the story would start to unravel. The funeral would be expected to occur within ten days at the latest, and neither he nor Harry had any idea how to blag that one. It would have to involve too many people and be unmanageable. As it was, Reedly's family had to be brought into the plan, and it would no doubt leak out from there at some stage.

'We all trust one person implicitly,' Vinnie said.

'Exactly,' Harry replied.

Vinnie knew it was a principle of intelligence operations that each person trusted at least one person with their life, knowing that they could tell that person anything. That person would also trust at least one person implicitly; but often it was a different person, and so it went. Vinnie had always found senior officers the worst offenders; they thought rank meant they should know everything. Vinnie had got himself in the soft stuff many times as a junior detective when he'd refused to tell a boss something which he actually didn't need to know. Need to know was based on need, not rank. Or "need to know, not nice to know" as he'd often said.

'Who's got the job of dealing with the press?' Vinnie asked.

'The chief's bum wiper – Russell Sharpe,' Harry answered.

They both laughed as Vinnie imagined the chief inspector being hounded over the next few days.

'Or to quote the chief "Sharpe can do it, he's got nothing else to do".'

They both laughed again, and then Vinnie iterated what Reedly had said to him about the possible motive coming from his work in Ulster during the nineties. He also told Harry about Christine's enquires and the ex-cop Bury who was feeding her.

'That's very interesting,' Harry said.

'I know, and if Reedly is correct in his guess regarding motive, I was wondering if you would sanction me setting up a meet with Bury through Christine? His historical knowledge might help to confirm or deny Reedly's suggestion.'

'Is he safe to talk too?'

Vinnie said that he was and explained Jimmy's phone call from the Costa del Sol.

'Ok, but only tell him the least you have to, and only that, if you are 100 percent happy with him.'

Vinnie nodded as he swung his car from the busy, but oddly named Watling Street Road, into the private entrance to the barracks, which had a guardhouse and closed gate. A soldier approached and as Harry spoke to him through his passenger window, Vinnie's phone rang. It was Christine. 'Can't speak for long,' he whispered as he took the call.

'Why didn't you tell me about Reedly?' Christine asked.

'Look, it's not what you think, I'm going to have to go,' Vinnie said as he watched the soldier return to his post and start to raise the barrier, 'I'll ring you later, promise, in fact I'll need to see you.'

'Ok, but I'm going to be busy until tonight, give me a ring then and we can meet up.'

'Will do,' Vinnie said, before ending the call and driving through the entrance.

'Christine Jones?' Harry asked.

'Yeah, I've not told her about Reedly, but have arranged to see her later.'

'Tell her the truth, Vinnie, but make sure she understands that she is the only one to know who is on the outside. I take it you trust her fully?'

Vinnie said that he did, and as he needed her to get to Bury, he needed to trade something with her. And he reminded Harry that they had total editorial control at the end of it over anything Christine would seek to broadcast. She'd not let them down last time over the Moxley affair, and in any event, she wasn't covering the murders now.

'Ok,' Harry replied, before directing Vinnie where to drive.

It was the first time that Vinnie had been to the barracks, and he was amazed at how big the place was, even though it was the Army's command place for the whole of the north west of England. He drove into the grounds proper and around a massive parade square before Harry passed on the gate guard's instructions to take the third left and pull over by the building with the red painted door. He'd also put a yellow car pass in the windscreen. As soon as they had parked up a red-capped soldier appeared through the red door to greet them. They followed him into a reception area where both their warrant cards were taken from them and replaced with signed visitor passes. The red-capped soldier then led them up a flight of stone steps and on to the far corner of the first floor in what clearly was a Victorian era building. In fact, all the buildings Vinnie had seen so far looked to have originated from the late 1800s.

The door at the end had Major Crompton's name on it, and one knock later, their escort led them in before disappearing back down the corridor. The room was massive, with a huge mahogany table facing the door with a large sash window behind it. Sunshine streamed in through partly open blinds. In front of the desk were a number of easy chairs around a light oak-effect table that looked modern, budget, and out of place.

Behind the desk was a small man in his thirties with short black hair, but with a considerably longer cut than their escort had had. He looked friendly enough as he stepped from behind the mahogany desk with his hand outstretched. Major Crompton introduced himself and gestured towards the light oak-effect table where a tray sat with a steaming teapot and cups.

'Tea ok, chaps?' the Major asked, and Vinnie and Harry both said that it would be very welcome, and introduced themselves.

Tea poured, the Major spoke first. 'I've good news and bad news.'

'Bad first, please,' Harry said.

'The bad is that we've identified the nominal you know only as Jason.'

'Isn't that the good news?' Harry asked.

'For you perhaps, but not for us, you see he used to be one of ours.'

'Ah, I see. And your good news?' Harry asked.

'We've no intel on the nominal you call Jack Quintel. And he definitely has never been one of ours. Even with a fake name our facial recognition software would have ID-ed his photo you emailed me. Incidentally, I put a call into some desk-jockeys I know in Whitehall and your man Quintel doesn't seem to exist.'

Vinnie already knew that there was no trace on any databases of Quintel, he'd never had a national insurance number, paid tax or drawn benefits. It had been one of Charlie Parker's objectives to obtain Quintel's DNA or a print if possible, but the poor man's murder and the subsequent fire not so very far from where they were now had put paid to that. But at least they'd got a breakthrough on Jason.

'Since I spoke to your officer at Preston this morning the phone's been red hot,' Major Crompton said, adding, 'well, ever since yesterday really when we were told about the grenade attack at the cemetery, awful business. It certainly appears that the anti-personal device used came from us or from the manufacturer. In fact, I've sent a sergeant over there this morning to check their inventories, but I know it's academic.'

'Why's that?' Harry asked.

'Because you wouldn't believe how much stuff we misplace or have stolen from us annually. It's been a bit of a hot ammo casing for us politically, and something we've been working on for the last six months. We've locked up ten serving and twenty-two retired servicemen and women, but that stays between us gents.'

Vinnie and Harry nodded and stayed silent, letting the Major continue.

Jason was Jason Moriarty, who had served six years in the Signals Corps before being discharged to an address in Preston, his home town. He was single and in his thirties.

Vinnie was starting to feel excited as he asked, 'Do you have a discharge address?'

'I do Inspector, but don't get a hard-on just yet. He was discharged six years ago and the address he gave then is now part of the new flyover they are building across the River Ribble at Ashton.'

Vinnie groaned, and Harry rubbed his head.

'Whole swathes of terraced streets were knocked down about two years ago when work first began.'

'What about pension payments?' Harry asked.

'Typical ex-signals man I'm afraid. His bank account is an on-line one and his link-address is a post office box, but I'm guessing you could do some obs on it, not that he'll visit it much, I suspect, if at all. We've had a peek into his on-line account, and the only transactions are his pension being withdrawn every month in several cash point withdrawals from all over the country. I'll give you a copy of all I have before you leave.'

Vinnie was impressed with what the major had achieved in only a couple of hours, but disappointed about Jason's address; but at least they now knew who he was. The major went on to explain that they were also very interested in helping them locate ex-Lance Corporal Jason Moriarty so they could find out where he and his mate were getting their hardware from. The Major said he understood that their investigation took primacy, but as he put it, "we want a go with him when you boys have finished your stuff".

They just had to find him first.

Chapter Thirty-Four

Christine Jones put the phone down from speaking to Vinnie and tried to understand what he'd meant by "it's not what you think"? Her inquisitive mind was racing, and as desperate as she was to ring him back, or give Harry a call, she resisted the temptation. On the plus side, he'd also said that he needed to see her later, and the thought pleased her. She was enjoying Vinnie's company more and more, and she was fairly sure he felt the same. Whether it was more than a platonic extension to their professional roles or not, she wasn't too sure, but she planned to find out. It had been a while for her and that aside, she was genuinely fond of Vinnie. But she didn't want to spoil things by getting it wrong. That said, she'd seen the look of concern in his eyes when she had told him of her scare at *The Blarney Stone*. It had seemed deeper than a friend's apprehension, much deeper. She'd have to wait a while longer.

She shook off the thoughts as she turned her mind back to the job in hand; her editor, June, had asked her to start pulling together her work on Northern Ireland since the peace process, into some sort of order, so they could start planning a schedule. It was an onerous task, especially as things were still live and very fluid, but she was sure that the programme's producers would be in turn putting some pressure on June. Probably Sally Ainsworth who'd been at their last meeting.

She laboured on and by two o'clock she was fairly happy that she had the opening nailed - it had pretty much written itself to be fair, outlining the history of the 1999 power-sharing agreement, its aims, an up-to-date summary of where things appeared to be now, publically anyway, and the programme's objectives. She stopped to eat a sandwich at her desk and her phone rang, it was Paul Bury.

'I just wanted to apologise for what happened the other night at the Blarney Stone,' he said.

'I was probably overreacting, but thanks. More importantly, have you any idea what actually happened?'

'I have, but could do with a face to face with you. How are you fixed this afternoon?'

Christine looked at the pile of work she had done that morning and decided it was time to get some air, plus she was happy she'd done enough to allow June to feed her lions, she'd email it to her before she left. 'Ok, what about the same place, in say, thirty minutes? Oh wait, I could do with running an errand on the way, is an hour and a half ok?'

'Perfect, the sun's out, so I'll see you in the rear beer garden again.'

That agreed, Christine ended the call and headed to the Ladies to freshen up and check her teeth for stray bits of salad.

Five minutes later she was off towards the stairs when Vinnie called.

'Sorry for being so brief before, but I'll explain when I see you, but suffice to say, we now know exactly who Jason is.'

'That's brilliant, look it's my turn to be brief now. I'm just off to see Paul, so perhaps we can meet up this evening, and chat proper then?'

'Excellent. Look I might need to ask a favour, as in do you think Paul would agree to meet me?'

Christine was taken aback slightly, then said, 'Not sure, probably depends on why?'

'Nothing to do with what you've got going on with him,' Vinnie said, before adding, 'It's just the suggested motive that Reedly's advocated. I thought with Bury's service in Northern Ireland he might have some historical knowledge, or even just an overview which might help, but I don't want to cock-up your relationship with him.'

'I'll ask him, but on two conditions.'

'Fire away.'

'If he agrees, I can be present?'

'Wouldn't have it any other way,' Vinnie replied.

'And what's the story with Reedly?'

'Later I promise, I just can't talk now.'

Christine could hear a lot of loud office chatter in the background to Vinnie's call, so believed him and said her goodbyes. She'd have to wait, but the suspense was eating into her.

*

'Don't lose the fucker again,' Quintel said, as Jason accelerated away from the kerb into the Manchester traffic.

'I'm sorry about before, but we are only one car, Boss,' Jason said.

'I know the traffic in this city is a nightmare, but if we pull this little stocking-filler off, we can probably start naming our own fees when the whole job is over.'

'Yeah, yeah I get that.'

'So stop being so professionally over-fucking-sensitive and don't lose the twat.'

Jason didn't answer and Quintel concentrated on keeping his eyes on the motor. It was three-up ahead of them slowing towards a line of traffic held by red traffic signals at a major crossroads.

'The sun is bright and more importantly, behind us, so as long we keep heading east they'll see rock all in their mirrors,' Jason said.

Quintel didn't reply; Jason was just trying to show off, or make up for earlier.

*

Five minutes after setting off, Christine jumped out of the black hackney carriage and asked if he could return in an hour. She had a quick house-call to make. The driver said he'd be back in exactly an hour for five minutes, but only if he was free. She paid him with a healthy tip hoping that would help, and rushed across the road towards a modern town house.

An hour later the black cab was there as promised, and fifteen minutes after that she was outside the pub with the bay window. She entered and checked the front snug, just in case, on her way past. It was empty. Even the main bar only had a few in it. They all had city suits on and looked like dinnertime drinkers who had decided not to bother returning to the office. She was surprised to see that she had beaten Paul to the pub on finding the beer garden/back yard empty too, apart from one suited-smoker just finishing a cigarette. Having popped her head out the rear door she about-turned and headed towards the bar as the smoker followed her back inside. For a second she smelt his nicotine breath as he followed on close behind her through the doorway. It had been seven years since her last cigarette, and the man's second-hand breath smelled lovely. But the brief pang went as soon as it had arrived. It was the best thing they could have done when they banned smoking from inside offices and other buildings, like pubs, or she would still be on thirty a day.

Christine bought a white wine for herself and a pint of lager for Paul and then headed back outside before sitting at the same table they had used last time. She left the seat empty with its back to the wall; no doubt Paul would want to take up his usual watchful position. Several sips of wine and a few minutes passed before Paul appeared in the yard. He joined her and took a quick slurp from his pint, before he thanked her and apologised for being late.

'The traffic is mental today,' he said, adding, 'had to drive like an idiot; reminded me of the good old days; still got it.'

'Wasn't too much better for me, I was just lucky to grab a cab as soon as I left the office, and the way some of them drive you'd think they were all ex your old mob.'

They both smirked and then she added, 'Anyway, I get the idea you've got something to share?'

'Yeah, I do. Last night McConachy thought he was going to meet a group of likeminded Republicans.'

'As in, we are all for power-sharing with the Protestants, but really want to kick them all out of Northern Ireland?'

'There the ones. But according to my source it was either hardliners, or even Protestants who were waiting for him.'

'I'm confused,' Christine said, and she was.

Paul went on to elaborate that publically McConachy was seen as a moderate. An ex-Republican who had now got into bed with the Brits and the Unionists and was enjoying the trappings of power. She got that. 'I guess being First Minister of the Northern Ireland regional assembly was as near to being Prime Minister of the Province as one could get. And power is a seductive mistress,' Christine said.

'Absolutely, but when the armed struggle ended, there were extremists on both sides who would never, ever agree to anything involving a compromise.'

'Understood,' she said. Then Paul added that if Christine was right, then McConachy wasn't the all-round appeaser that many, including the Westminster government, thought he was. That he is suspected of slowly but stealthily ensuring that senior positions are taken by Catholics. Catholics who still long for the Republican dream of a united Ireland.

Christine was really buzzing now. If what Paul was saying was true, the reverse discrimination theme of her proposed documentary went far deeper than the Police Service of Northern Ireland and a few local councillors. 'I don't suppose there is any chance of speaking to your source of information?' she asked.

'If you knew where I was getting this from, you wouldn't believe it. It's not from some old Protestant tout who is upset at the slow but pervasive power shift, as I witnessed before I retired.'

'I didn't really think about it, but that would have made sense,' she said.

'It's from someone firmly on the extreme side of the Republicans.'

'But why?'

'Precisely because they feel that McConachy is selling them out, and they want him out.'

'You're not suggesting they would kill him?'

'No, they'd not go that far. They know if they did that the Unionists would get the blame, and the more moderate in the IRA would kick off, and so then would the ex-Unionist terrorists in response, and all hell would break loose. They just want McConachy replacing.'

'If McConachy is, as we suspect he is, then why doesn't he simply let his ex-IRA hardliners know that he is really on their side?'

'Good question, perhaps, he doesn't trust them to keep his secret? Perhaps he wants to achieve his aims while appearing to be all things to all men, which will ensure he clings onto power. It's a political minefield.'

'So what do you think went wrong the other night?'

'I don't think my source has the control of things he claims to have. I think he set up the meeting, hoping McConachy would see it as an opportunity to meet some good old boys on the QT, but the good old boys had other ideas and someone then warned him off. I think the source was hoping I'd witness the meeting and then publically embarrass McConachy, but it got out of hand.'

'Are you sure your source, or tout, or whatever you call him, is trustworthy? No offence, I'm not trying to tell you how to do your old job.'

'None taken, but yes I do think he is becoming unreliable, but they all do in time. Especially the best ones.'

Christine finished her wine as they chatted more, but she was unsure exactly where this left her. Potentially, her scoop was getting much larger, but how to prove it? As much as she hated documentaries that asked the unanswered questions, she could see her project heading that way. Sally Ainsworth would no doubt think it too much to ignore. Christine could keep the programme to the police and at the local level that she'd originally imagined, statistics alone would almost prove the point – the numbers of Protestants replaced by Catholics in the police was obviously disproportionate. But to leave out a suggestion that the First Minister himself had an agenda aimed at slowly ousting and replacing all Protestants in key positions, it would be too much to omit.

However, she could do with something to back it up, at least enough to defend any lawsuit. As she mused about this she realised she'd forgotten Vinnie's favour, so quickly asked Paul.

'So you've told him about me?' Paul said.

She sensed his disquiet and spent the next few minutes reassuring him of Vinnie's credentials and trustworthiness.

'Aye you are. I suppose I'll have to meet your man now, if only to satisfy myself he's all you say he is. But what does he want?'

'Oh, it's nothing to do with what we are doing. In fact, he's no idea of what we are up to,' Christine lied.

'Go on.'

'He just knows of you and he is after picking your brain about something that allegedly went on in the Province back in the nineties, an overview, that's all.'

'They were certainly busy times back then, but why is he asking now?'

Now that she had Paul's tacit agreement about seeing Vinnie, she didn't want to explain too much, not that she knew it all, but she'd let Vinnie explain it face to face. She knew she had to say enough to keep Paul's interest, so just said, 'Oh it's something to do with a murder or attempted murder or something.'

She could see that she'd piqued his attention.

'Aye, right you are then, you may as well bring him here when it suits. Can I drop you off anywhere?'

Brilliant, Christine was chuffed, and she knew Vinnie would be pleased. She thanked Paul and said she'd love a lift back into the city centre, save her a cab fare, and they both got up to leave.

*

'There the fucker is,' Quintel said, squinting against the late afternoon sun refracting through the car's windscreen.

'Got it, but there's two of them now.'

'Just don't lose the fucker this time. As soon as they split, it'll be game on,' Quintel said as he slid further down the front passenger seat and Jason started the hire car's engine.

Chapter Thirty-Five

As soon as they left the pub Paul accelerated severely and took a series of left and right turns before braking hard to a stop and turning around to stare out of the rear window.

'What was all that about?' Christine asked as soon as they pulled up. She'd spent the last couple of minutes hanging onto the grab rail above the passenger door so as not to end up in Paul's lap.

'I thought we were followed away from the pub?'

'You could have warned me, or were you trying to get me on your knee?'

Paul smiled before he answered, 'Sorry, I just clicked into counter surveillance mode. But the thing is I felt like I was followed away from the hotel on my way to meet you. That was the real reason why I was a bit late.'

'And were we being followed?' Christine asked, as she too looked over her shoulder.

'When, before or now?

'Either,' she said.

'It doesn't look like it. The car I suspected of having followed us away from the pub looked like the same one I saw earlier. Same make, model and colour, but I didn't get a look at the registered number, so can't be sure - and it's obviously not behind us now.'

He turned to face Christine and the look on her face must have displayed what she was feeling.

'Look, sorry to scare you, it was probably nothing, it's easy to get paranoid in my old job, and I'm a bit rusty and a bit jumpy too, if truth be known.'

'Sure?' she asked.

'Sure, please ignore it.'

It took a further twenty minutes before they were nearing the centre, and Christine's nerves had settled by then. Her phone alerted her of a text message from her sister Lesley. She had a separate ringtone for both calls and texts from Lesley, as she knew she had her problems, and never wanted to miss a call from her. Lesley was five years older than

Christine, divorced and lived in a modern flat near to Piccadilly Gardens in central Manchester, it was where she'd called in on her way to the pub earlier. They weren't too close, but she knew Lesley sometimes suffered from bouts of depression and Christine was her crutch when needed. She was surprised to hear from her so soon though; she'd seemed fine when she'd left her. Which didn't bode well.

Lesley wasn't a morning person and was between jobs, which Christine knew so she sometimes popped in on her way to work, which didn't always go down too well, but at least she knew she'd be in. So, today she had taken the opportunity to pop in for a brew on her way to meet Paul. They rarely found enough time for each other as it was, and Christine felt guilty that she only saw her sister mainly when things were not too good. And to be honest, it was that biased view of only seeing her when she was down that probably kept her away at other times. Since she'd started popping in during the "tits down times" as Lesley called it, they had grown a little closer. Christine had made a note to self, that even when Lesley started work again, they should both make more time for each other.

What really surprised her though about receiving the text, was not just the fact that she'd only seen her that morning, but that she'd been on a total upper at the time, as she'd received a letter inviting her for a job interview at a city centre ladies outfitters, just what she was good at; talking about clothes and selling them.

Christine opened up the message which just read "need to see you, urgent, can you come round ASAP". Christine tried to ring Lesley, but her phone just rang out.

'You look tense, everything alright?' Paul asked.

'It's just my sister, probably nothing, she's got a job interview tomorrow and is no doubt getting stressed,' Christine said as she looked out the window to see where they were. 'Look, Paul, her flat's near here, can you drop me if I direct you. It's close to Minshull Street Crown Court.'

'Is there a car park near there?'

'Yes, at the side of the court, which is round the corner, why?

'Well, I could do with some fresh gear as I've been over here a little longer than I'd originally planned. If you direct me to the car park, will that do? Or do you want me to take you straight to her flat first?'

'No, it can't be anything too serious, I only saw her for a brew on my way to see you. I'll show you where the car park is. It'll only be a couple of minutes' walk for me from there.'

*

'I can't fucking believe you lost the bastard again. I thought you were a surveillance expert?' Quintel said.

'I was, six years ago, but we are just one car. In the Army we could have ten cars and two bikes just in one surveillance team,' Jason said.

'I know, I know, and the car did shoot off like a boy racer was driving it. Take us back to where we found the twat earlier.'

'What about the pub?' Jason asked.

'We'll try the other place first; it's just round the corner.'

*

Paul parked the car on the single storey car park at the side of Minshull Street Crown Court. He was lucky, Christine thought, probably got the last space. She said her goodbyes and headed off in the direction of Lesley's flat. Twice in one day, it must be a record. But she was slightly worried. Sometimes her sister would get really wound up about something which another person would think nothing off. That was the way with depression. But Christine knew that to the person concerned the problem was as serious as the person perceived it. The only plus being that if it was something minor, relatively speaking, then hopefully it could soon be put right.

The last serious wobble Lesley had was when she'd been made redundant from her job a couple of months ago, but she'd seemed fine since then. She'd enjoyed having the spring off, and was now ready to get back to work, which was why this morning's letter offering an interview couldn't have come at a better time. So what could have changed so drastically since an hour or so ago? She just hoped the interview offer hadn't been rescinded, that would do it for Lesley.

Christine finished her musings as she approached Lesley's flat. It was actually a small modern terrace with a kitchen and lounge downstairs and one bedroom and bathroom upstairs, but everyone called them flats. The front door had a half-glazed upper with a hardwood solid lower half with a letter box, laterally in the middle.

As she walked down the short path to the front door, she stopped in her tracks. The door was ajar. There was no sign of damage, or anything nefarious. It would be Lesley who left the door open, but the last time she had asked Christine to come round and had done so, she'd been on a real downer. As she'd explained later, she didn't know how long it would take Christine to get there, and she couldn't be bothered coming to the door to let her in. It hadn't made much sense to Christine then, other than to know that depression was an evil all-encompassing blanket which sapped every ounce of energy and reason from those it affected. Now she was really worried.

She quickened her pace, and gently pushed the door open whilst shouting, 'Only me, sis, be with you in a sec.'

Initially, she heard nothing. But then she did.

Chapter Thirty-Six

The noise was muffled, strained even, but somehow Christine knew it was Lesley's voice, not that it could be anyone else's, but she recognised it as hers. It came from upstairs. Christine bounded up the steps two at a time, crashing into the wall as the stairs split onto their second level. At the top she heard the noise again; it was definitely coming from the bedroom at the front. The door was closed. She grabbed the handle and rushed in. What she saw brought her to an abrupt halt.

To her right was a double bed and on it was Lesley, sat up with her back propped against the landing wall. Her hands were tied with a ripped sheet and silver gaffer tape covered her mouth. Her eyes were pleading, scared, but with a warning in them. They were looking through her in the unfocused way a drunk or a drug addict might look. Christine started to turn around, then she heard two clicks. One was the sound of the bedroom door being closed, and the second one was far more metallic. Her spirit sank.

She spun around as quickly as she could, only to have her fear confirmed. She was looking at the pointy end of a handgun, aimed at her chest. She looked up at the person who was holding it, which was when she received the greater shock.

'Sit down on the bed and put your hands on top of your head, we have some questions we'd like to ask you,' the gunman said.

Before she'd spoken to Dempster the other day, Vinnie had shown her two rough surveillance photos of Quintel and his sidekick Jason. Just in case they were paying their man a visit; she could make an excuse for her call and leave quickly. The photographs had both been taken at distance but she was sure that the large brutish looking man in his mid-thirties stood here with a gun in his hand in front of her, was the same man as Jason from the surveillance snaps. But what the hell was he doing here?

Christine did as she was told, guessing compliance was the only thing to do as she tried to make sense of what was happening and evaluate the threat. She wished she'd asked Paul to drop her off at the door now, she might have seen the door ajar before he drove off. Her mind struggled to compute what she was seeing. Why and how was Jason here? And if it was him; where was Quintel?

She didn't have to wait long to have the last thought answered. The door opened and in walked Quintel. He looked shorter close up than she would had imagined, and uglier, but easier to recognise from the photos. He took the gun from Jason and told him to tie her hands, which he did using some more of the sheet from Lesley's bed. She ignored him, keeping her eyes on Quintel and the gun. When Jason had finished, he stood back next to Quintel.

'This is definitely her?' Quintel asked.

'Yes, Boss. Hundred per cent. I got a good look at her when she reappeared from here earlier and jumped the cab,' he answered.

Christine's mind was straining to understand what this meant. They must have been here when she visited earlier, or had seen her when she'd left. Did that mean they had the house under watch? But why? Or had they been following her? Her heart sank as she assumed it was the latter. She was a TV news reporter, it would be easy to sit outside her office and wait, she'd turn up eventually.

'So, this is your sister, apparently? Quintel asked, adding, 'but you obviously don't live together, as there is only one bedroom. Unless you are into some weird incesty thing,' Quintel asked.

Christine's terror edged sideways slightly, with a flash of anger at the repulsive little man's remark. She ignored the question.

Quintel then walked over to the bed and back-handed Christine across the face, her cheek stung as her head swung to one side, and she could feel the heat increasing on that side of her face.

'Don't fucking ignore me,' Quintel said.

'Well ask me a proper question,' she replied, slightly shocked by her own boldness. She tensed for a further slap, but none came.

'Ok, here's a question; you've been sticking your nose into things you shouldn't have, why?'

Christine's mind raced once more, trying to read the subtext in the question: which things? Had this something to do with Dempster? It couldn't be anything to do with Paul Bury and her documentary, it must be Dempster. Then as if to confirm the latter, Jason spoke.

'Who was that fucker who drove you away from the pub?'

This also confirmed her worst fears, that she had indeed been followed. They must have tailed her from the office. Damn, she wished she hadn't called in at Lesley's now. God knows what this would be doing to her. She glanced at Lesley bound and gagged next to her, sheer terror in her pretty blue eyes.

'Just an old workmate, catching up. Look can't we sort this out, please I've not done anything.'

'Yes you have, you've been sticking your reporter's nose where it's not welcome,' Quintel said.

'It's my job to nose around, and if I've offended you in anyway, please just tell me where and I promise I'll leave it alone.'

'Oh you'll leave it alone alright, I can promise you that,' Quintel said.

This was definitely to do with her visit to see Dempster, and now she feared for his safety as well as her own. She just hoped they didn't know of her friendship with Vinnie. These guys obviously think they are clear away, just tying up loose ends perhaps? She had to say something. 'Look if this is about me going on the knocker in Preston after the fire, I only spoke to one guy, Dempster I think his name was, and only then because someone on the estate said he was "the go-to guy". But he was useless, he knew nothing.'

'Is there a back entry to here?' Quintel asked.

'Yes,' Christine answered before Quintel turned to Jason and told him to go and fetch the car around and then come back. Jason left and then Quintel put a further piece of gaffer tape on Lesley, but across her eyes this time. Dread coursed through Christine, wondering what it could be that Quintel didn't want her to see.

Quintel had put his gun down on the dresser at the foot of the bed whilst he used both hands on Lesley, and then he picked it up again and headed towards Christine.

He grabbed her hair with his free hand and pulled her head down in a violent jerk. Then she felt a searing pain on the back of her head, followed by darkness.

Chapter Thirty-Seven

It was gone four before Vinnie caught his breath. He'd spent most of the day sorting out actions – lines of enquiry to be issued as individual tasks – with Harry before turning to his covert enquiries. He'd made a series of phone calls trying to find someone in the Home Office or the Northern Ireland Office who remembered deputy chief constable Jim Reedly's work back in the nineties, when he'd been a detective inspector on secondment. Most replies had directed him to Carstair as the then Northern Ireland Secretary of State, but the dead don't talk. Harry had tried using his higher rank in a couple of calls to the Home Office in case Whitehall rank-snobbery had been a factor, but to no avail.

However, towards the close of play Vinnie had traced Carstair's old secretary, a woman in her late seventies now who had retired to the south coast of England. But a quick phone conversation had only served to confirm that 'Jim' had worked in the Province out of Carstair's office, before she started to ask "what was for tea"? Her husband then came on the phone to explain that the poor woman was suffering from dementia. He made his apologies and ended the call.

'How did you get on with the secretary?' Harry asked, so Vinnie explained.

'Ok, what next?'

'I could pay Reedly another visit and try to drill down into his memory to find who he might have pissed off the most, when he was justifying all those killings.'

'But?'

'But, I'd rather be armed with more info before then. I'm still not convinced Reedly's not rubber-dicking us.'

'Nice turn of phrase, Vinnie; but explain? Not the phrase that is.'

'Well, if Reedly was turning illegal killings – the ones where too much force was used – into lawful ones; and I say, if? Then he might not want to open up too much on the specifics of induvial incidents in case we stumble across a dodgy one. And let's be clear, if there are any dodgy ones, it will be from within that number that our killer will have come from.'

'Darlington voiced a similar concern when we last spoke, though he didn't quite use the same words as you.'

'Darlington knows Reedly well; does he think he's straight?'

'I think using terms such as straight or bent is too simplistic an answer, I mean it was a war in all but name, and the forces for good were under enormous pressure to gain any advantage,' Harry said.

'Granted,' Vinnie said, adding, 'ok, allowing for discretion on some of his judgements then when it came to writing a killing off as legit, or marking it up for investigation as a potential homicide. What does Darlington think?'

'He thinks Reedly is a bit of an arrogant "wide-boy", a "bullshitter", but basically honest. So where are you going to get the "more info" from?'

Vinnie iterated his earlier conversation with Christine, said he'd look her up tonight and hopefully he could get to see Paul Bury this evening, and see where that led. Harry agreed and said he'd be on his phone if Vinnie needed anything, though he wouldn't be going home anytime soon. He had a meeting later with the super who was running the investigation into Carstair's murder, together with the DCI from Manchester who was lead on the enquiry into the bombing at the cemetery at Blackley, where they would look for cross reference options. And then Darlington was expecting an update.

Vinnie wished him luck and was glad he was only a detective inspector, and suggested they grab some food from the canteen while they could. Harry agreed.

*

It was just after six when Vinnie arrived back at his home where he had a quick wash and shave and changed his shirt before aiming to link up with Christine. He tried her mobile several times, but each time it went straight to voicemail; it was either one hell of a conversation, or her phone was switched off, which would be a first. Then he tried her home landline and that ran out to answer machine as well. But he noticed that after the ringtone stopped and before Christine's personalised message kicked in there was a long musical interlude – several other messages. He wasn't the only one trying to track her down. As far as he was aware she didn't do the gym or anything like that which would explain her being incommunicado. He knew she had a sister, but didn't know exactly where, not that a visit there would take her far away from her smart phone.

Then he tried her office phone and was surprised, and relieved when her desk extension was answered. But the relief was short lived.

'Newsroom, June Jackson here.'

Vinnie recognised the name; it was Christine's editor, though he'd never met her. He introduced himself and was pleasantly surprised to discover that June knew who he was. Christine had obviously talked about him. He had known her last editor from when they had worked together on Christine's documentary about the hunt for Daniel Moxley, but that had been some time ago and June hadn't been there too long.

'I was hoping *you* might be able to tell me where Christine is?' June said, adding, 'she's been gone hours. I've even tried the hospitals in case she'd been in an accident. I'm starting to worry.'

Vinnie asked June what she knew and she gave him a brief rundown up until the point when she'd dashed out to meet her source, which Vinnie knew was Paul, but didn't let on. 'Have you tried ringing the source she was going to meet?'

'I would if I had his number.'

Things were obviously done very differently to the way the police would handle a source. He resisted the temptation to criticise. 'What about her sister?' he asked.

'Never thought of that, Christine doesn't tend to mention her much, but she might be on our HR files as next of kin, I know that neither of her parents are still alive.'

Vinnie heard the phone receiver bang down on a desk and waited a couple of minutes before June came back on the line. She gave Vinnie both an address in central Manchester and a mobile contact number for Lesley, Christine's sister, before passing her own number to Vinnie, and asked him to call her as soon as he had any news. She said she would do the same. He told her to leave it with him. He then tried Lesley's mobile first; it was switched off. The address wasn't too far away so he grabbed his Volvo keys and headed for the door.

Chapter Thirty-Eight

Pain wasn't possible in a dream, was it? Of all things that one could dream vividly, Christine was sure pain wasn't one of them. The throbbing from the back of her head was breaking the reverie she was in, drawing her into a transition from sleep towards consciousness. She could hear her own breathing, loudly. It sounded rapid and shallow. It sounded internal. As if she was listening to her own inhalation and exhalations from within. The pain grew worse and jarred her back to being fully aware. She opened her eyes. Still blackness surrounded her. Terror shot though her at the not knowing of her environment. Alert and tense now, she tried to calm herself as she learned more as her eyesight adjusted.

She could make out dark grey shapes, they were her legs. She was prone on one side, and her breath was bouncing off a hard object in front of her, explaining her earlier sensation. She felt her head, which was sore, and then reached out in front. The obstruction felt as if it was covered in carpet. She could hear a low constant droning noise beyond the carpet and all around her. She explored her space with her hands and realised she was totally enclosed. And the rumble, it was road noise. She realised she was in the boot of a car, but alive and relatively unhurt. She thought of Lesley, she hoped those two bastards hadn't harmed her. She would be severely traumatised as it was.

She heard muffled voices coming from beyond the carpeted partition in front of her. Not totally clear, but it was Quintel and Jason, she was certain of that. She cupped her hands around her forward facing ear as she strained to listen.

'Why didn't we just do her back there, Boss?' Jason asked.

'Two reasons; one, it would be easier to dispose of the body if we do her where we bury her,' Quintel said.

Dread coursed through Christine now at the realisation of her predicament. She no longer felt the pain at the back of her head, or acknowledged any discomfort from her physical incarceration. Dread and fear were tempered by the driven need to escape and flee. But why would these animals want her dead?

Quintel continued, 'And secondly, she mentioned Dempster. That made things personal. To her we are more than two random killers fulfilling a contract. She knows us, and I want to know how and why?'

Contract? Christine thought. Had she heard correct? Who would want her dead? Ok, her documentary might flatten a few pints of Guinness for those concerned, but this was taking it a bit far. She wracked her brains to think of all those she had spoken to over the previous weeks whom she might have upset.

'Any problems slotting her sister?' Quintel asked.

'Ah, I was meaning to tell you about that.'

'What?'

'I was about to pull the trigger when I heard someone banging on the front door, and I mean banging.'

'So?' Quintel said.

'Well, you were out back waiting in the motor, and it sounded like trouble. If anyone had come around the back you'd have been blocked in.'

'You saying it was the filth at the door?'

'Well, it didn't sound like the postie, so I legged it. Wanted to get the motor out as quickly as poss.'

'I thought you took off a bit smartish,' Quintel said.

Christine hadn't realised she'd been holding her breath until she exhaled loudly on hearing that Lesley was still alive, thank God.

Jason continued, 'You're not mad at me then, Boss?'

'No, if you are right and it was the plod at the door, they'd have come straight in on hearing gunfire.'

'That's what I thought,' Jason said.

'But you'll have to go back at some stage and sort it permanently.'

Christine shivered on hearing the last. The conversation ended then, and she tensed as she was slung to one side, again. She then spent the next few minutes searching her space for a weapon of some kind but wasn't having any immediate luck. She did notice a change from the road noise though; it was louder and more uniform. She also noticed that the car was staying on a straight course. They must be on a dual carriageway, or a motorway she reckoned. They were obviously going on a journey; it would give her more time to keep searching. Then she remembered her phone, but a quick search proved negative, not that she'd held out much hope on that one, so she returned to groping around the inside of the boot space.

*

Vinnie started with a gentle knock on the half-glazed door, but received no answer. He stood back to take in the narrow town house and noticed that the upstairs window curtains were closed. And even though it was still quite light outside, he could tell that the electric light in the room was switched on. The sun had disappeared over the rooftops behind him now and was starting to cast long shadows where he was stood. The electric light was clearly emitting around the curtains' edges. Someone in? Or had the lights been left on? He decided it was the former as the sun had only just gone over the rooftops; twenty minutes earlier and the front of Lesley's house would still have been bathed in sunlight. He knocked again. No answer.

He bent down and opened the lateral letter box which was in the centre of the door, and thought he saw a shadow cast down the staircase. Well, not a shadow as such, but a change in the ambient internal illumination. He called through the letterbox saying he was a friend of Christine's, he'd guessed what he'd seen was someone opening the upstairs door onto the landing, so knew someone was home. He held back from shouting "Police", as he didn't want to scare Lesley. Hopefully using Christine's name would be enough. Then he saw the light darken slightly. Had she returned to the bedroom? He stood up and banged louder this time, even if it scared her, he knew she was in and he had to speak to her. She'd obviously made a conscious decision to ignore the front door. He knocked once more. Nothing.

He banged again, louder this time, and was considering now using the "Police" line when he saw a shadow coming down the stairs. He couldn't see clearly through the frosted glass but it was definitely a "someone". He stood back and reached in his pocket for his warrant card, but noticed the figure turn at the bottom of the stairs and head toward the rear of the house. He bent down to the letter box again but got a shock when he looked through it. The figure was the back of a large man in casual clothes. Vinnie shouted but the man didn't look back - instead he started to run.

The front door swung open at the first kick, and Vinnie was about to tear after the man when he heard a muffled cry of anguish from upstairs.

It's inbuilt in cops that their first duty is to protect life; arresting offenders and preventing crime come after that. He bounded up the stairs and was in the front bedroom in seconds. He saw the originator of the cries bound and gagged on the bed, and presumed it was Lesley. He told her who he was and carefully pulled back the tape from her mouth first, but before he could ask her anything, she spoke.

'I'm ok, you've just missed them, go, go, they've taken my sister.'

Vinnie was down the stairs in seconds and through the kitchen and the open back door seconds later. He could hear a car engine revving and rushed to the gate which led into a narrow, single track rear alleyway. As he ran through the gate, he could see the rear of a blue saloon, possibly a Toyota, screeching out of the end of the back entry, and then turning left from view. He couldn't see the rear number plate clearly due to all the dust whipped up by the speeding car's tyres, but he did see two Zs together as part of the number. He considered running through the house to get into the Volvo to try and give chase, but they were long gone, and he needed to help Lesley. He pulled his mobile phone out and dialled three nines.

Chapter Thirty-Nine

Thirty, forty minutes passed, or was it longer? To Christine it felt like she'd been in there for a couple of hours, so she reckoned on an hour. She tried to see the time on her watch, but it was too dark. Then the car started decelerating and the turns, lefts and rights, resumed. She felt her heart rate quicken. Wherever they were going, they were nearly there. Then the car slowed some more, and then it stopped. She heard one of them get out and then heard the unmistakable sound of a steel roller shutter door. The car door shut and the car was driven into a building. The boot was filled with slices of light from around its sides and she heard the engine stop, and the car rocked as both men got out. She'd not been able to find a weapon earlier, so quickly used the extra light to search properly. Something moved under her hip. She could hear Quintel and Jason talking quietly, as if they didn't want her to hear, which she couldn't, but it struck her as daft as they'd talked normally when they'd been in the car. She paid no attention; she was more interested in why the floor had moved. Then it struck her, the spare tyre bay.

How could she have not thought of that before? She'd have to move fast, and she did, but desperately trying to do so without alerting her kidnappers. She found the tyre underneath a piece of hardboard which had been under the carpet she'd been laid on. And thankfully, what she was searching for was on top of the tyre and not beneath it. She quickly pulled the short-handled wheel brace out and put it in the inside pocket of her jacket. She then put everything back in its place and still had the presence of mind to pull her skirt down. She listened as her breathing slowly returned to normal.

She could only hear one voice now and it was Quintel's, he was talking in between pauses; he must be on the phone. And thankfully, he was one of those annoying people who subconsciously talk loudly when on a mobile. Those people annoyed her in normal life; but she was grateful now. She listened in.

'Look, it's only a small favour, not like the last one,' Quintel said, followed by a pause.

'And you were fucking paid well, don't forget that.'

Pause.

'There is someone who seems to know our business, and I want to know how, and how much?'

Pause.

'Of course I'm going to ask her, I just thought you might help me judge if she bullshits me.'

Christine felt a stab of fear as she heard Quintel pass her details and that of her employer to whoever he was talking to.

'I know they are supposed to report the facts, but you said the clowns had no idea where we are, or what we've done, apart from that undercover twat, Charlie or whatever his name was? The one you knew fuck all about. Yeah, yeah. Never mind that now.'

Christine was shocked, and then she heard Quintel again.

'But she mentioned one of my dogsbodies, and I thought you said they know fuck all – er, it was Dempster's name she used. She's obviously spoken to him, and he's not told me the press were sniffing around.'

Pause.

'Yeah, Dempster.'

Pause.

'You leave that twat to me, he's already had the hard word, and it's about to get harder.'

Pause.

'No, don't shit your pants; I'm not going to kill him. You just find out from the top pig what you can and ring me straight back.'

Christine then heard Quintel's voice lower again; he was off the phone and probably speaking to Jason.

'I know it might be nothing, but Dempster knows a lot about you, and that could lead to me.'

'Look Boss, Dempster's no hero, he might have had the press nosing around but so would a lot of scrotes on that estate,' Jason said.

'Yeah, but she obviously knows he's linked to us.'

'Yeah, that's a worry.'

'Look, I'm going for a shit; get the bitch out of the motor, and tie her to that chair, then we can have a little chat with her before we slot her,' Quintel said.

Christine heard two sets of footsteps, one going away from her, and the other getting louder. She kept her eyes shut and played dead as the boot lid opened. Through her closed eyelids she could see bright light invading her pupils.

'Wakey, wakey,' Jason said in a singsong way, just before he slapped her hard across her face, reawakening the sore nerves from the earlier strike at Lesley's. She couldn't help but cry out as she opened her eyes and blinked against the bright lights.

'Think I'm heaving you out of there? You must be joking. So get out, nice and easy, or I'll hit you properly.'

Christine moved as slowly as she felt she could get away with, as if she'd just come round. Jason stood back as she carefully orientated herself out of the boot space while trying to keep her skirt at a dignified length. She didn't want to give either of these monsters any ideas.

She took in her environment as quickly as she could; they were in a small one-car sized motor garage with work benches by two walls, and a door covered in oily handprints leading to somewhere in the rear. The walls were made of grey and blue breezeblock and the steel roller shutter door behind the car was closed, though she did notice a normal sized steel door next to it. It looked as if the lock on it was a Yale type one.

'Come on hurry up and get your arse on that chair,' Jason said, pointing to an orange coloured plastic chair in front of the car; the ones with a large hole at the back of the seat that had been all the rage in colleges and schools twenty years ago.

Christine walked towards the chair, her back to Jason, as she felt the wheel brace with the elbow of her left arm. She knew it wouldn't be too long before Quintel returned. She saw some rope thrown over the back of the chair. Jason obviously intended to tie her to it; it was now or never. She knew she was no match physically against Jason, so had to make the first strike count. She slipped her right hand into the inside of her jacket while her back was still to Jason, and took a firm grip on the cold steel shaft. As she turned to sit down she launched her attack.

She pulled the bar out as she swung around and kept her right arm swinging in a wide arc towards Jason's head, hoping the movement would enhance the power of the strike like some demented shot put thrower. She could see the look of surprise in Jason's eyes, but knew that the advantage would be short lived. The L shaped end of the bar – the bit that normally fastens onto the wheel nut itself – was the business end of her weapon and missed Jason's head as he started to react, pulling his head backwards, away from the arc of attack. But he didn't manage to get completely out of the way, as the end of the brace smashed into the side of his nose.

Christine heard the satisfying crack of breaking cartilage as her arm continued on its orbital path past Jason's head. He screamed out as a jet of blood shot from his nostrils down his front. He staggered backwards, dazed, and Christine brought her backhand into play as she returned the brace in a reverse motion. All those years playing tennis as a teenager were now paying off; she'd always had a strong return serve.

This time she stepped towards Jason as she struck and the end of the brace caught Jason squarely on the side of his head, somewhere near his temple, and he went down fast. She could see a nonplussed gaze in his eyes before he hit the ground. Euphoria and adrenaline coursed through her as she turned to face the door with the Yale lock. She was towards it before Jason was fully grounded. She dare not look behind her as she reached the door and started to turn the Yale lock and pull the heavy steel door open. She couldn't believe she'd done it, all ten stone of her against a large ape like Jason.

She pulled on the door as it started to open wider, and then she heard a deafening sound. A roar of gunfire, which seemed incredibly loud in the confined space of the garage. She heard it at the same time as she saw sparks fly off the door towards her and the door fly out of her hand back into its frame.

She frantically reached for the door once more.

Chapter Forty

By the time Vinnie had untied Lesley and removed the gaffer tape, the first of the cop cars arrived, followed by an ambulance which took a very shaken Lesley away. The local on-call DI was next to land and Vinnie quickly gave her the details of what happened and the background to it. He said he'd sort out a written statement later and send it to her but for now he was more worried about Christine. The local DI said the description of the vehicle including the part registered number had been circulated across the region. She said that an analyst would be playing around with the ZZ to try and identify all blue Toyota saloons which had a double zed in their number, but it would take time, and there might be quite a few nationally but hopefully only a few in the Manchester area. He just hoped it was a Toyota, he wasn't 100 per cent sure, but didn't say so.

'Why take her?' the local DI had asked. Vinnie only wished he knew.

Then the local DI's personal radio burst into life. CCTV at a nearby motorway junction had seen a blue Toyota with at least one Z in its number plate join the M6 north. The operator hadn't been able to see anything other than one Z, but would review the tape shortly. M6 North; Preston? They now knew Jason hailed from the city, it was thirty to forty miles away from Manchester, and he'd have contacts there. Vinnie said his goodbyes as the local DI's attention turned to preserving the crime scene, and he legged it to his Volvo.

Ten minutes later, he was on the northbound carriageway which was fortunately quite light of traffic as the rush hour was long over. He floored the motor and kept the speedometer in three figures. He had no idea exactly where he was going, but it felt good to be doing something. He put his mobile into the car's hands free Bluetooth device and called Harry, who was still at Preston having just finished his first meeting. He said he'd hang on there in case Vinnie needed any help. Preston is served by five motorway junctions and as Vinnie neared he was wondering which to take. Then he remembered Dempster, he wouldn't bother ringing ahead and spooking him, he would have a face to face with him; he might have an idea where they'd take Christine, if nothing else. But none of this made any sense. Though at least one thing seemed obvious; if they'd meant to kill her they would have surely done it at Lesley's, why go to the trouble of taking her with them otherwise?

Vinnie aimed for junction 31A which was the Longridge turnoff that served numerous commercial estates in the vicinity. It was also the nearest to Ribbleton, where Dempster lived. Then he got a call from Harry.

'Go ahead,' Vinnie said.

'CCTV has sighted a possible; it's a Blue Toyota with two Zs,' Harry said before giving Vinnie the full registration number.

'Seen leaving the M6 ten to fifteen minutes ago-ish at junction 31A.'

'I'm just approaching there now.'

'Excellent. I've also put a call into Major Crompton and he says according to Jason's old military personal file he had a relative who ran a small motor garage on an industrial estate near to junction 31A.'

Vinnie felt his mood soar on hearing this. Harry gave him the address and said he'd meet him there. He asked Vinnie to identify an RV nearby so they could have a stealthy look before sending in the boys and girls in blue.

Vinnie agreed, although his heart was telling him just to get there and get inside with no delay, but his head agreed with Harry. A covert recce was needed until they knew what they were facing. He just hoped they were guessing right.

Vinnie's first stop was at a large controlled entrance to the estate. It had barriers across the road in and out, but they were both up. He quickly identified himself to a bored looking security guard, who did say that the last vehicle to enter the site had been a blue one with two blokes on board, but more than that he couldn't say, but it had been about twenty minutes ago. He then gave Vinnie directions to the garage unit and five minutes later Vinnie pulled up short on a cul-de-sac which was off one of the main perimeter roads. It was poorly lit in the twilight, but Vinnie guessed it would perversely become easier to see as darkness fell properly and what lighting there was could take some effect.

He pulled up by unit 41B which was set back from the road. He could see that there were several units on both sides of the narrow road leading to a free-standing brick built unit at the end, with a large steel up-and-over door. Behind it was a thicket of established trees. He texted Harry his RV who rang him straight back, and said he had uniform on stand-by at Junction 31A awaiting confirmation and instructions. He told Vinnie to sit tight as he was only a few minutes away.

Vinnie ended the call and then turned the ringer off, before quietly alighting and walking towards the garage at the end, sticking to the shadows as he crept.

Chapter Forty-One

'I just hope for your sake that no nosy fucker heard that gunshot. Because if any security guard comes prying then their death will be down to you, bitch,' Quintel said.

Christine couldn't believe how her fortunes could change so dramatically in an instant. Getting the better of Jason had been more about good luck and surprise, she knew, but seeing the door shoot out of her hands like that had been a shock. She'd frozen on hearing the gun and the hesitation had cost her dearly. She tried to make her herself comfortable, but gave up. Jason had tied her to the chair with vigour. He was clearly embarrassed. He kept pacing up and down across the front of the car as Quintel addressed her.

'Tell me again about how you know Dempster, and don't bull me or your other cheek will match the red one.'

She repeated how she'd just been doing her job as a reporter, going on the knocker, and how someone had told her that Dempster was the local oracle. Christine had hardly finished her sentence when Quintel made good his threat with a stinging backhand across her face. It hurt like hell and would have knocked her onto the floor but for her restraints. She took a moment to recover the worst of the blow and then said, 'You should take up tennis.' She'd be dammed if she was just going to sit there and whimper in front of these bullies.

'What? Do you think this is a game? We'll see if you still feel like telling jokes when I hand you over to Jason.'

Christine glanced at the prancing Jason, moving like a tiger in a cage, and suddenly lost some of her resolve.

'I accept what you've told me, but why did you mention Dempster to me back at your sister's house? Why do you relate Dempster to us? Tell me that and I'll let you go,' Quintel said.

Oh God, what had she done? She thought. She'd no answer for that.

'And although I didn't see it, I'm amazed at how easily you took care of Jason. You are some kind of reporter?'

'I'm not a cop, if that's what you mean,' Christine said, adding, 'haven't you seen me on TV?'

'No I haven't, but I do know you are one of those nosy bastard types, and apart from sticking your snout into my affairs, which has come as an added shock, you have been nosing around into the affairs of others, haven't you?

This must be to do with the documentary, though she'd still no idea why, or how?

'You might be a reporter on the surface, but you could be some kind of police or government asset as well.'

'I told you, Boss, it was just a lucky hit, no finesse, she isn't no pro,' Jason said from behind her. She couldn't believe what Quintel was suggesting.

'Well, I'll just have to take your word on that, won't I?' Quintel said as he looked towards Jason.

'Honest, it's like he said, I got lucky; whatever you think of me, I'm just a nosy reporter, and I don't know any of your business, honest.'

'So who gave you my name if not, Dempster,' Quintel said.

Christine knew she had to be careful now, if she let Quintel suspect Dempster, he would be a dead man. She'd have to tell them something approaching the truth. 'Ok, look I just heard your name mentioned as a suspect by one of the cops, that's all. It wasn't Dempster, but I think the cops suspect Dempster of helping big villains, and you are obviously a top operator, so it's not such a stretch.'

'That still doesn't fully...,' Quintel started to say, before his ringing phone stopped him. He took the call, as he wandered towards the rear door. He listened for a while, and then said, 'So she could well know my name?'

Pause.

'Who is this Vinnie Palmer then...I see...ok,' then he ended the call.

Christine's heart sank on hearing Quintel speak Vinnie's name, but then calmed herself a little - it was obvious that his details were publically linked to the murder of Charlie and the fire, but who the hell was Quintel talking to? Was it Dempster? Was that little runt playing them all off against each other? She recalled Vinnie telling her how hard it could be sometimes running informants. "Like trying to train a cat" was how he'd explained it.

Then Quintel's phone rang again, he didn't look too chuffed as he looked to see who was calling, he sighed and then took the call. He turned his back towards her again, and seemed to be more cautious than when taking the previous call, whatever that meant. Then she heard her name and fear stabbed at her once more. She listened as Quintel raised his voice slightly, before he ended the call. She wished she hadn't.

'Of course I will, I know it's what you're paying me for. I'll do it now.'

Christine started to struggle against her ties as Quintel headed towards her with purpose in his step. She was about to scream for all she was worth when gaffer tape arrived from behind across her mouth. That distraction stopped her from seeing what hit her, but a vicious side-swipe to her right temple sent her into darkness once more.

*

'Thank you Jason, I was getting tired of listening to her whiny voice.'

'No problem, Boss. What did the man say?'

'Which one?'

'Both, I guess.'

'Our friend reckons she'll have got our name from this Palmer cop who is chasing us for doing that undercover rat.'

'Makes sense.'

'And they obviously know or suspect Dempster is on the payroll.'

'Do you want me to have another word with him?'

'No, Jason, I want you to kill the little shit, once we are all done here, but we have other business first, he'll wait. As for our paymaster, he just rings to state the bleeding obvious.'

'What about her?'

'I'm done with her now. It's time to complete the contract on her. Take her out the back into those woods and do her.'

'It'll be my pleasure, Boss.'

Chapter Forty-Two

Vinnie could see a shaft of light from under the roller shutter door as he approached. He stood very still and listened. He couldn't hear anything, which told him nothing. Should he wait for Harry? Probably. Then he heard a noise, a scrapping of feet, there was definitely someone in there. He glanced down at the concrete ramp which led under the big door. It was dry but there was a small pool of water where the ramp and the gutter from the road met. He could see drying tyre marks where a motor had been driven inside, through a puddle. It was all adding up. He decided to recce the rest of the single-storey stand-alone building, at the very least, before Harry landed. He checked his phone for any silent messages, but there weren't any. Where the hell was he?

Vinnie slinked around the perimeter of the garage, grateful for the failing light and the fact that the building didn't seem to have any windows. He stopped by the corner which led to the rear and peered around the edge. He immediately saw light shining out from the building towards a thicket of trees at the rear. The illumination was coming via an open rear door which was flat to the wall, probably a fire door. He was about to slide around the corner and creep towards the door when he heard a rustling sound coming from the woods. He froze and dropped down to a squat. Out of the gloom appeared a figure walking towards the rear door. It wasn't until the figure neared the entrance before Vinnie was sure. It was Jason. He was covered in what looked like sand, and was brushing his arms as he walked straight inside the rear of the building.

Vinnie hurried around the corner, worried Jason would close the door after him, but as he walked inside he just pulled it to and it clanged against its frame, but then re-opened an inch. When Vinnie reached the apparently closed door he saw that it was a fire door and that the lateral bar had dropped open wider than the door itself, which was why it hadn't shut properly when Jason had pulled it closed behind him. He half expected Jason to realise and the door to suddenly open again only to close properly, but nothing happened. It was a piece of luck Vinnie couldn't risk waiting to share with Harry.

He slowly pulled the door open expecting light to flood outwards once more, but he found himself in relative darkness. Inside he could see an inner door six feet ahead which was closed. Light seeped from underneath it, from where he guessed was the main unit space. Then he heard a voice. One he recognised from listening to the dead undercover officer - Charlie's - tapes from his meetings with Quintel and Jason. It was Quintel.

'All done?'

'Yeah, I didn't want to risk using the gun so did it quietly?' said a second voice from those tapes – Jason.

'How do you mean? You've been quick,' said Quintel.

'We've got away with the sound of gunfire once, so I didn't want to risk shooting her. She was well out of it when I buried her. She'll not be waking up. Luckily there's been some ground work done out there, looks like they are putting a sand base in to soak up the water. Loads of pre-dug trenches.'

Vinnie's heart nearly stopped. He quickly drew his handgun and opened the inner door and stepped inside to face a very surprised looking Quintel and Jason.

'Who the fuck are you?' Quintel said.

Vinnie quickly glanced around before he spoke. No sign of Christine. There in front was the blue motor with the two Zs, and in front of that an orange plastic chair with rope laid across it. 'Police, so don't try anything stupid, and keep your hands where I can see them.' But as he spoke, both men had already separated, each now at a forty-five degree angle to him. 'Where's the woman you kidnapped?'

'I take it you must be Palmer?' Quintel said.

Vinnie was taken momentarily by surprise with Quintel using his name, but he kept moving his gun arm's aim in an arc between both men.

'Where is she?' Vinnie said, as he focused on Quintel for a second, before aiming his gun at a stationary Jason.

'You can go and join her if you like,' Quintel said.

And in the instant of distraction Quintel's chilling remark caused, Vinnie heard a thunderous noise coming from Jason's direction. He instinctively turned towards it and felt a jet of hot air race past his right ear, followed by the dull thud of something burying itself into the wooden inner door behind him.

As he pulled the trigger of his own gun, he saw the gun in Jason's hand as the recoil of his arm ended. Jason was in the process of taking aim once more.

'You missed the fucker,' he heard Quintel say as he kept his focus on his target this time. He saw the blue yellow flash of fire discharge from the mussel of his Glock as he also saw blood erupt from Jason's chest. More flew from his back at the same time, and splattered over the bonnet of the Toyota.

Vinnie felt as if time had nearly stopped, even though everything seemed to have happened at once. Focused in a tunnel of concentration, he watched as Jason fell backwards. His gun clattered onto the concrete floor before his body landed. He ran over to Jason but before he could feel for a pulse, he saw the lifeless glazed stare from his soulless eyes telling him all he needed to know. It was a look he was sure he would never forget. A quick feel at Jason's left carotid artery confirmed he was dead.

Then time caught up as blood started to pool from underneath Jason, and Vinnie swung around with his gun arm outstretched once more towards where Quintel had been standing. But no one was there.

Chapter Forty-Three

The sound of the gunfire in the enclosed space of the garage was still ringing like tinnitus in both of Quintel's ears as he ran through the woodland. Such a pity that he'd had to leave his gun in the boot of the car, not to mention the car itself. But he'd had to take his chances while that daft copper stared at his handiwork. He knew from what Jason had told him in the past just how inaccurate handguns were unless used really close up. There had probably been about twenty feet between them; the cop just got lucky; twice.

He could see what Jason had meant earlier. Running through the foliage, he saw several trenches dug, some empty and some part-filled with sand, with large piles of building sand all about. It was no doubt to do with flood defences, water table levels or whatever to guard against all the rain they seemed to be suffering from since the globe got warmer. But looking on the bright side, but for this, Jason would probably have not got back before the cop had arrived. And as his gun was in the boot of the car, it could have been his claret and flesh plastered all over. Quintel liked to think of it as the survival of the fittest rather than chance, or good luck. The natural order of things. As useful as Jason was, and as good as his company also was, it was simply the way. Poor Jason, though it would mean more dosh for Quintel. His only regret was having had to leave that copper Palmer back there; he'd have loved to have had the opportunity to do him, just for the fun of it.

It didn't take too long before he was through the woods and down by a brook, which did look very full. He knew this place would be crawling with filth in a few minutes, and that also meant filth dogs, not to mention helicopters, no doubt. He couldn't do too much about the pigs in the sky, other than to hope for some cloud cover, but he could frustrate the dog filth. He jumped into the brook and went in up to his waist. He'd clamber through it for as long as he could bear it. As far as he knew, water always ended scent trails. Then he felt spots of water falling on to his face, and smiled to himself, another stroke of the royal order of things; not luck. He made his own luck.

*

'Armed police. Drop your weapon and put your hands on the top of your head. Then kneel down. Do it now.' The voice behind Vinnie demanded.

It wasn't the first time this had happened to him; he hoped it didn't become a habit. Christ he didn't have time for this. At least the cops' arrival brought him back to the here and now. He did as he'd been told but added who he was and that his warrant card was in his inside jacket pocket.

'That won't be necessary officer, I can confirm what he's saying,' said Harry.

Vinnie turned around, relieved to hear Harry's voice, and saw that the three armed cops behind him were now lowering their weapons. He stood up, but before he could say anything, Harry continued.

'When I said "locate an RV and wait", which bit of that did you not get?'

'I—' was as far as Vinnie got.

'You nearly got yourself killed, and now we have one dead suspect and the other one on his toes, thanks to your insubordination. I should suspend you right here and
now,' Harry finished.

Vinnie could see how angry Harry was by the redness of his face. He half expected him to start rubbing his head next.

'Boss, I'll explain why later, but we haven't got time for this now. You've got to help me search. It might already be too late,' Vinnie said, and then explained how he had seen Jason returning from out back covered in sand, and the conversation he'd overheard him have with Quintel.

'Come on then,' Harry said, and Vinnie followed him out the back door as he told the uniform cops to secure the scene and to get others to start an area search.

'What about the dog units?' the cop who challenged Vinnie asked.

'Preserve the immediate route from the back. And suggest when they arrive to get a scent from inside the car. Get a second dog to run a trail from the boot of the motor; just in case they had Christine, er I mean the kidnap victim in there. We are going to need all the help we can get.'

'Got that, sir, they should be here any minute.'

174

'Good,' Harry said adding, 'but no one else goes in there apart from the paramedic to confirm death.'

Vinnie and Harry then took a circular route from the back door. Vinnie led and retraced the way he'd initially approached the rear of the unit from, until they were at the building's edge, and then he ran towards the trees at the rear. In a couple of minutes the trees thinned out to a glade which ran towards a brook. A digger sat unattended by several piles of sand, tons of the stuff, and all around were a variety of long trenches. Some half filled with rocks, and others filled completely with sand level with the grass. They both came to a standstill and Vinnie looked around for recent signs of disturbance, but the whole place was a mess, and the rain which was now falling was just adding to it.

There must have been twenty or thirty ditches, some short and some long. Where to start?

'We are going to need some help here, it could take ages,' Harry said.

Before Vinnie could answer he heard someone approaching from behind. He turned to see a uniformed dog handler with an Alsatian on a mission. His hopes raised a little, but were tainted with the fear of what they might find. The dog and handler powered through the clearing and headed straight for the brook.

'Picked up two scents from the car, Boss. Driver's seat went straight to the deceased, and this is from the passenger seat,' the dog handler said.

Vinnie's heart sank.

'What about the car boot?' Harry asked.

'My mate's got that but her dog's only showing interest in the chair,' the dog handler shouted over his shoulder as he raced towards the stream.

Vinnie had a crushingly bad feeling about this now. He could see it in Harry's eyes too. That bastard Jason must have carried Christine out of the unit. He knew now this was no longer a rescue mission, but a recovery one. He knew how much he liked Christine, and how his fondness had been deepening at a fast rate. But the thought that she was gone hit him far harder than he could have imagined. He was glad he'd disobeyed Harry now, even if it meant Quintel had escaped. They'd catch him eventually. He was just glad he'd had the chance to kill that bastard Jason. Any post-operative shock he'd first felt in the garage was long gone. Replaced with a primeval rush of morbid satisfaction.

Harry broke his thoughts as he approached Vinnie and handed him one of two spades he'd found by the digger.

'I know you two were good friends, so if you rather not…,' Harry said.

'It's ok, Harry but thanks. I just want to find her, and grant her some dignity, and two sets of hands are better than one. We need every spare uniform going after Quintel.'

'Looks like he's jumped into the water, Boss,' the dog handler shouted back from the banks of the brook. 'I'll track up and down both banks for a while, to try and pick up where he gets out.'

Harry acknowledged him as they each started to dig at separate trenches.

After only five minutes Vinnie was wet with sweat and his clothes on the outside were becoming damper as the light rain started to fall heavier.

'Time to stop, Vinnie,' Harry said as he glanced up at the sky, 'we'll cordon the whole place off and get a full search team in here first light to do it properly. If she is here, and remember, we still don't know for sure, then I think we are well past the time where she could be still alive. He probably, you know; first anyway.'

'I think we should turn a search team out now and get them to carry on with lighting, just in case.'

Harry looked tired as he paused before nodding, and then said, 'I suppose it's still an if, Vinnie. I mean you didn't hear Jason say he'd *actually* killed Christine?'

Vinnie could feel anger rising through his weary body, but reached deep within himself to control it. He reminded Harry about hearing Jason say something about not wanting to use his gun.

'Not good,' Harry said, adding, 'we'll turn a search team out and wait here until they arrive.'

'Thanks, Harry, but until we find a body, there has to be hope.'

'I'll use that line if they whinge about the cost, which they will.'

Vinnie nodded as he picked up the spade and continued to dig.

Chapter Forty-Four

Christine opened her eyes, or had she? The last thing she remembered was blackness. The first thing she saw now was blackness. She opened her eyes to blackness. Well, it seemed black; perhaps it was a dark blue. It was hard to say. Was this reality? She felt numbness all around, its edges softened in keeping with her vision. But was it vision? Was she seeing? Or was this a dream? Could it be something else altogether? All these questions flooded through her in an instant. Then in a further moment stretched in time, she realised she was breathing. She must be alive. She breathed deeper, but had to spit something from her mouth. As the extra oxygen fed her senses, her thoughts started to crystallise. As that second fleeting moment ended, clarity coursed through her with a searing pain from the back of her head, as her senses started to attune. It wasn't too bad, but bad enough.

She realised she was prostrate. She started to turn, spitting something out again. Loose grit or sand she realised. She was able to turn easier than she might have expected. The sand enveloping her was loose, but it weighed down on her nonetheless. As she turned, the blackness stayed. Was she up or down? She panicked for a second, until she realised the sand, now against her back, was firmer than that on her front. She must be the right way round now. It brought hope but it was still mixed with terror, like some caustic cocktail. She felt cold, very cold, but could still sense perspiration all over her. She opened her mouth to scream, but more sand fell in, she spat it out and tried to raise her arms instead. She felt some leverage, but it was tough going. Fear was winning, and she desperately tried to keep calm. Tried to retain her focus as she reached upwards.

*

Ten minutes later and lighting rigs arrived, as did the crime scene investigators. Harry had a quick word with the CSIs whilst the illumination kit was put in place. Vinnie carried on, but was mightily relieved to see the lighting kick in. The lamps were powered by a portable diesel generator, and Vinnie could feel the heat from the bulbs warming him. It spurred him on. It had also stopped raining now, which helped. He stood back and looked at the ground they had covered and the vastness of the task ahead. Vinnie had started to think that Harry was right, looking at the size of the area: the search team were on their way, perhaps he should wait until they got here. Then a uniform cop approached, he was one of the armed response vehicles' crews. He offered Vinnie another Glock handgun, saying, 'Your own gun's been bagged and tagged, sir. Here's a replacement. If you'll just sign this form.'

Vinnie did as instructed and put the weapon away in his shoulder holster. It would probably get in the way now if he carried on digging. Then he shook his head at himself, and reached for the spade once more.

*

Christine kept scratching away at the sand, but as soon as she made any progress more fell in to fill the gap. But at least she knew she was facing the right way now. She also realised that the sand was damp. This seemed to make it harder to shift, but it had created air pockets. She kept her head to one side and took advantage of the trapped air, even though it was in short supply. She stopped for a rest, her arms now feeling like lead. She needed to rest, if only for a moment. Then she felt suddenly becalmed in a strange way. The terror that she'd been fighting had all but ebbed away. An eerie serenity numbed her all over. She realised she was no longer cold.

Then a crazy thought hit her; was this it? But instead of fearing an answer to her question, the very consideration of it seemed to remove all of her remaining terror. Peacefulness and extreme tiredness were taking over now. She knew the answer, but wasn't afraid. Sleep was coming, but it would be more than sleep. She opened her eyes for what she knew would probably be the last time and could now see shards of light. Daggers of brilliance confirming her thoughts. She welcomed the release. As she closed her eyes again; one last thought raced across her; she saw Vinnie's face and wondered, what could have been?

Chapter Forty-Five

Quintel couldn't believe his luck. He could hear a filth dog, but it was in the distance and definitely going the wrong way. It had been behind him, he was sure of that, which was why he'd stayed in the water. He could barely feel his legs now, but the noise had definitely done an about-turn. He clambered to the side and climbed up the muddy embankment. It was only then he realised just how cold he was. His shivering was almost rabid in severity, and his trousers were stuck to his legs as if they'd been vacuumed packed on to him. But none of that mattered, he was free.

He'd long passed the perimeter of the industrial estate and could see houses up ahead. He didn't know the area as well as Jason, obviously, but he could see the street lights marking out the main road back into Preston through Ribbleton. He knew exactly where to go to get himself sorted out; his infrastructure, albeit limited in Preston, would pay off nonetheless. And he could clear up some business at the same time.

*

It had been taking a long time to clear each trench. Vinnie was worried about thrusting the spade in and hitting Christine's body. If she was here, he was starting to accept the unthinkable. But the thought of hitting her with the spade, it would feel horrendous; like a fresh assault on her. So he'd been using the ditch edges, feeling his way in before scooping the sand out. And this way, when he hit the bedrock below, he knew what depth he was playing with.

He'd just started another ditch, a short one, and had gone down about a spade in depth when he felt something. His stomach churned as he threw his spade to one side and frantically used his hands to excavate the wet sand. Then he saw it sticking up; a hand. A woman's hand.

'Harry, here,' he yelled as he grabbed hold of it. It was cold, very cold, but not ice cold. But how cold would be too cold? He noticed Harry arrive, who started to dig with his fingers on the opposite side to where the hand was.

Harry was directly opposite to him; he was looking for the other hand.

'Found it,' Harry shouted, as Vinnie took a firm hold of his hand's cold wrist. His heart broke when he recognised the watch on the end of the arm he had hold of.

'Oh God no,' he exhaled as he pulled hard on the arm.

'Again,' Harry shouted as they both tugged in unison.

This time the loose sand gave up its hold and the top half of Christine's body broke free from the grit. Her head lolled forward, lifeless, as both he and Harry got a firmer purchase under each armpit and each heaved a further time in unity.

Vinnie rose from his knees as he pulled Christine's body from the pit, her head rolling from side-to-side as he and Harry managed to pry her entire body clear of the grave. They hauled her forward as her shoeless feet dragged loose ground behind; it was as if some demonic tentacles were trying to reattach their grip.

Over onto clear grass, they gently lay Christine's avatar down. Neither man had spoken. Then Vinnie realised his right hand was wet with sweat, but not warm like in his left palm; it was cold but definitely moist. It had been his right hand which he'd used to grab Christine's wrist. What this realisation actually meant he wasn't sure. Then he got his answer.

Christine coughed, and then spat out some sand.

'My God, she's still alive,' he screamed, as he watched Harry feel for a pulse. A touch arbitrary he thought, but probably instinctive.

'Weak, but definitely there,' Harry said.

Vinnie quickly put Christine into the recovery position and checked that her airway was clear. It was, bar some residue sand and grit which he scooped out with his finger. He put his cheek to her face and could feel her breath on it, gentle and slow, but regular, like a sleeping child might expel onto a caring parent's ear.

He could hear Harry on his radio calling for an ambulance. Vinnie still couldn't quite believe that Christine was alive. She'd seemed so dead when they'd dragged her from the earth, not a moment too soon, he was sure of that.

She coughed again, more forceful this time, and then inhaled sharply. Vinnie watched as she slowly exhaled and inhaled sharply again. Several respirations later, and Christine slowly opened her eyes, her gaze looked befuddled at first, but then clarity came.

'No,' she shouted, before seeming to take in her surroundings, as if waking with a nightmare still active. Then she seemed to focus on Vinnie' face before smiling and calming. She started to sit up and Vinnie helped her.

Once steadied, she looked around before returning her stare to Vinnie, 'You took your bloody time didn't you?'

Vinnie laughed and then threw his arms around her and kissed her gently on the cheek.

'Hey steady on,' Christine said, before coughing and then continuing, 'help me to my feet before this sand-musk drives you crazy.'

Vinnie couldn't believe it. Thank God they hadn't given up. He didn't know how much longer Christine would have lasted down there, and didn't want to contemplate it. Once her gyros had stopped spinning he and Harry helped her to Harry's car. She had come around remarkably quickly considering, though complained of a searing headache, and Vinnie could see that her hair was matted with blood at the back of her head; accentuated by a large swelling. Jason had knocked her out and probably thought he'd killed her, or that she'd die in her sleep soon enough once buried.

The medic arrived and said she would have to spend the night in hospital in case she'd suffered concussion. A normal precaution Vinnie knew with any head injury, but the paramedic was as sure as he could be that her skull hadn't suffered a fracture. He also added that the rain probably saved her, cloying the sand together as it did, and providing small pockets of air for her to breathe. She probably wouldn't have lasted much longer though, he said, in fact from what she'd described, she must have been very close to death.

An icy blast pierced Vinnie on hearing him say this. He was just so relieved he'd got to her in time, with not much harm done, physically, anyway. He couldn't even begin to imagine what it had been like for Christine when she had awakened; he just hoped that the memory of it didn't trouble her for too long. But only time would tell.

'How's Lesley?' Christine asked as she was being helped into the back of the ambulance.

'Don't worry, she's safe and well,' Vinnie replied, adding, 'do you want me to tell her you're ok?'

'Please, but don't mention what's happened. She'll have enough going round in her head after today. She'd only worry. Tell her I'm busy at the police station and I'll ring her later. I'll ring from the ward.'

'OK,' Vinnie said, adding, 'I'll be up to see you after. I've got a back-up pay-as-you phone in the boot of my car. I'll charge it up and bring it later.'

'Thanks and thanks. You're my hero, Vinnie. I'll never forget what you've done tonight.'

Vinnie could see her eyes welling up as she disappeared from view into the rear of the ambulance. The emotion of what she had been through was obviously starting to hit home. Seeing her become upset hit him too and he had to steel himself, so as not to join her. Then Harry's arm appeared around his shoulder.

'Come on, Vinnie, we've got a lot of writing to do now, and please ignore my earlier bollocking. We both know what would have happened if you'd waited. Not that you knew that of course,' Harry said, finishing his sentence with a smile on his face.

Chapter Forty-Six

Thirty minutes later and Quintel was banging on Dempster's front door. No reply. He stood back but could see no lights on, even though he was sure there had been some illumination edging from behind the closed upstairs curtains as he'd approached. Twat was hiding. He couldn't be arsed buggering about while he half-shivered to death, so he took a step back and booted the door in. It flew open on the first kick and as Quintel entered he heard movement upstairs. He closed the door behind him and immediately started to feel the warmth of the house start to de-chill him. It would take a while until his bones felt warm again; and probably much longer to get used to the smell.

Seconds later, the person responsible for the foul emissions came racing down the stairs, but slowed to a halt near the bottom when he saw it was Quintel.

'Don't worry, I'm not the filth. You will still need a new front door; but I guess you are used to that.'

'Mr Quintel, what's happened to you?'

'Shut up and find me some dry clothes, and they better be clean ones.'

Five minutes later, Quintel was wearing what he assumed was Dempster's Sunday best – a clean silver shell suit. He felt like an oven ready meal, but it would do. The trainers were a size too small, but would have to do until he could buy some fresh kit tomorrow. Now he needed a gun, but before that he needed a car. He told Dempster to go and borrow a motor from one of his pond life friends, but told him not to nick one, he needed clean wheels. He'd pay Dempster for it via the usual on-line account to include a heathy bonus. Or so he told him.

As Dempster was about to set off, he made him leave his mobile phone behind and asked where the nearest phone box was? Dempster looked confused.

'I need to make a secure call, and I don't want you to make any calls,' he explained, though the confused look on Dempster's face didn't alter. He then grabbed Dempster by the throat and pushed him up against the wall in the hall. 'If it had been up to me, I'd have been tempted to "off you" in that garage in Leyland. But Jay vouched for you, so don't let him down; or I will. Got it?'

Dempster nodded frantically and then asked, 'Where is Jay?'

'Just go,' he said, and he did. Quintel hadn't quite decided what to do with Dempster. Initially, he'd thought he'd take what he needed and then kill him, but he might still have his uses, for a while anyway. Once he brought the motor back Quintel would pay the shithead in Blackpool a revisit to re-arm. He considered asking Dempster to set up a meet with a local supplier, but he didn't really trust Dempster not to fuck it up. Knowing his history he'd probably introduce him to another undercover cop. No, Blackpool would do, it was only twenty odd miles away and would probably prove a safer place to hole down in the short term, rather than be right under the local plod's nose. It was certainly a more cosmopolitan town with its transient population. Though why anyone would want to holiday there was beyond him. It seemed full of gays, stags and hens to him.

As soon as Dempster had gone, Quintel found the phone box at the end of the street and texted the client the details as per his annoying security protocols. When the phone eventually rang, he answered it and spoke first, before rent-a-rant could get started. 'There's been a slight hitch.'

'What the fook does that mean?'

A redundant question Quintel thought as he hadn't yet given him a chance to explain, so he ignored it and carried on saying all that happened. When he had finished there was a surprising pause before the client responded.

'What a total fuck up.'

'Well, it was doing your little stocking-filler that brought it all on top.'

'So it's my fault is it? You cheeky twat.'

Anger was raging through Quintel now, but he knew he had to reign himself in; too much money was at stake. He paused, breathed and then spoke. 'Sorry, it's just been a trying day. But there are now no problems; I'm in the process of re-equipping myself through my embedded infrastructure,' he started, thinking it put Dempster and the Blackpool shithead on a grander scale than they deserved. Adding, 'And once I'm sorted out, which should be by tomorrow, I'll be ready for your main target, whoever that is?'

'I'm not paying you for removing the nosy reporter.'

'She *is* dead. Mission accomplished. But when the full contract is completed and there have been no further problems, I'll invite you to reconsider, but I won't hold you to it if you still feel the same,' Quintel said. After all, what was an extra ten grand when he was going to be getting a hundred grand now Jason's half was his.

'Too fooking true you won't. Look, the main man won't be easy to get at, are you sure you can complete it alone?'

Quintel knew it would be harder, but how hard could it be? Unless the target was some VIP, which he was sure it wasn't. He told the client not to worry. The line then remained open for what seemed like an age before the client spoke again.

'Look, sort yourself out but do nothing for the next twenty-four hours or until you hear from me again.'

As Quintel still didn't know the identity of the main target, he could hardly do anything else, but resisted the temptation for sarcasm, and just said, 'Ok.'

'Where will you be when I want you?' the client asked.

'Blackpool, probably, unless I have to leave for an unexpected reason, apart from a quick trip to Manchester.'

'What's in Manchester?'

'We hid the spare grenade when we left with the reporter; operational security, so I'll need to retrieve it.'

'Excellent,' the client said before ending the call.

Quintel wondered about the delay while he walked back to Dempster's house. He just hoped it was to do with the availability of the target or other logistics. But one thought troubled him; he hoped the client wasn't thinking of sending him a replacement for Jason. That could potentially cost him fifty large ones.

*

Two hours later, Quintel was driving a shitty Nissan Primera that looked like some of Dempster's relatives had been sleeping in it, but it would do, though he might have to get it valeted by one of those Kurdish run car washes that seemed to be everywhere nowadays.

He'd just had an interesting visit to the address off Central Drive where Jason and he had called at a few days earlier. This time the cocky little shithead couldn't do enough to help – especially given that currently he only had one good hand - he gave Quintel a boxed unfired Glock 17 pistol and loads of ammunition for free. Quintel said he wouldn't be bothering him again and he'd seemed relieved. The gun had come with two barrels; one of which had been cut at the end with a dye so a silencer could be screwed onto it. Or flash eliminator, as Jason would have called it. The cocky twerp had also thrown in a used silencer which fit.

Quintel tried the composite pieces out and found it remarkably easy to change the barrels and then fit the silencer. He had never used a silencer before but understood why they were called Flash Eliminators when he tried it out before he left. The flash was totally eliminated, as was the annoying cocky twat, whom neither he nor anyone else would ever be bothered by again.

Now it was time to find a hotel before it became too late. He didn't fancy sleeping in the motor.

Chapter Forty-Seven

Vinnie had just about started to feel warm again by the time he and Harry had finished writing their witness statements covering the day's events. It may be springtime but the temperature could still vary massively from one day to the next, especially as night time came. Harry had finished his deposition first and made a welcome brew. Vinnie finished his and sat back to take a sip.

'I still can't work out how or why Quintel and Jason came after Christine?' Harry said.

'I've been thinking about that too. At first I wondered whether it was something to do with the exposé she'd been working on, but I don't see how?'

'What was that again, exactly?'

Vinnie then briefed Harry as fully as he could.

'Well, if she did piss someone off suggesting the Catholic Republicans are getting more than their fair share of the peace cake; one, it's a bit extreme taking out a reporter, which you would think would only highlight the issue; and two, one hell of a coincidence that the disgruntled ex-IRA member concerned would hire Quintel and Jason to do it. Apart from anything else, they've got plenty of their own assassins or ex-assassins to use.'

'Exactly, and you know I don't believe in coincidences.'

'Or fairies, I know. So what then?'

'Dempster perhaps?'

Vinnie then told Harry how he'd asked Christine to do a random call on his behalf soon after Charlie had been murdered, and how they had discovered that Dempster had been the snout that introduced Charlie to Quintel and Jason.'

'Still doesn't add up,' Harry said.

'Nor to me. Look, I never got the chance to speak to Christine's source, nor Christine for that matter. I'll nip up and see her at the Royal Preston Hospital, give her this spare phone,' Vinnie said, removing an old Nokia from the desktop charger in front of him, adding, 'Have a quick chat and get Paul Bury's number from her.'

Harry looked at his watch, which prompted Vinnie to do the same; 10.05 pm.

'I'd come with you, but it's getting late and Darlington is waiting in his office to see me, so give her my best and keep me updated,' Harry said.

Vinnie said he'd ring him later, unless it got too late, and reached for his Volvo keys on his desk.

It only took ten minutes at this time of day to reach the vast hospital at the northern end of the city, and once he'd shown his warrant card he was soon walking down the main corridor of ward twenty. It was designed with bays containing four beds in each and he found Christine sat up by a window. She'd just finished using the trolley telephone and smiled as he approached. He sat down next to her bed and she spoke first.

'What, no kiss this time? It was the sand musk thing after all.'

Vinnie stood up and kissed her gently on her cheek. 'Better?'

'I was only kidding, but if it works?'

Vinnie asked her how she was, and she told him she should be released the following day. X-rays confirmed no fractures, just a small scalp wound, which they'd fixed with butterfly stitches, and a nice bump; but the painkillers were doing their job. 'It'll be a while before I can visit the hairdresser again though,' she added with a smile.

Vinnie gave her his spare phone and she thanked him. Her phone was in a million pieces back at Lesley's. He told her that he'd given Lesley a quick call as soon as he'd reached the office in Preston, and Christine thanked him, saying she'd just spoken to her and she seemed remarkably ok. Vinnie looked around and even though all the occupants of the other three beds seemed asleep he suggested they should talk some more in the day room.

As expected it was empty, and Christine told Vinnie all that had been asked of her, and thought it must be something to do with Dempster. He told her that they'd checked Dempster's address on their way back to the nick, just in case, though it would probably be the last place Quintel would go. 'And if he had, I'm confident Dempster would have belled me,' Vinnie said.

'What did he say?'

188

'Nothing. The house was all in darkness and there was no answer at the door. A neighbour confirmed he was out, had been all evening.

'But I've had another thought, a darker one; what if it is to do with the feature you are working on? I mean, how sure are you about your source, Paul Bury?'

'It would be a bit of a—' Christine started to say.

'Coincidence, I know,' Vinnie said, finishing off the sentence.

'And don't forget, Quintel did ask me why I'd mentioned Dempster's name?'

'You may have just hit a nerve when you used his name, but in the absence of anything to the contrary, I think you're right, so the threat's over. But just to be on the safe side, why don't we keep you under the radar?

'Without getting too elaborate, we could keep you out of the public eye and put out a press release saying a body has been found where you were...,' Vinnie said, not wanting to use the word "buried".

'It's ok, you can say it. No, I'm cool with that; in fact you don't have to say anything straight away.'

'True; it can take us a couple of days to "find you",' Vinnie said, adding, 'and even then we can say that the body is unidentified. Should buy us plenty of time to make sure the threat is over and that it was all Dempster related.'

Strategy agreed, Vinnie asked Christine for Bury's phone number, which thankfully she'd noted down in her diary. She told him that Bury had agreed to meet Vinnie so a call from him shouldn't spook him.

'What if he asks about me?' she added.

'I'll say I can't reach you, use that as a need to see him urgently. But first I think we both need a good night's sleep.'

Vinnie walked Christine back to her bed but stopped her while they were still alone, in the corridor.

'What's up?' she asked.

So he told her. He was wracked with guilt that this horrendous ordeal which she and Lesley had been through was all because he'd asked her to knock on Dempster's door. He said he would never forgive himself.

Typical Christine, she said that they couldn't possibly have guessed these unintended consequences, even if there was a link. And in any event, it all ended ok thanks to Vinnie; so he'd made good by any fault he was wrongly feeling.

He smiled, and thanked her for her words. He then felt a deep connection between them in the short pause that followed, but then broke it by saying that she should ring him as soon as she was discharged and he'd come and get her. He'd ring Paul Bury in the morning and hopefully set a meet for the afternoon. He pecked her other cheek, and said, 'Don't worry, Christine, I promise you I'll catch Quintel.'

'We'll catch Quintel together. I'm signed up all the way after what he did.'

Chapter Forty-Eight

Quintel checked the regional news channels over his fried breakfast, but they weren't giving much away. Spoke of a fatal shooting the night before, of a suspect who had already opened fire on a police officer. The chief constable of Lancashire, Brian Darlington, had said that the incident had been automatically referred to the Independent Police Complaints Commission to investigate. There would be a full press conference at twelve noon. There was no mention of finding the kidnapped TV reporter. Jason must have buried her well, bless him. In fact the bulletin he watched had made no link between the two incidents, which the recovered motor would no doubt provide. The filth were obviously keeping that little gem back for now. He could understand why, though. If they mentioned that the recovered car was the one believed used in the earlier kidnapping of one of the media's own, they'd be ragging Darlington non-stop.

Quintel smiled. There was a chance that plod wouldn't find her body at all. They might know the car was the one used, but they had no one to ask about it. It was probably as well that Jason hadn't survived.

After breakfast, Quintel went shopping in Blackpool and bought a holdall and some fresh clothes, the sooner he could get out of Dempster's favourite tin foil suit, the better. He'd already drawn too many sideway glances since booking into this four star hotel in Blackpool's South Shore district. Clothes sorted, he soon found a car wash place and had the motor cleaned up, the smell of Scandinavian Pine effectively masked the musk of whichever dirty bastard Dempster borrowed it from.

He then hit the M55 motorway which led to the M6 and then to the M61where he headed south towards Manchester until he came off at the Bolton West services. He had to walk over the bridge to the northbound side to retrieve the hand grenade Jason had stashed behind a tree the previous day. He was glad he'd got Jason to show him, in case they ever became split up; he was always thinking.

He was then going to head back to Blackpool, when he had a change of mind. He couldn't do anything until the client told him who the main target was, so he had a better idea. He'd head to Birmingham and go and see Jason's ex-army mate. He didn't have his phone number but felt sure he could remember how to get to the house. He'd met him with Jason, so there shouldn't be any problems. He fancied a further grenade and could do with a back-up gun. The only one worth having from the cocky twat he'd seen in Blackpool was now under the spare wheel in the boot of the Nissan.

It was late afternoon before Quintel arrived back at his hotel, all sorted. The Birmingham man had asked where Jason was, and Quintel wasn't sure he quite believed the load of fanny he'd given him as an excuse, but he'd still sorted him out.

He was now the proud owner of a second grenade, and a second Glock, and loads of ammo. He'd leave all the hardware in the boot of the car, safe in the knowledge that no one would want to nick that shit heap. But to be on the safe side he parked it on the hotel car park under a lamppost, where he could see it from his room. Then he headed to the hotel bar.

Three beers later and the client was texting him. Quintel had noticed a pay phone booth in the hotel lobby, so texted the details to the client, who told him to ring 'A'. The client picked up on the first ring.

'Did you get your logistics sorted today?' he asked.

'Yeah, all good, including some extra help,' Quintel said.

'Extra help? Who the fook are you involving now?'

'No one. I mean extra-hardware type-help. But why would it matter who or how many people I use?

'Where are you?'

'Why?' Quintel asked without answering, the client was seriously trying his patience.

''Cause you sound like you're in a public place.'

'That's where public phones are,' Quintel said, no longer being able to resist some sarcasm.

'Nar, you clever twat, I mean I can hear a lot of background noise.'

Quintel explained where he was.

'Right, well, be careful you're not overheard.'

Quintel opened his mouth to answer, but thought better of it so said nothing.

'You still there?'

'Yes, I'm here.'

'It's good you're fully tooled up, it'll help.'

'You didn't answer my question about why it would matter who I use, if anyone, to complete the contract,' Quintel said.

'And you never answered my question.'

Whether it was the three bottles of lager, Quintel couldn't be sure, but this bloke was really getting on his tits tonight. He dug deep, sighed, and answered. 'I'm not in anyone's earshot.'

'Good, now don't repeat what I say. My name is Bobby McKnowle.'

He said it in an arrogant way. Quintel wasn't sure if it was supposed to mean anything, or was just another example of the client's general big-headed attitude, so he just said, 'Ok.'

'And the reason you don't need any more staff is because I'm going to come over and take Jason's place, so I am.'

Quintel hadn't seen this coming, the last thing he needed was this ranting hothead getting in the way. As best as he could, he tried – without losing his rag – to talk McKnowle out of it, while stuffing the last of his one-pound coins into the slot. He reminded McKnowle that by coming over he was putting himself on offer, after all that was the whole point in hiring Quintel in the first place.

'I know you are right,' McKnowle said.

This admission took Quintel by surprise; he wasn't used to him backing down so quickly. Actually, he'd not known him to back down at all. But his elation was short lived.

'But I won't get in the way, and I still want you to do the business. But with your man being out it gives me an opportunity to join you. I know I'm taking a risk, but if you'd any idea how much and over how long that bastard has made me suffer, you wouldn't begrudge me this. And if it's the money you're worried about, don't.'

Quintel had to admit the thought of being back to 50K had flown through his mind, 'It's not that,' he lied.

'You can have it all, and I'll not be taking issue over the reporter with you, so that's 110 large, and I'll throw in a bonus,' McKnowle said.

Quintel had to admit the figures were stacking up nicely, but the thought of McKnowle chewing his arse wasn't a nice one. Then he sighed again, one of resignation this time. 'Ok, you're the boss, but we do it my way?'

'Absolutely, I'll only help. You're the man, I just want to watch if I'm honest,' McKnowle said, before telling Quintel that he'd text him his flight details later, he'd need picking up from the airport the following day.

Call over and Quintel headed back towards the bar. He wasn't quite sure why McKnowle had revealed his name over the phone. If he wanted him to know it, he could have waited until they were face to face. In fact, why tell him at all; an unnecessary risk. There must be a reason but he'd no idea what?

He churned the name over and over in his mind. It didn't mean anything, but there was a nagging familiarity to it.

Chapter Forty-Nine

It was late by the time Vinnie had arrived home, and he was starting to feel pretty jaded. All he wanted to do was shovel a microwaved TV dinner down his neck together with a couple of bottles of that French lager he liked, and then hit the sack, but he knew he should give Harry a quick ring first.

He waited until he'd eaten and then put a quick call into his boss. He propped Harry with the suggestion about keeping Christine under the radar for a few days, supported by the disinformation he'd discussed with her at the hospital. Harry was up for it and said he'd get on it tomorrow. The chief's office was going to release a brief statement early on with a full press conference due at noon. The timing would work well and Harry would personally attend the briefing to support Darlington.

The call over, Vinnie considered another bottle of lager as his mind was still racing, but as active as it was, the heavy blanket of fatigue was starting to win the battle. He headed for his bed and once there, he laid musing, not so much about the events of the day, as dramatic as they had been, but more on the shock he'd felt at the depth of his feelings towards Christine. They were certainly becoming more entrenched than he would have otherwise admitted to himself. He fancied her, yes, but this was something stronger. He then thought about his estranged wife, also called Lesley, from whom he'd soon be divorced. It was after the race against time to recapture the escaped killer Daniel Moxley that had brought things to a head. It had been true to say that they'd had problems before that job exposed the depth of them, and as much as he had loved her, what she had done was unforgiveable. But that was in the past. Mentally, he had moved on, though it might take a while before he could talk to, or use another Lesley's name without first thinking of his ex-wife.

When all this was over, he would make a serious play for Christine. He hadn't expected to feel like this about anyone, not for a long time, but the thought of nearly losing her had certainly crystallised his feelings towards her. Plus, she loved the Blues.

*

Vinnie woke up feeling mentally refreshed but still physically tired, though he wasn't sure why that should be; bar some frantic digging he hadn't done much exercise the previous day, though emotive strain always seemed to knock him sideways a bit, physically. That would be it. He'd be fine after two cups of coffee.

Thirty minutes later, he tried ringing Paul Bury. It just rang straight to answer machine. He didn't leave a message. He then treated himself to a rare breakfast of toast and marmalade and tried the number again. This time it rang out – it was turned on – but eventually rang to the answer machine nonetheless. He left a message, but was careful. 'This is the person who you agreed to meet via a mutual friend. We have a shared past, though mine is still active, please call back, I'll be by my phone.'

That should do, it would tell Bury who he was but mean nothing to anyone else who might listen to it. He didn't have to wait long for a call back.

'You'd be Vinnie then?' the voice said.

'Yes, and you'd be PB?'

'Aye, call me Paul. How can I help?'

'It's to do with a murder I'm deputy SIO-ing. Reggie Carstair. Used to be secretary of state for Northern Ireland, back in the day.'

'Aye, I heard he'd been slotted. But it was a long time since he worked in the Province, not sure how I can help.'

Vinnie deliberately didn't mention the attempts on Jim Reedly; he didn't want to say too much, not at first. 'It's just background really, but it is sensitive. I could do with a face to face, if you don't mind?'

'Will our mutual friend be coming?' Bury asked.

'No she's a bit indisposed today, though I do hope to be seeing her later.'

'Her phone's off. I've just tried her.'

'I know, it got broke. When she gets a replacement she'll no doubt bell you. When I see her later, I'll remind her to.'

'Ok, fair enough. If you are Vinnie, you'll know where to meet me. The back yard in two hours,' Bury said, before ending the call.

Fortunately, Christine had told Vinnie about the pub where she'd met Bury, so he knew about the small rear yard turned beer garden. This guy was certainty cautious.

*

196

Two hours later, Vinnie was enjoying the spring sunshine while nursing an orange juice in the beer garden when a tall, imposing man in his late fifties came through the pub's back door and came straight over. They were alone and the man quickly introduced himself, as did Vinnie.

'Sorry for all the cloak and dagger stuff on the phone, but I have to be mighty careful. Has Christine told you anything of our business?'

'No,' Vinnie lied, as Bury sat down with his back to the garden wall, and placed a pint of Guinness on the table.

'Good. It's just that when I met her yesterday, I was sure I'd been followed away from the hotel. I've spent the last two hours making sure I arrived here without an escort, so I have.'

'Change your hotel.'

'Already have.'

Vinnie wasn't too sure why a documentary about how Catholics are now being better treated in public office than Protestants – if true – would warrant the sort of attention Bury was suggesting, but he took his word for it. Or at least believed that Bury believed it.

'Anyway, you wanted to talk about Carstair?'

'Yes please,' Vinnie said, and quickly brought Bury up to speed with details of the murder, keeping to the facts which had been made public, which wasn't much. 'Did you know him, personally?' he asked.

'Aye, as did all senior officers in the RUC – Royal Ulster Constabulary - and as politicians go I have to say I always found Carstair one of the better ones. But why are you looking back then for your killer, or motive? That was back in the nineties. He must have made many enemies later on after he became home secretary, or is there something you're not letting on?'

He had a point Vinnie thought, why then? So he fed a bit more into the conversation. 'Did you ever meet an English DI on secondment to your old force, a man by the name of Jim Reedly?'

'Ah. Nar I understand. No, I never met Reedly, but I knew of him,' Bury said, and then went on to outline what he knew of Reedly's work in examining killings by the police or army.

'It can't have been an easy job,' Vinnie said.

'Poisoned chalice, that's for damn sure. But if you think Carstair's murder relates to back then, why has whoever it is waited twenty years to extract revenge?'

'A good question to which I don't know the answer. It may be that they had to wait until he retired from public office to be able to get anywhere near him?'

'But surely former home secretaries get security for life?'

'They do,' Vinnie said, and then explained that the level of such security would be drastically reduced, unless Intelligence identified a specific threat. 'But in any event he's been retired several years now, so it makes no sense not to attack as soon as he left office,' he added, destroying his own theory.

'Plus, it's one hell of a grudge to keep alive all this time,' Bury added.

Vinnie just nodded and then took a drink of his juice.

'I take it you're going over all the files relating to Reedly's job, if that is where your killer comes from?'

'As best we can, but a lot of paper records were destroyed after the peace process was signed, which is why I was hoping you might be able to help, or perhaps if you can't, can you point me in the direction of anyone who can?' Vinnie said.

Bury sat in apparent contemplation for a minute as he took all the top off his pint of Guinness. 'What about Reedly?' he eventually said.

'Trust me he has wracked his brains,' Vinnie said.

'I guess he's a target too?'

Vinnie then realised that Bury couldn't have seen the news put out about Reedly not surviving his injuries from the bomb blast at Blackley. He dearly wanted to tell Bury about the misinformation, and also about the earlier attempts on Reedly's life. It was not that he didn't trust Bury, he did, and found him quite charming, but it was all about need to know, and Bury only needed to know what Vinnie had told him. So he stuck to what had been released. 'I'm afraid Reedly is dead,' Vinnie said, and then explained about the attack at the cemetery, keeping to the script of Reedly's faked demise.

Bury looked shocked. 'That's a dreadful shame, so it is,' and then added, 'You could have used him as bait; and if your theory had been right, you'd not have been waiting too long, if I know those Provo bastards,' Bury said.

As if Bury could see the surprise on Vinnie's face, he continued before he could comment.

'Yous have to understand, that in the world we worked in back in the troubles we had to take risks sometimes, most of the time. Do the unexpected. Nar I know those Provo boys would expect me to play dirty, but they'd have not been expecting yous over here to do that. No offence.'

'None taken,' Vinnie said. It was an interesting idea, and not one he'd previously considered. But of course Reedly was not dead, so it could still be used. Of course they'd have to explain to the press the little problem of how he made a miraculous recovery from his mortal wounds. That said, he still couldn't see the deputy chief constable of Greater Manchester Police being too up for hanging his bollocks out of the window and saying "come kick these boys, I'm waiting".

'It would have proved or disproved your theory, so it would have,' Bury said.

'Apart from the fact that he's dead, logistically it would have taken some serious resources,' Vinnie said, wondering why they were still discussing what on the surface was just a hypothetical theory. He wondered if Bury really suspected that Reedly was still alive.

'Ah, away with you. I used to get that sort of rhetoric all the time when I was working. It would have been expensive, yes; but I'm telling you it wouldn't have taken long. And would have worked out a lot cheaper than a murder investigation that dragged on for months or longer.'

It was as if he knew Reedly was alive and was egging Vinnie on to consider his proposal. Certainly, regarding the finances, he did have a point. But Vinnie knew neither Harry nor Darlington would want anything to do with such a plan. Bury had clearly worked in different circumstances and during very difficult times.

Vinnie thanked Bury for his help, and said he would get Christine to bell him later. He also asked him to give what he'd said some thought, in case he could remember a potential suspect, even if it made no sense why he or she would wait this long.

'I take it you've checked those in Prison, no offence,' Bury asked.

'Yeah, a lot were released early as part of the peace process and we've got a team tracing the others. But apparently, there have been none released in the last eighteen months, which is the timeframe we are using, though we will broaden that if needed. What about me speaking to anyone else?'

'Not safe for you to be asking those sorts of questions. You'd get nar answers anyway, but let me make a couple of calls; I'll bell you if I come up with anything.'

Vinnie thanked him again and left.

As he reached his car his phone – which he'd set to silent during his meeting – vibrated in his pocket. It was a text from Christine, ready for a lift home. Just before he reached his car he turned around and took in his environment. There was no sign yet of Bury following him out of the pub, and as over-cautious as Vinnie thought he was, something in the way he spoke gave his concern credibility. Vinnie then spent a couple of minutes checking out all the parked cars, and recesses on the street. There was no one about. He headed to the driver's door of his Volvo.

Chapter Fifty

Quintel had been enjoying his Full English breakfast until the text message from McKnowle informed him of his arrival later at Manchester Airport's Terminal Three, on a Ryan Air jet from Dublin. He also asked him to source two pay-as-you-go mobiles for them both to use during the operation. He told him to wait in the arrivals lounge and he'd find him once he was through customs. At least he hadn't bothered with his A and B payphone bollocks this time. Though he'd much prefer that, rather than have to endure him personally over the next few days. He was the client, and he had said he mostly wanted to observe and wouldn't get in the way. Quintel knew he'd have to lay out the ground rules when he saw him. That said, he still didn't know who the target was, or why? Though the latter wasn't too important; he was just intrigued.

After breakfast he asked reception for directions to the nearest mobile phone shop and went and bought two disposables as requested. He put them both on charge in his room and preloaded each's number in the other's phone memory under the initial A for McKnowle in his, and B for him in McKnowle's. He'd appreciate the A and B theme, and then he scratched the screen of his with the car key so he knew which was which. He then checked and cleaned both guns, as Jason would have done, and then removed the rounds to give the loading springs in the magazines a rest. Jason had always advised doing this when the gun's readiness was not needed. A worn spring in a magazine was apparently one cause of ammo load failure. And it was something to do. At midday he packed everything up into the holdall he'd also bought that morning and headed to the car. On his way through reception he reserved a second room for McKnowle and then went to the Nissan and stored everything back in the boot, together with the grenades. Time to head leisurely towards the airport.

He arrived at the multi-storey carpark at Terminal Three at 1.30 pm and had a leisurely late lunch in one of the food outlets in the arrivals hall. At 2.20 pm he checked one of the screens again and saw that the short flight from Dublin was due in any minute. He checked that his personal mobile was on, and then glanced up and saw that the flight status on the large info screen had changed to "Landed". He made his way to the Information Desk and waited.

Twenty minutes later, a stream of passengers started to filter through and one in particular stopped and looked around before settling his gaze on Quintel. This must be him; they had never met before but this was him. A man in his early sixties, Quintel reckoned, but he was short, with a thin build, and balding short grey hair to match his prison-like pallor. He was not half as imposing as Quintel had expected, but then sometimes the shorter in height and stature a person was, the shorter their fuse. He made directly over to Quintel and introductions over, Quintel gave him his disposable phone and charger.

'Good, now turn your private one off and don't use it again until we're done. And no personal calls on these ones,' McKnowle said, adding, 'now let's get to whichever shithole town you've booked us into. I want to discuss the dirty bastard you are going to kill.'

Once away from the airport, Quintel tried to engage McKnowle in a bit of light conversation to ease him in, but he was having none of it, so Quintel went straight in. 'You said on the phone, that you'll not interfere, that you only want to watch.'

'Aye so I did, and I'll be staying out of your way when it matters, but things change.'

'What do you mean by that?'

'Well, now I'm here, you can make use of me, make the hit easier.'

'How exactly?'

'I'll telt yous later, but suffice to say; with me I'll be able to get you nearer to the target when it matters, but for now just drive will you, Jackie-boy.'

'"Jackie-boy"?' Quintel was sure it was going to be a trying few days.

*

En route to the Royal Preston Hospital, Vinnie called into the Preston office to give Harry a quick rundown of his meeting with Bury.

'So not too much help then?'

'Not really, but insightful in some ways. He's obviously operated as a tricky bastard in the past.'

'You are not seriously suggesting I try and talk Reedly into putting his arse in the firing line and then try and talk Darlington into authorising it?'

'Suppose not, it's just a thought I guess, another way of approaching it, but it may come to it if all else fails.'

'In your dreams.'

'How are we getting on with identifying possible targets?'

'Pick any one from many. But how do we know for sure that Quintel's not finished and is now on his toes?' Harry said.

'I hope he is, as harder as that makes it for us in tracing him, at least we'll know it's over. I guess the only way to know is to find out if he's still about.'

'All possible intelligence sources are tasked and out and about looking for any mentions of him, but so far nothing. Which perversely might turn out to be a plus,' Harry said, adding, 'how much do you trust Dempster? You know he's told his handlers that he wants no more to do with them.'

'Understandable really, but he promised me if Quintel made contact, he'd let me know that at least.'

'Believe him?'

'As far as one can. Look, I've got to collect Christine from the hospital shortly and take her back to Manchester.'

'Where to? Not that I expect she or her sister are in any further danger now,' Harry said.

'Agreed, as long as Quintel thinks she's dead, and to be honest, even if he knew she was still alive, would he be mad enough to risk trying to finish her off? He'll know we will be all over her and Lesley,' Vinnie said, cringing to himself slightly on using Lesley's name.

'So, where are you taking her?'

'Back to her place, where her sister has been temporarily moved to. There is no suggestion that her address is compromised.'

'What about Dempster?'

'I'll pay him a visit later on this evening, just to keep him warm and remind him of our arrangement.'

'Why not bell him?'

'No, Harry, his sort always has a better recall of things when you are stood in front of them.'

'Fair enough, keep me posted.'

'Will do,' Vinnie said, before heading off to collect Christine.

*

Quintel was nearing the junction at Preston where the M55 motorway to Blackpool starts from the M6 which they were currently on, when McKnowle broke the silence Quintel had been enjoying.

'I forget how fookin busy your roads are over here.'

'Yeah, well it is rush hour now,' Quintel said as he decelerated yet again down to about thirty miles per hour.

'Nar your man Jay's gone, who've you got left on the team?' McKnowle asked.

'Just a local busybody who thinks he's the go-to man.'

'Will you need him again?'

'Depends on who the target is?'

'Arr don't be worrying about that, I'll be giving you all you need on that front.'

'Well, I guess I won't be needing him then.'

'And afterwards?' McKnowle asked.

'I intend to re-locate abroad and stick to this line of work, but only after I've had a suitable break, of course.'

'Of course,' McKnowle said, adding, 'so this guy's no part of your team, then?'

'To be honest, I've been in two minds whether to off him or not once we're done,' Quintel said.

'Excellent, Jackie-boy. I was hoping you'd say that. I won't be wanting any loose ends, so I won't. The shit'll be thick enough when it's done as it is. It'll be like eight layers of shite with an extra layer on top.'

'Meaning?'

'Meaning let's go and do the fucker, nar. It'll save fucking about later, it'll keep the filth well-busy, so it will, and it'll get us out of this bastard traffic.'

'Ok, you're the boss,' Quintel said as he noticed the half-mile marker board for junction 31A and switched his left-hand side indicator on.

Chapter Fifty-One

Quintel drove to the estate where he knew Dempster lived, but there were no signs of life at his home address. Jason had been his first point of contact, but he remembered Jason once saying that Dempster spent a lot of his time at the local labour club. The sat nav took them there and he pulled up outside, but set back. The club was a typical sixties-built concrete-fronted shithole with metal grills dressing the outside of the windows. It was towards the end of a cul-de-sac, which was where they were parked, with high privet behind them. Quintel used the cover to grab both handguns from the boot. As he gave McKnowle one of them, he saw the man's eyes shine as he turned the weapon over in his hand.

'It feels good to handle one of these again,' McKnowle said.

'Been a while?' Quintel asked.

'Twenty or more fookin years thanks to those bastard Brits – no offence.'

'None taken, I'd been meaning to ask you about that, I take it you were locked up?'

'Prison? I wish. It was much, much worse than that I can telt you, but it'll have to wait 'till later. I tell yous over a pint.'

Quintel was intrigued as to what McKnowle meant, but also glad the ensuing rant that would undoubtedly accompany the story would wait until later. They had work to do.

The pub was clearly open as several low-lives trudged into the bar, none of whom were Dempster. He didn't want to put his face too much on offer, so after ten minutes decided to give him a ring. It might spook him, but he couldn't hang around here all day. He obtained the number from his private phone and rang it from his pay-as-you-go. Dempster answered quickly.

'It's Mr Quintel here, Dempster, I'm in Preston and I need to see you.'

'Oh, er ok Boss, I'm not at home at the mo, but can be there in five.'

'I know, I just called. Place looks empty, you've not moved since the other day, have you?

'Er yeah, I got evicted but I'm squatting further down the same street. Is everything ok? Is the car ok?'

'Yeah, now it's clean. Look, I was a bit sharp the other day, especially after what had happened, and I need to keep good people like you on-board, so as I was passing I thought I'd call and give you a bonus.'

Quintel thought he could hear the greed in Dempster's reply as he trotted out the house number; 101. Though Quintel did note a pause before he said the actual number, 'You sure?'

'Yeah Boss, I'm outside there now.'

Quintel told him to wait there and ended the call. He then put the address into the sat nav, and it was as he thought; the numbers only went up to eighty-nine in odds and eighty-eight in evens. Lying bastard. But the street would no doubt be correct, if indeed he had moved at all. He fired up the car engine, 'If they were quick' he thought.

But before Quintel could pull away, the front door of the club swung open and Dempster came out at full pelt. 'That's the bastard,' he said, pointing him out to McKnowle.

'Ten feet past,' Mcknowle ordered.

Quintel did so as stealthily as he could, though he doubted Dempster would have heard them above the pounding of his own feet on the pavement. He drew past him and before he'd fully stopped McKnowle was out and Dempster ran into his right fist before he had chance to stop himself. Quintel reached across and opened the back door, and McKnowle had Dempster in, with himself next to him before he had any time to react. Quintel accelerated hard away from the kerb, the force of which caused the front passenger door to slam shut. He glanced in the mirror and could see the look of fear in Dempster's eyes as McKnowle aimed his gun at him.

'Who the fuck are you? Dempster eventually managed.

'I'm the new Jason, and you'd be as well to mind your fookin mouth,' McKnowle said before he pistol-whipped him across the side of the head.

Quintel saw a look of pure joy in McKnowle's face as he struck the terrified Dempster. Perhaps it wouldn't be too bad working with McKnowle after all.

'Sorry sir,' Dempster said, adding, 'where are you taking me?'

'Just for a little ride into the country, I just want to ask you about a news reporter called Christine Jones before I pay you your bonus,' Quintel said as he watched Dempster's expression via his driving mirror. It had turned from fear to dread. He'd touched a nerve.

'Are you sure?' Vinnie said as he approached the roundabout leading to the M6 motorway at Fulwood, north Preston.

'Look, I'm really fine now and it'll save you a lot of time toing and froing from Manchester later. Plus, I'm looking forward to having a drink with you afterwards. I reckon I owe you one,' Christine said.

Vinnie didn't argue with her as he drove all the way around the roundabout and headed back towards central Preston. He'd head straight to Dempster's house and hope he was home. If not, he'd probably be at the local club at this time of the afternoon. The address wasn't far from the motorway junction and although traffic would be heavy on the A6 road back into Preston, he knew a quicker route.

He was glad that Christine hadn't suffered any real physical problems, but for her head being a bit sore. She was certainly made of stern stuff; unless she was hiding it? But if she was, she was covering it well. He looked forward to spending the evening with her, and his call on Dempster wouldn't take long. He either knew something, or he didn't. But a personal visit would hopefully keep the relationship going if nothing else.

He drove around the north-eastern end of Preston's outer ring road and soon neared Dempster's estate when his phone announced the arrival of a text. His phone was lodged in the Volvo's centre console and as he was driving he was going to leave it. Then he decided just to have a peep to see who the message was from, in case it was Harry. When he saw the caller's ID he slammed on the brakes.

'What's up?' Christine asked.

'Dempster,' Vinnie said as he pulled the car to a stop and picked up the phone.

'That's a coincidence,' Christine said, adding, 'and before you say it, I know you don't believe in them or fairies.'

Vinnie read the message and said, 'Well, here's another one for you; Quintel's just rang him and is heading to a joey house number on his street. Come on.'

Vinnie pulled away from the kerb and headed straight for Dempster's road, hoping to find a lost Quintel looking for a house number which did not exist. Christine sat up in her seat as she gripped the grab rail above the passenger window. 'Is it far?' she asked.

'Just around the corner,' Vinnie said as he pulled off the main road onto the leading entry road into the estate. He knew Dempster's street was off to his left and started concentrating on the road signs. He mulled over Dempster's text as he drove, "I'm in club. Quintel on way to see me. I gave him wrong house number – 101 – said I'd flit. Thought I'd got shut of him, should have told you before, sorry. Need your help".

'What did you reply?' Christine asked, breaking Vinnie's thoughts.

'He said he was in his club, so I just texted "Leg it". If I know about the club, you can assume Quintel does.' But it was the "before" bit that troubled him. For right or wrong reasons, Dempster had been holding back.

Vinnie was halfway down the road and knew the club was in a cul-de-sac at the end. He half expected to see Dempster come legging it past them, when he saw the road they were after twenty metres up ahead on their left. He started to brake hard, when Christine's shout made him flinch.

'Vinnie, Vinnie stop, turn around, I'm sure it's them.'

Vinnie had already pulled into the street and on checking his mirrors saw a blue saloon flash past the back of them going in the opposite direction, exiting the estate. He asked Christine what she had seen and she said she was sure she saw someone bundling a man into the rear of a blue car, and that someone looked very much like Dempster. 'Sure?' he asked her.

'As sure as I can be.'

Vinnie had learnt a long time ago not to disrespect one's first thoughts, and threw the car into a violent three-point turn. As much as he loved his Volvo, the one fault with it was its poor turning circle and his three-point turn became a five-point one on the narrow street. Once going forward again he turned right into the road they'd just left without stopping. Two-hundred metres ahead he could see the road's T junction with Ribbleton Lane – a major thoroughfare in and out of the city.

At the T junction he looked left and right but all he could see was traffic, and no blue cars with three on board. He was minded to turn right towards the city centre for no particular reason other than he knew he had to make a snap decision if he was to have any chance. Then he thought, where would *he* take Dempster? He turned left and headed towards the small town of Longridge. Industrial estates and countryside were aplenty on the eastern side of the city. He passed his personal radio to Christine and asked her to hold the transmit button down as he shouted into it as he drove like an idiot. He forced a third lane in between the on-coming and apposing traffic. He just hoped they were going the right way.

Chapter Fifty-Two

Quintel disregarded the garage unit, as handy as it would have been, too hot now. So he turned left after that industrial estate and headed towards junction 31A of the M6. He wanted somewhere rural for their little chat with Dumpster as he liked to call him, but also somewhere handy for the motorway. The only hassle with this junction was that it didn't allow traffic to head north, and Blackpool was north. He'd have to go south and do an about turn at the next junction. Still, safer than hanging around local roads, as sure as he was no one had seen them lift Dumpster, you could never be a hundred percent.

'You've had a few minutes to think since I dropped that nosy slut's name on you, so give, Dumpster,' Quintel said as he drove off the main road down a narrow lane which led to a dead end.

'I just know she came around on the knocker, after the fire, that's all. Honest. I told her shit as I knew shit.'

Quintel didn't say anything. He stopped the car and McKnowle pulled Dumpster from the back seat, out and around to the front of the car. There were open fields spanning all around with no one in sight. He could see the motorway in the near-distance and hear its traffic noise, which was remarkably loud. He wasn't really bothered about Dumpster's relationship with the news reporter, after all she was dead; it was just something to say to engage the idiot in conversation.

'What are we doing here?' Dempster asked, his words trailing off.

'Giving you your bonus, like the man said, and making sure we can trust you in the future,' McKnowle cut in.

Quintel could see a half-look of relief dance across Dumpster's face, as he rushed to spit his words out. 'Count on me, Mister, Mr Quintel knows he can trust me. I'll be of proper use, and you know I'll never grass.'

Quintel didn't know why, but doubt suddenly entered his head. True, having scared the crap out of Dumpster – more than once – he would probably prove to be a safe asset. It also crossed his mind that by giving the filth another murder to look at might not just tie up the cops as McKnowle had suggested, but actually bring a whole lot more on-board.

210

Was it added grief he didn't need? McKnowle must have read the indecision on his face as he said, 'Your call, Jackie-boy, but you know my feelings.'

Fuck it; he'd give him a chance. 'I want you to turn and face the other way, and count to a hundred while we do one. And consider this a warning should you ever stray onto the straight and narrow,' he said.

'Yes, sir, enough said,' Dempster said as he turned around.

Then Quintel thought about how that undercover bastard – Charlie – had nearly been his undoing. He pulled his gun out and shot Dempster through the back of his head at point blank range.

He felt an inherent thrill rush through him as he watched Dempster's face explode away from his head and land on the grass four feet in front of him with a thud, before his body had even hit the deck. He hadn't been sure where the fault lay that led to Charlie, and irrespective of what Jason had thought, he had to blame someone.

'Change of plan?' McKnowle said, as they climbed back into the motor.

'Toss of a coin, but I never liked the arrogant shit. Thought too much of himself,' Quintel replied.

'Time to fuck off then, wees got ourselves a busy day the morrow, so we have,' McKnowle said, as Quintel reversed back towards the pleasantly name Bluebell Way and its route to the M6.

*

At least fifteen minutes passed before Vinnie pulled over to think. They had seen several police cars going in both directions, all with their "Blues and Twos" on, but there had been no sign of the blue car with Dempster, Quintel and A.N-other on-board. There'd been a couple of possibles, but they had turned out negative. He tried the garage, just in case, but the scene was still closed with a bored looking PC stood outside.

'After causing all this fuss, I do hope I'm right,' Christine said.

'Stick with your first impressions, they are usually correct.'

'What about his house, would he go back there?'

'Probably not, but I heard Harry on the radio before sending a car there just in case.'

'I'll be honest with you, since we pressed the launch button; I've hardly been able to decipher much of the chatter coming from your radio. It all sounds like gibberish.'

'You get an ear for it,' Vinnie said, just before his phone rang. It was Harry.

They gave each other a quick update and then Harry cut in with something else. 'You'll not believe it, but there's been another murder.'

'Never,' Vinnie said.

'A day or two ago over in Blackpool. I've only just heard about it chatting to Darlington,' Harry said.

'Who's got it?'

'Not our unit, that's why I've only just heard about it.'

Vinnie knew that the whole point of creating the Regional Homicide Unit was to extend resources from the five forces in the region into one pool. But the last few days had been unprecedented, with the killings of Charlie, Carstair, the milkman Devers, and not to mention the attempts on Reedly and Christine. Plus there had been a couple of normal day-to-day jobs in Salford and Liverpool. One was a domestic which had been solved pretty quickly – jealous boyfriend - but the other looked like a turf-war job which could prove a lot harder to resolve. 'Who is doing it then?' Vinnie asked.

'Darlington has asked for mutual aid and a team from West Yorkshire are in Blackpool as we speak.'

'Who is the deceased?'

'That's the bit that worries me.'

'Go on.'

'A local backstreet gun dealer. Shot at point blank range probably by his one of his own weapons.'

'And you think maybe Jason and Quintel are connected?'

'Could be them tooling up?' Harry said, adding, 'if they are as organised as we suspect, then they'll change their hardware with every job.'

Vinnie was glad Harry had chosen the word "organised". He hated it when villains were described as pros, but that aside he knew Harry had a fair point. It was a bit of a coincidence and Blackpool wasn't that far away. Then he remembered the "Kiss Me Quick" hats they'd been wearing at the Leyland hotel. With everything that had been going on he forgotten all about them. 'What have you told the SIO over there?'

'Just enough to keep a dialogue going, but they've got no suspects yet,' Harry said.

Vinnie said his goodbyes and told Harry that they would stay in the area a while longer before leaving the continuing search to the locals - and in any event he had to get Christine home.

'Don't worry about me,' she said as soon as he was off the phone. She also asked what Harry had said and Vinnie told her.

'Just a hunch,' she said, as soon as he'd finished.

'What?'

'Why Blackpool?

'I've been wondering that. It might just be that that is where Jason knew they could go to get some guns.'

'Why kill him?

'Seen their faces?'

'No honour among thieves then?'

'They're not thieves.'

'You know what I mean. But if you wanted to re-arm and needed somewhere to hole down, somewhere away from Preston or Manchester, but with easy access to the motorways, where would you go?' she asked.

'Not too far from where the guns were. You might be onto something?'

Christine smiled and Vinnie said he'd ask Harry to push through the action – line of enquiry – for checks with Blackpool hoteliers with Quintel and Jason's mugshots, to be run as a priority. But he warned her about how many hotels and guest houses there would be in a seaside resort like Blackpool.

'All the more reason to hole down there,' she added.

As they had chatted Vinnie had driven and drifted generally towards the motorway when a thought hit him. If they had used the motorway to escape then it made sense they would have used Junction 31A. Which would send them the wrong way if they were headed to Blackpool. But if he and Christine cut across local roads, they could pick up the Blackpool motorway – the M55 – at Junction 32 of the M6, which is where he'd been headed before they'd decided to pay Dempster a visit. He just hoped they still had Dempster with them. If they'd dropped him off before they'd left, he'd have no doubt belled him by now.

Vinnie explained his hypothesis to Christine as he drove like an idiot again. Once on the M55 he screwed the guts out of his car's 2.4 litre engine, and ten minutes after joining the motorway he parked up by a roundabout at its end. The road carried on after becoming a single carriageway two-way road, and they had a good view of its traffic. It was a long shot but at least they were doing something. Vinnie settled back into his seat to concentrate on the road as the engine tinkled a childlike tune as the motor cooled.

Chapter Fifty-Three

'I think you and me will get along just fine, so I do,' McKnowle said as Quintel gunned the motor south on the M6.

'Why'd you say that?' Quintel asked.

'The way you offed Dempster. I looked into your eyes.'

'Meaning?'

'No emotion – you'd have made a good volunteer.'

Quintel had already guessed that his client McKnowle was an ex-terrorist of one variation or another, but had never wanted to pry, especially over the phone. Now was his chance. 'Volunteer? I'm guessing you're not talking about helping out in your local library?'

McKnowle laughed before he answered, 'The Provisional wing of the Irish Republican Army. Or PIRA, the Provos or just, the IRA. I used to be one of its senior commanders.'

Quintel had all but guessed the organisation, but was shocked to hear of McKnowle's high status. 'Wow, I'm honoured that you have deemed me a suitable asset to use.'

'No offence Jackie-boy, but I've got no idea who the fuck I can trust back home nowadays, the majority have either gone soft, or are too busy sticking their tongues up the Brits' arses.'

'I'm obviously glad you picked me, but what of your hard-core? There must still be some guys you could have used?'

'I'm fucking hard-core, but the rest, well, most of them were nutters back in the day. I don't even know them now.'

Quintel stopped the conversation as he concentrated on leaving the motorway at the Preston central junction – 31 - and navigated them back onto the M6 north. The junction had come at a bad time in their little chat and had broken the rhythm. He was intrigued to ask more, but noted that McKnowle was now just staring out of his passenger window. Quintel remained quiet as they passed the junction they had initially joined, and were soon at 32 where the M55 to Blackpool started.

The M55 was a lot quieter than the M6, as it only went to one place, and as he relaxed more, Quintel couldn't resist carrying on the conversation. 'I hope you don't mind me asking, but you said you'd been away for a long time. Because of the Brits. I just assumed that you'd been in the nick, if you don't mind me asking?' Quintel, tensed, half expecting McKnowle to launch into one of his rants, but he didn't.

'The fookers tried to lock me up but they could never catch me, and as a member of the Army Council I didn't get involved too much with the Active Services Units, so was pretty much off-limits,' McKnowle said calmly, before adding, 'Though every now and again I would show up with one of the Belfast ASUs just to keep my hand in. I enjoyed it and missed it if I'm honest.'

'I take it the job went bad?'

'Did it, the fucking Sass were waiting for us.'

'But you didn't get nicked?'

'They'd no intention of nicking anybody. Those SAS bastards. They just opened up and a fookin huge firefight ensured. All the óglachs were killed, except me.'

'"Óglachs" what the fuck is that?'

'Irish for volunteers, Jackie-boy, not every fucker kills for money, like you.'

Quintel didn't want to nose too far, too soon, but had to pose the unasked question, 'So what did happen to you?'

'We're at the end of the motorway, so I'm guessing wees are nearly here?'

'Yes, not far. Our hotel is in the South Shore district, not far from here.'

'In that case we'll chat later.'

Quintel didn't argue as he steered the motor from the end of the motorway and took the first exit from the roundabout. What he had learnt about McKnowle had certainly intrigued him; he was one serious mother, and he was starting to figure out who the final target was. They had obviously seriously pissed off one serious bastard in McKnowle. That said; if his hunches were right he'd have to tread carefully, he'd only get one go at this, he was sure of that.

*

'Vinnie, look. That's it. It's gone the other way from the roundabout.'

'You sure?' Vinnie asked, as he fired up the Volvo.

'Couldn't see the driver, but I'm sure the front seat passenger is the guy who bundled Dempster into the car. He looked out his side window. Straight at me.'

Vinnie slewed his car across the road as he headed to the roundabout, knowing he'd have to go all the way around it to get to the same exit that the blue motor had just taken. 'No offence, Christine, but you said earlier you couldn't describe the guy apart from "a small white man in his sixties".'

'I couldn't, but now I've seen him again, I'm sure.'

'How come?'

'I can't explain it. Just the look of pure evil on his face. Like a permanently etched countenance of hatred. Now step on it.'

Vinnie did, and just hoped he wasn't damaging his motor, he was paid an allowance to use his own car, which wasn't as wonderful as some thought. It didn't seem to matter when you were screwing the guts out of a firm's pool car. Fortunately, he got a clear run onto the roundabout and left it in the offside lane of two as an urban dual carriageway opened up in front of him. There were a few cars in the nearside lane but their outside lane was clear. He asked Christine to keep an eye on her side so they didn't flash past the blue car by mistake. His plan was to follow it discretely until he could arrange an intervention by – ARVs - Armed Response Vehicles. He asked Christine to repeat her trick with his radio as he shouted into it.

They soon approached a further roundabout with no sign of the targets' vehicle, and as they hadn't passed any turn-offs they were still in play, at least until this next roundabout. The advance warning sign told Vinnie that there were four exits from it. He would pick the straight ahead option, the third exit.

Then as he started braking heavily on the approach, he saw it at the same time as Christine screeched. The blue car was an old Nissan in the nearside lane and it entered the roundabout twenty-five metres ahead of them. He saw part of the vehicle's registered number – SP02 something, something, something. A 2002 model. He came off the brakes as he shouted the update into the radio. An ARV was making ground from North Shore he was told, and the Force Incident Manager in the force Control Room had authorised the use of weapons. 'Shit,' he shouted, as he slammed the brakes back on. A slow moving heavy goods vehicle was now blocking his access onto the roundabout, not to mention his view. He glanced to his left, and was fairly sure the Nissan hadn't taken the first exit, so he drove around the back of the artic and undertook it. He received a blast from the driver's horn drawing attention to them, but he'd had little choice. As he passed the wagon there was no sign of the Nissan. He picked the third exit, the effective straight on, named Progress Way – which he hoped was an omen – and floored the accelerator.

Vinnie raced along Progress Way until it became Squires Gate Lane and they passed the site of the old Blackpool Airport, but still nothing. They had passed many junctions since they had lost sight of the Nissan; it could be anywhere now. He slowed down and thumped the steering wheel in frustration. 'So bastard close, but so far.'

'You did all you could,' Christine offered.

'I know, but?'

'But nothing, at least we know they are in Blackpool, whether just to hole down, or for something more sinister, it's more than we knew ten minutes ago.'

Vinnie knew she was right and appreciated what she was trying to do, but if they went on to kill someone else now; it would weigh heavy on him. He thanked her and took the radio from her and brought the Control Room up to date. He then pulled over; it was time to ring Harry. But before he did, he turned to face Christine and said, 'You sure there was only the driver and front seat passenger in the car?'

'Sure. I know what you're thinking; but he could have been on the back seat slumped down, or even in the boot, God forbid; I know what that feels like.'

Vinnie signed as he dialled Harry's phone, he only hoped she was right.

Chapter Fifty-Four

It was gone eight by the time they had all eaten their fish and chips supper, and settled down with a beer. Vinnie just wanted to collapse into the armchair in Christine's flat and sink a few while letting go of the day's stresses. He was pleased to see Lesley coping well after her ordeal, and she seemed happier to be staying with her sister until Quintel was caught. Christine had warned Vinnie before they landed that Lesley could be up or down, especially after what had gone on, but seemed relieved when she greeted them with a smile on her face.

'Why don't you make a night of it?' Christine said, adding, 'you can crash on the settee, or you could have a threesome with me and Lesley? What do you reckon, sis?'

Vinnie could feel the heat in his face as he laughed, 'A rose between two thorns? I wouldn't risk it, but the settee offer sounds perfect,' he answered, and then ducked to miss a low flying cushion.

'Hey,' Christine said.

'Yeah, hey,' Lesley added as a second cushion flew past Vinnie.

'After all you've been through, it should be me treating you two to plenty of drink in some swish restaurant,' Vinnie said.

'I'm ok, I'll let you treat my sister, she's been through much more than me,' Lesley said.

'Why do you think I'm plying you with free booze? I'm just making sure your bill goes through the roof. I don't do back-street bolt-holes, well, unless I'm paying for myself, that is,' Christine said.

'Well, joking apart, when we get a chance, dinner is on me,' Vinnie said.

'Sounds great,' Christine answered.

'I'm off to the kitchen, while you two carry on flirting, I mean pleeease. But if you need a top up, say now,' Lesley said.

They both said they'd love another bottle of lager each as Vinnie's phone rang. 'Hello Frank,' he answered.

'Just to let you know that the locals have stood down their search in Blackpool, no sign of the car or Quintel,' Delany said.

Vinnie had guessed as much by now, and said, 'Hotels?'

'I've got a DS and two DCs on it, but it's a long list. I hope they weren't just passing through.'

'ANPR?'

'The part number is logged in, but it'll be hit and miss even if the motor passes one of the fixed-cameras sites.'

'What does Darlington say?' Vinnie asked.

'Can't get hold of him which is unusual, so I've had to leave a brief update with Blister.'

'Who's blister?' Vinnie asked.

'Oh sorry, it's the chief's nickname for his staff officer.'

'You mean the lovely Russell Sharpe?'

'The same.'

'But why Blister?' Vinnie repeated.

'Because, according to Darlington, he only appears once all the hard work is done.'

Vinnie roared with laughter while seeing Christine's puzzled expression watching him. He said his goodbyes and said he'd see Harry in the morning.

Christine laughed when Vinnie explained to her what Harry had said.

'God, you cops don't half stick it to each other,' she added.

'Only for those who deserve it, and don't tell me journalism is any different,' Vinnie said.

'You got me there. We have our fair share of Olympic Torches,' Christine said.

Vinnie laughed, the police also had their share of 'those who never went out' too. Perhaps their two professions were not that different after all. Then his phone rang again. It Christine's editor June ringing to ask if he'd had an update from the hospital on Christine. He apologised profusely for not letting her know sooner that she'd been discharged and made it sound as if he'd just arrived at Christine's flat straight from hospital. He accentuated his words and saw Christine nod her tacit understanding, before he handed the phone over to her.

'Just about to ring you, June, sorry I didn't get chance sooner,' Christine said.

'No don't be daft, you've been through enough,' June said, adding, 'are you sure you are ok, you know hospitals can't wait to clear beds nowadays. Perhaps we should do a feature on it.'

'I'm fine June, really, and the staff there were first class.'

'Ok, I'll drop the feature idea, but I've had your man on, he said you'd been due to ring him some hours ago and was becoming concerned.'

'You mean Paul?

'Yeah, Paul Bury.'

'What, he gave you his full name?'

'Yeah, said he was starting to worry.'

'He hadn't struck me as the worrying kind.'

'Something about being followed? I'm damn sure you don't tell me all you should, Christine Jones,' June said.

'Honest, it was nothing, I promise to fill you in properly tomorrow.'

'Ok, you're off the hook, but ring your source back.'

'I'll give him a bell; I've had no access to a phone until a minute ago,' she lied.

'No need to explain; only he's just rung again and said he needed to talk urgently.'

Christine thanked June and said she'd keep her updated. She told Vinnie quickly what June had said, before using her new mobile to ring Bury. It rang out to answer machine with an automated message. She said who she was and asked him to call back on this number. She didn't have to wait long.

When he rang back she gave him an abridged version of what had happened, in case he had been tailed the previous day, but she was sure it was her who had been followed, probably from her office to Lesley's.

'So, glad you're safe nar, but are you sure you're ok? Bury said.

'I'm fine, bit of a sore head but ok, thanks for your concern,' Christine said.

'As glad as I truly am, I'm selfishly glad too, if you're up for it?'

Christine wondered exactly what Bury was about to say, and asked, 'Depends what you mean?'

Bury laughed, and then said, 'Sorry, I mean a bit of work. Any chance of meeting you tomorrow?'

'Sure, why?'

'It's the main man, I know where he'll be later on tomorrow, if you're still up for an ambush?'

Christine said that she was and arranged to meet Bury in the morning, but this time at the coffee shop near her office. She then rang June straight back, not just to update her, but to ask her to sort out an outside broadcast unit.

'I'll need to speak to Sally, but I can't imagine she'll want you to ambush the First Minister of Northern Ireland, without due cause and provenance.'

Christine expected this, and knew they needed some proof from Bury in the morning, but knew also what great TV it would make. June agreed to have a camera and sound team on standby all day so they could use them at a moment's notice, and Christine promised to get what they needed from Bury. She pointed out that he knew their terms so assumed that he had what was required. She'd known better than to ask him more over the phone.

She quickly brought Vinnie up to speed and asked if they could postpone the evening. He said he fully understood and in truth could do with getting up to Preston as early as possible the following day. He said he'd taken up enough of her time as it was and didn't want to get in the way; they both had jobs to do. She loved this about Vinnie, no edge; her job was just as important to him as his.

'There's just one problem, though,' Vinnie said, as he prepared to leave.

'What's that?' she asked.

'Aren't you supposed to be missing, with just an ever so slight hint that you're dead?'

'Shit. I forgot. What now?'

'Don't panic, I'll get Harry to release something to the press office tomorrow saying that the 'hostage has been found fit and well'. Then at least your family can stop having to pretend. We can say you were found unconscious but are fine now. No one needs to know the details. And as your name hasn't been released publically it shouldn't create too much of a media storm for you.'

'Will he be ok with that?'

'He'll have to be, you have your job to do.'

'Won't that put you back at risk,' Lesley interjected, 'I mean if that madman hears that you're alive?'

Lesley had said what she herself had not wanted to think, but Christine had her job to do. They discussed it further and Vinnie suggested that they prepare the press release but hold back until Christine knew for sure what she was doing. No reason to out herself prematurely if the decision was not to ambush McConachy. If they just ended up covering an address or speech or whatever, she could sit at the back with Bury and observe. She could get a junior to sit at the front and ask the usual questions.

That agreed, she kissed Vinnie softly on the cheek and watched him walk away a while before closing her door. He'd keep, but for now she was buzzing with what might play out tomorrow. It was good to be back doing what she loved; she'd leave the cops and robbers stuff with Vinnie for now.

Chapter Fifty-Five

Quintel was at the hotel bar for nearly an hour after they had eaten. It was gone eight now and McKnowle had said he'd only be a short while; he had some calls to make. Quintel figured he obviously had another phone with him. Eventually, the thin, haggard looking oddity that was McKnowle came rushing into the bar. He wondered what the other customers would make of him; someone's granddad, probably. He certainly didn't have the appearance or aura of an ex-terrorist. Not that Quintel had met one before. That said, who would know that he himself was also a dead-hearted killer.

'Sorry 'bout that, Jackie-boy,' McKnowle started.

'I wish you wouldn't call me that,' Quintel said.

'Oh away with you, it won't be for much longer, nar.'

'Sounds encouraging.'

'Get us a drink and we'll find a corner.'

So suitably refuelled Quintel chose an alcove with a crescent shaped seat set away from the main bar.

'Right you are,' McKnowle started, 'I had a chat with one or two boys over here that I still trust, just locals you understand, not volunteers. And they've sorted out an O.P. for us to use the morrow.'

'Is er "the morrow" game on day?'

'Oh no, but we need ta build up arh reconnaissance.'

'Where's the O.P?'

'I'll telt yous when we are on arh way, not before, no offence. But it's a small office cum flat above a shop, that much you can know.'

'Where are the owners?'

'Ah the owners of the shop and flat have decided to take a short vacation, so they have. Same again?' McKnowle said, and headed to the bar without awaiting an answer. He was back a few minutes later with two more drinks.

Quintel knew better than to ask McKnowle about the target yet, so concentrated on the man's fascinating past. 'You said you'd tell me where you'd been, the last twenty years, or however long it was?' he said.

McKnowle put his arm around Quintel's shoulders and pulled him in close with a strength that surprised Quintel, before whispering in his ear, 'Back in the day over the water, had you been asking these questions, you'd have been made as a tout of the Brits and would had been sent to have a chat with one of our Security Officers, and there never was a more ruthless set of bastards than those guys.'

He then let go of Quintel and roared with laughter, before adding, 'Nar would you look at yous, I'm only feekin joshing you, Jackie-boy.'

Quintel sighed in relief. There was something alien about McKnowle, and his laughter had an unhinged tinge to it. 'I meant no offence,' he said.

'None taken. I'm just readjusting to living by today's rules. Different times.'

'I don't follow you.'

'Oh course you don't. It's not the nick that those Brit bastards put me in, it was a living hell. I've spent the last twenty years, until recently, suffering Locked-in Syndrome. It's taken the last two years to learn how to freekin walk and talk again.'

Quintel sat back, amazed at what McKnowle had said. He only had a rough idea what was meant by Locked-in Syndrome, but he needn't have worried as McKnowle was off and running. He just sat back and listened. McKnowle told him how on one of his unannounced visits to an ASU – active service unit - the plan had been to shoot and kill a 'Proddy-dog' – Protestant – as he returned home to his wife and two teenage kids at their mansion home out in the countryside, west of Belfast. The 'Proddy-dog' whose name McKnowle couldn't remember, apparently owned a large office cleaning company who had the sole contract to clean all the police stations and some other civic buildings in Ulster. The plan was to assassinate the man as he arrived home for the crime of taking the Brit's money, and to send a message to anyone else who fancied getting rich working for the enemy.

'So what happened?' Quintel asked.

'I wanted the ASU to kill the bastard's family too, so I did. They'd been enjoying the wages of sin, and the message would have had all the more meaning.'

'Does that mean the ASU didn't agree?'

'Let's just say I had to remind the soft bastard who was leading the ASU who the feck he was talking to.'

Quintel replenished their drinks and McKnowle continued. He told him how that when they were getting into position they received the warning that the target was approaching, and at the last minute all hell broke loose. 'Go on,' Quintel urged.

'Those Sass bastards were everywhere, jumped up out of the feckin ground, so they did. Two of them materialised out of a feckin hedge, the same hedge I'd took a piss in five minutes earlier, would you believe.'

'Sounds like you had no chance?'

'They had dropped everyone but me and the ASU commander in seconds. I ran at the bastards firing, and then went down. A round sliced through the top of my neck at the back of my head damaging the Pons,' McKnowle said, before leaning forward to show Quintel a lateral welt of twisted scar tissue about three inches long, which was under his shoulder length hair at the back.

'What's a Pons?'

'It's at the base of the brain stem, and it's taken all these years to gradually repair itself. Connections slowly re-established themselves. Nar, I'm not saying I'm not grateful, but it's the never knowing.'

"We live by it, so we die by it" Quintel thought, but instead said, 'I think I'd have rather died.'

'Aye, I thought that many times later on. But back to the night, I was laid down but wide awake. I felt no pain, nor anything else for that matter. I couldn't move a muscle. Eyes open, starring up. They must have thought I was unconscious, but I could see and hear everything.

'The ASU commander had legged it and two Sass had gone after him. That left two with me before one left to go and see the Proddy-dog. But before he did they had a quick chat about me.'

Quintel was hooked on the story now, not sure whether to believe it all, but guessed it was probably all true. 'What did they say?'

'One examined me and told the other I was alive but noted my neck wound and added that I was not responding to painful stimuli.'

Quintel asked what that meant.

'It meant, they reckoned I was either unconscious or paralysed. One wanted to finish me off, but the one who was obviously in charge said no.'

Quintel was surprised to hear this, and asked, 'What, the leader of the troop wanted to save you?'

'The feek he did,' McKnowle said, before realising his rising tones were starting to draw attention. He paused and returned his voice to normal. 'No, he didn't. He said as my eyes were open I couldn't be unconscious. He then stuck his knife in both my legs to prove I was paralysed. I never felt a thing. Then he told the other soldier to call a medic on his way to see the Proddy-dog.

'I was laid there and the bastard lent over me and said, "I want you to live the rest of your life as a fucking vegetable; death is too good for scum of your depth. You even give terrorists a bad name." He probably thought he was talking to himself, but I heard every word alright.'

'I thought about little else for the next few months.'

Quintel was starting to see where all of McKnowle's rage came from now, and asked, 'What happened next?'

'Next, I spent twenty years hearing, seeing, but never moving.'

'Wasn't there an inquiry? Quintel asked.

'Aye, a sham sack of shite by that bastard Reedly working as Carstair's bitch, so it was all covered up.'

Quintel wasn't too sure what McKnowle meant by that, but he said that if he'd get him a double-Irish whisky to finish the night, he'd explain. And as Quintel rose to head to the bar, McKnowle said, 'And tomorrow when you can clap eyes on arh main target, it'll all make sense.'

Quintel was convinced more than ever now of whom their main target was. He knew the man would be twenty-odd years older but still would be a formidable adversary if they didn't get it right first time. He was glad about the O.P. now; reconnaissance was good. He was halfway to the bar when Mcknowle shouted.

'And none of that Scottish shite; Irish Jackie-boy, Irish.'

Chapter Fifty-Six

Christine had slept fitfully and was relieved when her alarm went off. At least her head had stopped pounding and she was now glad the evening had drawn to a premature end, as far as her sore head was concerned; a hangover wouldn't have helped. Lesley was already up and was again brighter than she'd have expected. 'You seem in a good mood again?' she asked.

'That nightmare at mine the other day has given me some perspective on what's not worth worrying about.'

Christine was glad to hear this; it would be nice if a positive became the legacy.

By 9.30 am she was sat in a window seat of the coffee shop near her office. It was busy with office workers but most were buying 'to go'; there were only a handful of people seated. She'd taken the liberty of getting two lattes and hoped Paul wouldn't be too late. Then he walked in with a genuine look of relief and joy on his face. She quickly gave him a fuller version of her ordeal, setting the scenes but without too much detail.

'I hope I'm in no way responsible, for this?' Bury said.

He explained. He wondered if it had anything to do with her trip to *The Blarney Stone*, or his suspecting of a tail on him. She smiled on hearing this and reassured him that it was not. She explained how she had been followed from her office. All that out of the way, she asked him what had come up?

'The First Minister is due to give a speech or something later today.'

'Well, if he is, then our office will already know all about it.'

'Aye, but I've got proof that he has been systematically removing pro-Brits from senior positions, all the while whilst playing the game. In fact today's address is just another example of his "look at me, aren't we all just the best of buddies nar".'

'Well, if we are even thinking about ambushing him, it better be pretty good.'

Bury then took a small Dictaphone from his pocket, which had earbuds attached, and handed it to her.

'Just press play,' he said.

'What is it?'

'The last senior officer still in place in our squad who was signed up to the power sharing but has not had his contract renewed,' he started.

'Another Protestant?'

'Surprisingly no, a Catholic, which probably makes it worse, for the likes of McConachy.'

'And I'm guessing he's been replaced with a suspected Republican sympathiser?'

'That he has; nar press play.'

Christine did. And what she heard was a very brief, but heated exchange between two men. Both addressed the other by their titles, which was handy. The First Minister of Northern Ireland and an assistant chief constable. Once the ACC is told his services are no longer required he accuses McConachy of arranging his demise.

"It's up to your chief who his top team are, not me," McConachy says.

"He's already told me that you were behind it," the ACC says back.

"Well, I do have to have confidence in your chief and his decision making."

"I suppose once you've got control of NIUCS and the PSNI (Northern Irish United Crime Squad and the Police Service of Northern Ireland) the regional government will be next?"

A pause followed and then the ACC carried on, "Then you'll no doubt tell the Brits to fuck off and declare a union with the south?"

"How fucking dare you. Get out of my office."

"I'm going McConachy, but as we are here alone at least have the bollocks to stare me in the face and tell me the truth."

"Those wankers in Whitehall are so blinded by their desire to make power sharing work; they fall over themselves to keep me sweet. I have no more intention of making that work than I would in keeping scum like you in office. We will be victorious; and those British bastards will need a visa to drink my piss."

Christine was utterly stunned by what she was hearing, and glanced at Bury's smiling face, as she listened in. McConachy continued his deranged rant.

"And you being Irish and a Catholic are the worst of the worst. So now you know what you thought you knew. I Hope it eats away at you. Now get out before I have you thrown out."

"Thank you," the ACC said.

"What the fuck for?"

"You'll find out." Then there was a click and the recording ended.

Christine pulled the earbuds out and handed the kit back to Bury. 'When was this?'

'Two days ago. The guy is a friend of mine. We shared our views and after I went he started taking note. Started taking precautions. This is the very Dictaphone he took with him to see McConachy. That's one reason I've been frantic to get hold of you. Now will June sanction our little ambush?'

Christine knew that June would. This was gold. This would become TV gold. This was why the press and the media in all its guises had to remain free. This was why she got out of bed in the morning and did the job she did. This would be the scoop to end all scoops.

'Come on Paul, I can't wait to see June and the producer Sally's faces when they hear this.'

Chapter Fifty-Seven

After breakfast McKnowle insisted that they take everything with them, and not just the holdall with the hardware in, everything, just in case they didn't return. They "were operational now, approaching the wet end" as McKnowle had put it. He even insisted they empty their room bins and wipe down things they had touched. The guy was definitely an old pro and Quintel respected that.

By 10 am they left the hotel and were walking towards the old Nissan, Quintel was relieved to find it still there, and five minutes later they were on their way to Preston. Quintel suggested they go via a different route and picked the A586, which pretty much runs parallel to the M55. He told McKnowle it was good tradecraft to vary their routes, which McKnowle accepted. He has glad, as he knew he couldn't tell him the real reason, not that it would matter for too much longer.

En route Quintel picked up where they had left off the night before. 'If I'm guessing who the final target is, would I be far wrong if I said he was present on the night you were shot all those years ago?'

'That much I can confirm, Jackie-boy, you'll be clapping eyes on the bastard soon enough, so you will.'

'So where are we headed?'

'A row of shops near to Fulwood Barracks in the north part of Preston. It's a huge place off a road called Watling Street Road which itself is off the main A6. Head for the centre and find the A6,' McKnowle said.

This was further confirmation of what Quintel had previously thought. 'We'll have to be careful near there, they'll have security everywhere.'

'Aye, that they will, which is why we are meeting a local sympathiser in a nearby side street, so he can show me the best way into the flat,' McKnowle said, before he gave Quintel the details of the side road which was off Watling Street Road. Considering McKnowle had been off the manor for twenty years, he appeared quite well-connected.

Fifty-five minutes later, Quintel parked the Nissan in the side street where a middle-aged man in a leather jacket was waiting for them. He watched as McKnowle greeted the man with a hug but couldn't tell whether they actually knew each other, or whether it was just a case of belonging to the same club. They had just disappeared around the corner when Quintel's private mobile rang.

'Are you alone?' the caller started.

'Yeah, but be quick.'

'They're releasing a press release saying they have found the unnamed kidnap victim alive and well.'

Quintel was taken aback by this. Jason said he'd done her and buried her, how could she have survived that? 'You sure?'

'Hundred percent.'

As annoying as it was, it didn't really matter from his point of view, that cop Palmer had already seen him as it was, and after this final job was over he wouldn't be hanging around. The only problem would be if McKnowle heard about it. He thought she was dead, an extra ten large ones rested on his belief in that. Quintel instinctively turned the car radio off. 'Ok, thanks for letting me know, it shouldn't be too much of a problem.'

'If you are thinking of finishing her off, you'd be taking a huge risk trying to get near her now. That cocky twat Vinnie Palmer who is hunting you, is all over Christine Jones like a love sick puppy.'

'I not fucking stupid, and don't forget you are paid to keep me informed, not to give advice.'

'Just saying,' the caller said.

Quintel ended the conversation by telling the caller not to ring but text until further notice. If he felt they needed to speak, he was to say so in a text and Quintel would ring him when he could. He then set all the alerts on his phone to vibrate only.

Then his new phone rang and McKnowle told him to grab the holdall and leave the car where it was. He directed him to a back alley which ran behind the shops. He told him to make his way to the last gate.

*

'Sorry I'm late,' Harry said as he rushed into the SIO's office in the incident room at Preston.

'No worries, Frank, it gave me chance for a fried breakfast. This canteen does do one of the best police breakfasts going,' Vinnie said.

'Thanks for that. I've just had to make do with tea and biscuits in the chief's office.'

'How is Mr Darlington?'

'Not a happy camper today. He'd just come off the phone to Reedly when I arrived.'

Harry had rung Vinnie earlier telling him to get in ASAP, said he couldn't speak over the phone but that it was urgent, which had proved a little baffling when he found the office empty. But it did explain why Harry didn't want Vinnie to pay Reedly a visit en route as he'd suggested. 'And was the chief's chat with Reedly productive?'

'No. He said he'd come up with a list of ten possibles whom he might have seriously pissed off back in the day, but our intel cell has apparently eliminated them all,' Harry said.

'Ah, that explains Darlington's displeasure.'

'I only wish that was true,' Harry said, before closing and locking the office door. He then made his way to his desk before continuing. 'You remember when I couldn't get hold of the chief to brief him about you chasing the Nissan in Blackpool?

'Yeah,' Vinnie said.

'Same thing happened with the press release re Christine. Both times I had to sort it out via the Headquarters Press Office. Via the chief's office.'

'Ok.'

'Well,' Harry started, while also starting to rub his head.

'They've not fucking named her, have they?' Vinnie said, cutting in.

'No, nothing like that, but Darlington had been expecting a pre-arranged telephone update from me without having any knowledge of Christine, or indeed any idea of what was in the update .'

'So?' Vinnie asked.

'So he made himself scarce on purpose so I'd have to go through his staff officer.'

'Russell Sharpe?

'Blister indeed,' Harry said. And then he explained.

Apparently the chief knew about the sighting of the Nissan in Blackpool as the Force Incident Manager had mainlined into him, which was normal procedure anytime armed response vehicles were deployed. What Darlington had not previously told Harry was that for some time he had suspected a leak at senior level. 'What, from the Press Office? Vinnie asked.

'He didn't know for sure, but he's had someone working inside his own staff office looking for the leak,' Harry said.

'So Blister is one of the good guys after all,' Vinnie said, almost feeling disappointed. Harry just carried on. Apparently, they had a suspect and had covertly put a live cell-siting on the individual's phone. Subsequent analysis proved that soon after Vinnie had given chase after the Nissan, the suspect had rung a mobile number cited in Blackpool and left a voice message warning that the cops were "nearing in on you, in Blackpool".

'Whose number was rung?' Vinnie asked.

'It can only be Quintel's, but it keeps being turned on and off so it is proving difficult to locate.'

'Whose handset made the call?

'That's the tricky bit, it is a pool phone owned by Lancashire Police but of whom anyone in the Staff Office or Press Office have access to,' Harry said.

'No wonder the chief's not a happy chicken. So what happens now?'

Harry told Vinnie that the chief had spoken to the Home Secretary and requested an urgent warrant of interception – a phone tap – or line, as they called them, on the basis that there was an imminent threat to life, as in Quintel's next target. Vinnie knew that obtaining a phone tap by normal channels took months but also knew that in emergency situations where life was in danger it could be done in a matter of hours. 'I'm guessing the Home Sec agreed?'

'Well, he agreed to put a line on the mole's phone as we could prove it had been used to tip off Quintel, but he refused the request for a line on Quintel's phone itself.'

'Why the hell not, after all it's Quintel who is providing the main threat, not the mole?'

'They don't grant lines easily as you know, but until we can prove that it's Quintel on the other end of that phone the Home Sec won't sign. He said it could be anyone's phone, as the police were probably chasing a lot of folk on that particular night in Blackpool.'

'How long will it take to put the line on, if and when we prove that it's Quintel on the other end?' Vinnie asked.

'Not long,' Harry answered, adding, 'they have most things in place to throw the switch, we just need a bit of luck.'

Then Harry's phone rang and Vinnie didn't pay too much attention as he sat back and absorbed all that Harry had just said. That was until Harry smashed his fist onto his desk, before ending his call, and turning to face Vinnie with a huge grin on his face.

'That was Darlington, bingo. The bent police handset has just put a call into the same number, only this time it was switched on and caller and recipient had a conversation.'

'What was said?'

'The caller told the recipient that Christine was alive.'

'The absolute bastard,' Vinnie said.

'The recipient was obviously Quintel, so London are now in the process of hooking up a live line on that phone too, which incidentally is somewhere in north Preston.'

'Shit.'

'Shit indeed,' Harry said.

'Any news on who the mole is?'

'It can only be one of two people, because when I rang with the press release about Christine, only two people were made aware. The person I spoke to and the press officer whom that person passed the info to.'

'But anyone could have heard the press release and then rang Quintel?' Vinnie said.

'They could in five minutes when it goes out, but in any event, Christine's name isn't being used in it. She's just being referred to as an "unnamed kidnap victim". '

'So if that puts the press officer in the clear, who did you speak to in the chief's office?' Vinnie asked.

'The on-call Staff Office representative.'

'Who was?' Vinnie asked, the suspense unbearable.

'Chief Inspector Russell Sharpe, no less, or Blister to his friends.'

Chapter Fifty-Eight

Christine was sat in the scrip edits room, with Paul Bury next to her on one side of the long, light wood table, and the programme's producer Sally and her editor and the documentary's director June across from them.

'Before you play the Dictaphone let's watch the opening to get us all back in sync,' Sally said. They all turned to face a large TV on a high stand, with casters which always reminded her of the ones they had in high school. Christine knew that neither she nor June needed any syncing; it was for Sally's own benefit, as she had so many half-done programmes on the go at any one time.

The title was 'One for you, and one for me', with the tagline, 'How fairly shared, is the power-sharing in Northern Ireland?' Over the last few weeks Christine had been busy fine tuning some of her pieces to camera and she knew June had pulled most of the programme together with those and her pre-recorded interviews. They just had the final conclusions to film so it ran like a visual dissertation. After the opening credits the first scene was of her walking down a very well-known road in Belfast with Loyalist Protestant social housing on one side and Republican Catholic ones on the other.

"My name is Christine Jones, and I'm strolling down a road known locally as 'The Slayer's Path'. It's where two sides of the community live in relative peace now. The Protestants known as 'St George's Men' on my left – after the English flag of St George – and the Catholics, known as the 'Dragons' are on my right." Christine always hated watching herself on the telly; some reporters loved it, but she was not one of them. She thought she looked a bit pale. "But how fair is the share, in the new power-sharing of Northern Ireland's regional government?" The opening went on to set out the two arguments asking had too much grace been given by one side to the other, or was this just paranoia? The Deputy First Minister of the Northern Irish Assembly was a Protestant and staunch Unionist, whereas the First Minister himself was a Catholic Republican whom many accused of previously being an active member of the IRA. This was something that Mathew McConachy had always denied, stating he had been a member of their political wing but no more.

Sally paused the recording and asked Paul to play the tape, which he did.

Christine enjoyed the look on both Sally and June's faces, and when the recording ended Sally asked if Paul had a deposition from the officer proving the provenance of the recording. Paul said that he had, and opened a folder in front of him and handed some papers across the table. 'Here's his written statement,' he said.

Sally read it and passed it to June, who spoke for the first time after reading it and putting it on the table. 'Fucking hell; have we got an ending, or what?'

Christine laughed, and the others joined in. When order returned, Sally spoke. 'This is huge and will have potentially major consequences.'

Christine worried that Sally was thinking of allowing McConachy a right of reply prior to any broadcast. She needn't have. The strategy they then agreed was that McConachy's visit to the North West was too good an opportunity. The ambush was on. Paul was to remain in the background as an observer in case anyone turned up that they should know about. 'I can do covert,' he said.

Christine, with a soundman and cameraman, were to do the ambush with a choice of words that Sally would quickly have run past the in-house lawyer first, and then she was to record McConachy's comments in response, and if in the negative as presumed, to ask if he had ever used his influence personally to have officials removed from office.

'Record his denials but with no follow ups,' Sally said, continuing, 'we get that on tape and then the night before we air, we can give him his right to reply then.'

'Garden path the fucker,' Paul said.

Christine joined the others in looking quizzically at him.

'An old CID interview expression,' he said, adding, 'We'd take the suspect on a path of denials so there can be no doubt what he or she is saying, and then hit them with the evidence.' He gave the example of finding a print or DNA at a crime scene, say, in someone's house that had been burgled, and making sure the suspect couldn't suddenly remember having visited the place once ages ago, after being hit with the evidence.

237

'Exactly,' Sally said, 'that way, he'll be none the wiser to exactly who or how we know.'

'He'll be "garden pathed" to within an inch of his life, don't you worry about that,' Christine added.

'Ok, let's get cracking, he's due to give a speech outside an Irish community centre in Manchester in two hours' time,' Sally said.

Chapter Fifty-Nine

Quintel found the last gate as described at the end of the rear alley by a brick wall. He was glad it was only five minutes from the car, as the holdall with all its goodies was starting to become heavy. Inside the rear yard he could see a half-glazed kitchen door ajar, which he closed behind him.

'Upstairs, Jackie-boy,' McKnowle's voice boomed, and Quintel joined him in the front bedroom of what looked like a bedsit-come-office above a computer repair shop. Over by the window was a scruffy two-seater settee and a table. The window looked about four feet wide and had dirty net curtains covering the glass.

'Where did you say the occupants were again?' Quintel asked.

'A little tied up on an unexpected vacation,' McKnowle said.

'Won't the shop being closed draw attention?'

'Apparently not. According to the man, the place is run by a couple of nancy-boys who are either out all day fixing people's porn riddled laptops, or are up here letting life imitate art. I'd be careful where you sit, Jackie-boy,' McKnowle said before roaring with laughter. Quintel gave the two-seater a miss and sat on a picnic chair next to it.

'Nar, would you look at that,' he said.

Quintel did, and got his first glimpse of the British Army's North West Headquarters of some Brigade or other. It was a huge place situated on the busy urban thoroughfare that was Watling Street Road. The Barracks was set back slightly as the road curved around its perimeter at a set of traffic lights, where a further road joined and formed a sort of Y shape. McKnowle said it was within sight of Deepdale, which was Preston North End's football ground. And according to him, the oldest league football ground in the world. 'I didn't know you were an English football fan?' Quintel asked.

'Not English, just football,' McKnowle said.

Quintel took his time weighing up the topography of the area, as Jason might have said. The entrance was set back from the road accessed by a short driveway which had a barrier and sentry to protect it. 'This isn't going to be easy,' he said.

'Piece of piss,' McKnowle answered.

'So where is our target actually going to be, and when?' Quintel asked.

'He'll be stood at the end of that driveway, but by the road itself.'

'That sounds pretty exact information.'

'Always make sure you have good intel, and we've got good intel.'

'Your local sympathiser?'

'Aye.'

Quintel further looked at the plot and knew that from this distance a handgun would be useless. As the proverbial crow flew, they must be thirty or forty metres away, more if you considered their elevation. He suddenly became aware of McKnowle looking at him.

'I knows what yous arh thinking, Jackie-boy, but do yous remember me telling you that I wouldn't get in the way?'

Quintel said that he did.

'Well, all you have to do is sit around the corner in that old Nissan of yours and I'll call you on when arh man's in place.'

'Then what? Drive past and try and hit him with a handgun?'

'No, but I do want you to drive past and lob one of those grenades at the fooker; that should do it. But just the one mind, use the second one on the motor when you ditch it. I'll fuck off from here and meet you somewhere. See, I won't be in the way, but I'll have a fookin good view of the bastard getting what he's owed.' Then McKnowle launched into one of his unhinged laughs and Quintel took a further look out of the window.

The Irish bastard might be a psychotic madman, but his plan should work, he thought. Not even an ex-SAS trooper would survive that. 'So we get a look at him today, but when are we doing it?' Quintel asked.

'Need to know, and yous now needs to know. The fooker will be here in a couple of har's time. Then we do the bastard.'

'How will I know him?'

'No worries Jackie-boy, he's giving a talk first and then will come forward ta answer questions, so there will be plenty of time for yous to see him and get ta your motor. I'll call yous on when he comes forward, it'll be easier for yous then. Like I say; a piece of piss.'

*

'So what happens to Blister now?' Vinnie asked.

'The chief has authorised a full surveillance on Blister in the hope that they can collect further evidence of the scumbag's duplicity,' Harry started.

'I never liked the weasel,' Vinnie interjected.

'And,' Harry continued, 'to hopefully lead the team to Quintel. A full firearms authority has also been granted and there are three gunships – ARVs running behind the surveillance team. There's just one problem.'

'What's that?'

'The little shit's gone sick and isn't at home, nor is his own car.'

'Bollocks,' Vinnie said before asking, 'What about Quintel?'

'His phone is switched on so the live cell-citing still has it somewhere in North Preston; the last mast it pinged off was near the football ground.'

'When will the line go on?'

'Dunno, hopefully soon.'

'Do you think Quintel's final target is today?' Vinnie asked.

'Anyone's guess, but there seems to be a lot of activity going on.'

Vinnie said he'd take a run up to the north end of the city and see if he could spot the Nissan, that was if Quintel still had it. He couldn't think of what else to do, well, not until the line on Quintel's phone went live, then they had a chance. Harry agreed and said he'd stay in the office and await Darlington's call, and coordinate the surveillance team's activity.

Chapter Sixty

The Manchester community centre where McConachy was due to speak outside was on a quiet side street not a million miles from *The Blarney Stone* pub. Paul told Christine not to look for him but he would be close enough should she need him for any reason. She got the impression that he was rather enjoying himself, sneaking about in the shadows. There were two TV channels set up outside to cover McConachy's address, so she and her two-handed crew blended in well. Fortunately, both the soundgirl and cameraman had not only worked together many times, but had both worked on her programme several times so knew the backstory. The press brief was that McConachy would give a short address before taking questions, which was when she'd strike.

A little after eleven a motorcade of two plain cars and two marked police escort vehicles swung majestically into the street. The cop cars' blue lights were flashing but with no sirens. A lectern had been set up at the roadside and a number of uniformed police community support officers and two cops held back the handful of locals who had turned out for a nosy. There were more press and TV knocking about than actual members of the public.

Five minutes later and Christine got her first look at McConachy in the flesh; he was not as imposing as he appeared on TV. He was a man in his late fifties, of small build and only about five foot five inches tall. He walked with a pronounced limp, almost dragging his right leg behind him as he stood in front of the podium and tapped on the mike to test it.

'I don't have too long before I head off to make my full address,' McConachy started, 'but I wanted to pre-empt what I will say later, here first; in this small piece of Ireland on English soil, it seems fitting, and in-keeping with all the marvellous initiatives that are now taking place in Northern Ireland since the peace process gave us the power sharing we all enjoy today.'

'You getting all this?' Christine whispered. Both her crew nodded.

'A lot has been said about the dropping of investigations into the actions of paramilitaries on both sides of the political divide during the troubles, even though these events were considered acts committed within a war, and so therefore should not be treated as crimes. Indeed, it is the pardoning of those convicted which was a cornerstone of the peace agreement in the first place.'

Christine couldn't hold back. 'Christine Jones NWTV, is this why you are choosing the UK mainland to say this? To protect yourself from any backlash?'

'If you'd let me finish Miss Jones,' McConachy replied. But the short exchange had allowed her and her crew to edge to the front, which was all she needed.

'As I was saying,' McConachy continued, 'In order to silence the critics of this policy, I want to announce today that I have agreed with Whitehall that all similar investigations into historical atrocities committed by the British Army and the Royal Ulster Constabulary – as it was, before it became the Police Service of Northern Ireland - will also be dropped so that we might all move forward.'

Any hope Christine had of ambushing McConachy on the totally different subject she had in mind soon became impossible. After dropping the bombshell he just had, the remaining press and media surged forward with a thousand questions being asked at once. McConachy silenced them as he took to the mike again. 'I appreciate you have a lot of questions for such a historic announcement, but it might be better at the next venue where there will be more room. I'm sure you'll all be off over there in a mo. Thank you.'

And with that McConachy was swiftly ushered back to his car. 'Shit,' Christine said, as she felt a hand on her elbow. She turned to face Paul. 'You hear that?' she asked.

'Sure did, come on, let's get to the next venue before the pack.'

Five minutes later Christine was a passenger in Paul's hire car as he put it through its paces. 'You after me landing in your lap again?' she asked.

Paul just grinned as he concentrated on his driving; both of her crew were in the back seat, Paul said it would be quicker in one vehicle, which it would. Though by the look on her cameraman's face he was probably wishing he'd put his camera in the boot now as he tried to cocoon it on his lap while the car slew around several corners.

'Didn't see that coming, talk about wanting to appear all things to all men,' Paul said.

'That'll enrage his lot,' Christine said.

'Aye, they'll see it as another example of him rolling over to let the Brits tickle his tummy,' Paul said.

'Smokescreen though. Did you note his choice of language?' Christine said.

Paul just gave her a quick quizzical glance.

'When he's describing what the terrorists did during the troubles – and he really means the IRA but can't say it – he talks about "acts committed within a war" and "should not be treated as crimes", but when he talks about what the British forces did, it becomes "atrocities".'

'Well spotted,' Paul said.

'He probably doesn't even realise it himself.'

'Anyway, how do you intend to play it at the next venue?' Paul asked.

'We need to get in first, before the hoo-hah goes up at the end again. And, it'll spoil his "historic moment". It just depends if you can get us there before a fully equipped police escort?'

'Better believe it; anyway it's not that far.'

Christine glanced at Paul as he concentrated on throwing the car's occupants from side to side with what was obviously an involuntary smirk on his face. Now she was sure he was enjoying himself.

Chapter Sixty-One

A crowd had been gathering for a while now, Quintel noticed. It was up to about fifty he reckoned and was being held back by a cordon of police where the driveway to the barracks' main entrance met the pavement which abutted the road. A lectern had been set on the pavement and a second one was being set up near to the sentry at the entrance to the compound. 'A couple of those fuckers look like the press,' Quintel said as he glanced at his watch; 11.30 am.

'Don't be worrying about that, you'll be through before they know what's hit them,' McKnowle said.

'How do you know where the SAS escort to - whoever the fuck will be talking - will be? I mean I know an escort is an escort, but we've only got one crack at this, it could all become a bit fluid,' Quintel said.

McKnowle turned to face him with a puzzled look on his face, which seemed a bit spooky as the sun came out at that very moment and threw a spotlight on his face, giving it a ghoul-like quality.

'What Sass escort yous on about?'

'Well, I just assumed the target was ex-SAS.'

'And why would you be thinking that, Jackie-boy?' McKnowle said, his voice with a sharp edge, and his countenance taking on an even harsher look.

'It was just with you saying the target had been at the scene where you got shot, all those years ago, that's all,' Quintel quickly said, and noticed the look on McKnowle's face ease a little.

'Arh, I did say that, didn't I?'

'Look no offence, but I'm going to need to know which fucker to throw the grenade at?'

'So you arh. Fair enough,' Mcknowle said before glancing at his own watch. 'The target isn't one of those Sass twats, though I'd love it to be, but there is no way of ever knowing who they were. I've had to settle with Reedly and Carstair instead.'

Quintel still didn't quite understand the relevance of Reedly and Carstair; he hadn't needed to, but was now intrigued. McKnowle clearly saw this and explained. He told Quintel all about the British strategy of justifying the security forces' "murders" of the IRA's volunteers up until the late nineties. How Carstair had been the government minister who brought in the policy and how Reedly had been the detective inspector charged with executing it. Quintel now understood his hatred of them.

'I spent twenty years in that hell-like state, while those two bastards covered up the Sass's actions. I had thought about asking you to kidnap them first so I could try to torture the information out of them, but I realised not even they would have known the Sass's true identity. It would have been all that "Soldier A and Soldier B" bollocks.'

'So who are we looking at today?'

'I telt you properly afterwards, no offence, Jackie-boy, but what I can telt you is that the target was the ASU commander on the night I was ambushed and left for worse than dead.'

Quintel hadn't seen that coming. Now he understood why McKnowle couldn't use one of his old terrorist killers to do these jobs. There would have been no problem with Reedly and Carstair, but a fellow member of the IRA? And an active service unit commander to boot. 'Forgive me, Bobby, I hope you don't mind me using your first name?' Quintel said.

'Only in private, but no worries.'

Though Quintel now knew why McKnowle had gone outside on this job, and why Reedly and Carstair had been targets, he still didn't know why the ASU commander was, so he asked, 'Is it because he didn't want to do all of the man's family, and left you on your own after the ambush went down?'

'Either of those reasons in themselves would be justification enough, Jackie-boy, but it runs far deeper than that, so it does,' McKnowle started, and then opened up again like he had done at the bar the previous night. He went on to explain that he was actually a very, very senior member of the IRA's ruling Army Council. He didn't say he was at the top, but Quintel wondered if he had been. McKnowle told him of his hard-line views and that he would never have approved with the whole peace process that the paramilitaries on all sides eventually agreed to with the Brits. As far as McKnowle was concerned the war was still on now that he was free from his medical incarceration.

'I'm taking care of my own business and then I'll start the war again,' he said.

'So why the ASU commander?' Quintel asked again.

'After he legged it and I was carted away, he wheedled his way into the Army Council and eventually took over as a major influence within it. Something that would never had happened if I'd still been on my feet. The arrogant twat used to visit me in hospital to tell me how well the peace discussions were going. He was freeking pleased with himself. Thought I would be too. I had to just lie there and listen to it.'

No wonder McKnowle was such an angry man, Quintel thought, so he knew to go lightly now. 'Maybe he thought you would have approved?' Quintel offered.

'Approved, approved,' McKnowle said, adding, 'that bastard knew. He was taunting me, taking the piss, rubbing in the seniority he had gained. If I'm to restart the armed struggle, he'd have to die anyway; it just so happens that it's also personal.'

Quintel glanced out of the window and noted more activity building up outside. McKnowle also turned to face the window, before adding, 'It doesn't look like it'll be long nar, best you check the kit.'

Chapter Sixty-Two

Vinnie was getting tired of aimlessly driving around looking for any sign of the old Nissan. He knew that the part- registered number had been logged into the ANPR – automatic number plate recognition – system, but with it only being a partial, it would be hit and miss whether a roadside or vehicle born camera would pick it up. In fact, the more he learnt about Quintel, the more convinced he was that he'd have ditched the motor by now. Even if he hadn't initially been aware that he'd been clocked in it in Blackpool, that bent bastard Blister would no doubt have made sure afterwards. He'd also taken a ride to Blister's address, which was also in the north of Preston, but made sure he didn't get too close. He spotted a surveillance vehicle parked up near the house keeping watch, so veered off before he passed the address. He'd not heard from Harry since he'd left the nick, which must mean no good news. He eventually pulled up into a small car park opposite Preston North End Football Club's Deepdale ground on the one side and a huge inner urban park called Moor Park on the other. He noticed that it was past 11.30 am as his phone rang. Harry.

'Hi Harry, is the line on?'

'Unfortunately not yet, and to make matters worse, Blister's turned his phone off.'

Brilliant, Vinnie thought, the phone they really needed intercepted – Quintel's - was turned on, but with no interception, whereas Blister's was being intercepted but he'd turned it off. 'Is the cell-citing still active?' he asked.

'That much we still have, and according to the last update a few minutes ago the handset is still somewhere in north Preston. But the reason I'm ringing is that I've just spoken to a local uniform superintendent who seemed harassed because of a last minute security issue he'd been given.'

'What kind of issue?' Vinnie asked.

'He says some ex-IRA terrorist is due to make a speech set up at short notice; or short notice to the cops in Preston, anyway.'

'Whereabouts?'

'Very near to where you were headed. Outside Fulwood Army Barracks.'

'Why, is he just trying to wind up the military?'

'Probably,' Harry said, adding, 'I've put a call into our friend Major Crompton, and have our intel cell ready once we get a name.'

'How do you mean?'

'The uniform super wouldn't tell me who it is, which is fair enough from his point of view,' Harry said. Always the diplomat, Vinnie thought, he'd have taken a more brutish approach.

'But I'm hoping Major Crompton will surely know, and then we can do some research.'

'What about Darlington?' Vinnie asked.

'On voicemail, probably in a meeting, and I daren't go through his staff office; we don't know whether Blister was working alone or not.'

'Any news on that slime ball? I'd love to have five minutes alone with him after what he's tried to do to Christine.'

'I'll pretend I didn't hear that Inspector, but no, to answer your question, but he's got to return home sometime. Anyway, for now can you keep the area around the barracks warm?'

Vinnie said that he would and ended the call before firing up the Volvo engine. He also noticed that the sun had come from behind the clouds at last.

*

'There the fucker is. It's been a while since I saw that ugly face peering over me with his rancid breath, but that's him so it is,' McKnowle said.

Quintel took a long look at the man as he got out of a plain car, and was relieved to see the marked police escort vehicles all sod off as soon as they'd dropped him. He started to head up the driveway to the podium near the gatehouse as McKnowle had said he would. This guy certainly had some pretty sharp intel. Quintel studied him and wasn't particularly impressed by the man's demeanour, and voiced as much.

'Don't be conned by physical appearances alone, he's been a bad man in his time, before he turned into the traitor that he now is,' McKnowle said, adding, 'some of the meanest Sass I've ever come across were the meekest looking; not all muscles and noise like the Paras and the

Marines. Just mean, dirty, sneaky bastards, and ASU commanders were the same.'

Quintel noticed that their target was wearing a light grey summer suit, which also helped mark him out from the crowd. 'Ok,' he said, 'I'll not mistake him, all five foot four of him, so I'll head to the motor, bell me when we're ready.'

'I telt yous what, Jackie-boy, I know I said I'd keep away, but nar I've set eyes on the twat, I'll come with yous.'

Quintel wasn't entirely surprised by this; in fact it gave him an idea. It would mean parking on the main road to get a long distant view of when their man made his way to the podium by the pavement, but it would greatly increase their chances of success. 'Ok, he said, and then threw the car keys at McKnowle, and added, 'You drive and I'll throw the grenade. But we'd better get moving, it looks like he's about to start the first part of his address.'

Chapter Sixty-Three

Vinnie drove past the Barracks twice, once from each direction. He had approached the Y shaped junction from the top right of the Y. The Barracks themselves were set back on a bend with a large grass verge separating the street from the perimeter road. Vinnie could see a large crowd of sixty or more being held back by a police cordon on the wide pavement, next to a podium set up by the entrance road to the barracks. On his second drive past he saw a second lectern set up on the entrance road to the Barracks by the sentry post. He didn't know if the ex-IRA terrorist had permission to do his address there or not, but guessed he had by the bored look on the sentry's face. He turned right at the junction and headed back towards the football ground where he'd turn around and try and find somewhere to park. His phone rang, so he pulled over. It was Harry.

'I've just had Darlington on and Major Crompton. This must be it. The ex-terrorist is thought to have been on a job years ago in west Belfast but escaped. Nothing could ever be proved, but when I dropped the name that Darlington gave me on Crompton he just said, "I'm unable to confirm or deny your speculation, but if he's linked to your targets already attacked, then…,"'

'What does that mean?' Vinnie asked.

Ignoring his question, an excited Harry continued, 'I've spoken to Reedly and run the name past him, too, and, bingo.'

'In what way?'

'He remembers a job where the security forces intercepted an ASU kill team. Two were killed, one escaped, and one was seriously injured. The two who were killed were adjudged to have been so by virtue of "Justifiable Homicide".'

'Good of Reedly to only remember this now.'

'Well, that's the thing; he'd discounted it as the injured terrorist – who incidentally was a very senior member of the Provisional IRA – never recovered from his injuries, he was left in a paralysed state known as Locked-in Syndrome. He apparently hated the man who is speaking today.'

'Why?'

'He took over his role and became a leading light in the peace process, and there's more, much more.'

Vinnie could see the links now. Carstair and Reedly because of their adjudication – rightly so – that the terrorists who had died had been stopped about to commit murder. But more so with today's speaker, a man hated by the man behind Quintel. 'So who is the man behind all this?'

'He's called Bobby McKnowle,' Harry said.

'But why now after all these years, and who is doing it for him?'

'McKnowle himself is behind it and the reason for "why now"? is easy. According to our intel team McKnowle recovered his muscular movement a couple of years ago and has since made a full recovery.'

'Shit this is it,' Vinnie said.

'Can you get in close and look for any sign of Quintel and McKnowle; I'm guessing he was Quintel's passenger the other day. I've got the three gunships that were behind the surveillance team making ground to join you.'

'Ok, Harry, no probs. Has Quintel's phone been lined-up yet?'

'Imminent I'm told and Blister's phone is still off, I'm afraid.'

'Last question, Harry; who is the actual target then?'

'You won't believe it, Vinnie,' Harry said, and then he told him.

*

Quintel picked up the grenade he'd bought the other day from the guy in Birmingham. He guessed either would do, but this one looked newer and Quintel hoped that would make it more effective. The lesser of the two – if indeed there was any difference – would be plenty explosive enough to destroy the Nissan afterwards. He kept the two hand guns under his coat until he was back in the car, and handed one to McKnowle who slipped it in his pocket before starting the engine.

McKnowle drove away from the Barracks before turning around and re-approaching. He pulled over fifty metres short as they took in the scene. The crowd was growing larger and their white-haired target in the light grey suit kept strutting up and down the driveway between the two podiums. He eventually settled at the one by the sentry, away from the crowd.

'Typical of the arrogant bastard to say whatever the feckin ejiot has to say away from the crowd, and then to do a photo opportunity afterwards. Grandstanding bastard, so he is. We'll wait until he's started, all the attention will be on him then. You ready, Jackie-boy?'

Quintel looked at the grenade in his hand and looked up at their target, before saying, 'Don't worry about me, just get me as close as you can.'

He was going to enjoy this.

Chapter Sixty-Four

By the time they were approaching the scene of McConachy's main address, Christine was feeling decidedly car sick. 'We should be the only press here, well, the only TV hopefully.'

'Why's that?' Paul asked.

'As no one was expecting him to drop any bombshells, most channels, or those who were bothered, thought they could get away with covering the first address only, and now thanks to your skill behind the wheel, they'll all be playing catch up.'

'Not lost it,' Paul said, adding, 'it looks like it's not easy to park around here, I'll drop you three and join you after I've ditched the motor.'

Five minutes later, Christine had managed to push her way to the front of the crowd. People naturally gave way to a camera crew coming through, apart from other camera crews that was, but they were the only ones here yet. She could see McConachy walking between two lecterns; one by the cordon by the road and a second one a little way down the driveway to the main entrance to the Barracks. She could only imagine why he'd picked Fulwood Barracks to make his grand speech. She watched as the silver-haired man in his light coloured suit seemed to settle by the lectern nearest the gatehouse. She also noticed he walked exaggeratedly straight. Probably trying to cover up his limp.

'If he's going to do it from there, then we will need to be closer,' the soundgirl said.

'Come on them,' Christine answered, adding, 'but do it slowly, like it's pre-arranged.'

The three of them walked slowly up the short driveway to where McConachy was stood, clearly preparing to start his address. He only seemed to notice them as they drew to a halt a couple of feet away. He'd been engrossed in his notes or whatever he'd been reading.

'Turning,' Christine whispered to her crew, who both repeated the word.

'Outside Fulwood Barracks, take one – Action,' she said, facing the camera before turning back to face McConachy.

'I'll be doing press interviews by the roadway in a few minutes, if you can wait 'till then,' McConachy said.

'Christine Jones, NWTV. Mr McConachy we have evidence that you, although appearing to be pro-power sharing with other political groups, have in fact behind the scenes been systematically removing any Protestant or pro-Unionist from public office.'

'What the hell is this?'

'In fact, you have replaced such senior figures, including within the police service, with Republican sympathisers in a secret plan to eventually usurp the British Government, isn't that true?'

'What rubbish is this?'

'The fact that you plan to announce today that you are ending investigations into the actions committed by the forces of law and order, is simply a smokescreen to your true political agenda.'

'Get these out of here,' he said, turning to two minders who were stood back from McConachy.

'Actions, which only this morning, you still described as "atrocities".'

'Get that camera,' McConachy barked at his minders.

Christine told her crew to run as she stepped forward to block the advancing minders in an effort to give her crew a head start. She knew she'd gone further than June had told her to, but she couldn't help it.

*

Quintel could see the three-person TV crew head up the driveway towards their target as McKnowle spoke. 'We go now while McConachy is distracted, so get ready.'

It was the first time McKnowle had used their target's name, not that it made any difference, it still meant nothing to him. Quintel wound down the passenger window and held onto the grenade tightly as he pulled the safety pin out.

McKnowle drove at normal speed as they approached. Then, as they neared, Quintel got a side-on glimpse of the woman in the TV crew asking the questions. It was that bitch Christine Jones. What was she doing here? And then he smiled to himself. He could kill them both in one go and McKnowle would never be the wiser. Both jobs completed, no problems. Money in the bank.

'Get ready,' McKnowle said, adding, 'I'll slow right down as we pass the back of the crowd, every fucker's watching that twat. Make it a good one.'

Quintel reckoned their target would only be between fifteen and twenty metres away at the most. If he hit the driveway at five metres prior or better, it would be good enough. He remembered at Blackley cemetery when Jason had told him about the three meter zone – within that there was no chance of survival.

He turned to face the window as the car slowed down, and kept a firm hold of the blue painted weapon in his right hand.

Chapter Sixty-Five

Vinnie had turned back onto the main road that the Barracks were on, done a U-turn, and was headed in the general direction of the A6 for a further drive past. He slowed down, as he wanted to be able to take it all in, see if anything had changed since a few minutes ago. The crowd were slightly larger and First Minister McConachy was stood at the podium nearest to the Barracks. He had grey hair with a suit to match. It looked as if he was being interviewed by a three-person camera crew. McConachy was waving his arms aggressively; he guessed the interview wasn't going too well. He'd got quite a shock when Harry had told him that this ex-terrorist was now the First Minister of the Northern Irish Assembly. No wonder the local uniform superintendent was harassed at having this dropped on him at the last minute, and no wonder he was coy with Harry as to the man's full identity.

Although this had to be the target, and acknowledging the fact that according to what Crompton had told Harry that he had took over from McKnowle and had then taken the IRA in a different direction, there had to be more to it. McKnowle had spent God knows how many years fermenting his hatred of McConachy, a man whom he once must have stood with as brothers-in-arms. There had to be more.

Vinnie slowed as he started to pass the back of the crowd, albeit from the opposite side of the road, scanning their backs, looking for anything that could construe the start of a hostile act. His last contact from Harry had been to tell him that the ARVs had arrived and were decamping in a side street, their instructions being to mingle among the crowd.

He looked forward again and then saw it. The blue Nissan approaching from the opposite direction. It too was starting to pass the back of the crowd. It too was slowing. He was fairly sure that the driver was the same man who'd been the car's passenger when he and Christine had seen it in Blackpool. That must be McKnowle. And he was sure of whom today's passenger was, Quintel. And he was winding his passenger window down.

Fifteen metres between them and not a moment to lose, Vinnie hit the accelerator of his Volvo as hard as he could and aimed at the front of the

Nissan. It was all he could do in the time. He glanced back at McConachy and saw two of the camera crew running away and the anchor, a woman, being bundled by two minders back towards the cordon by the road. She had her back to him.

He turned back to face the Nissan and braced himself for impact. The front of his car missed the front of the Nissan, as McKnowle must have seen the threat at the last minute as the car swerved. Vinnie didn't have time to alter his course and the front of his car hit the driver's side of the Nissan. Horns blazed all around from other motorists as the crowd turned to face them, Vinnie saw a blue object fly out of Quintel's window in a looping arc towards McConachy. His own window was down and all he could do was shout 'grenade,' as he watched the small round death-giver fly through the air.

He then realised that the grenade was going to fall short. The collision between the cars must have altered Quintel's aim. Vinnie was horrified as he realised that the grenade was now headed towards the crowd. He wasn't sure in this time-lapsed moment whether people had seen the approaching object or heard his shout, or both, but some had reacted and were fleeing in all directions, star-bursting across the lawn perimeter with some running wildly into the road. Then Vinnie saw the TV anchor turn around. It was Christine. What the hell was she doing here? Then remembered what she'd spent months working on.

Vinnie felt sick as he realised what his intervention had done. The grenade was past its highest point and heading straight towards Christine. Time caught up as he helplessly watched in horror as the device landed at her feet.

Chapter Sixty-Six

Christine tried her best to stall the two burly minders but knew she was no match for them, but what she had done was to buy her crew a couple of vital seconds, and they were off and through the crowd before they could be stopped. Job done. She stopped resisting as the two goons frog-marched her to the outer cordon by the pavement and then gave her an unceremonious shove towards the main gathering. Then she heard an almighty crash, a road accident beyond the crowd. She couldn't see the vehicles clearly because everyone had turned to look, but two cars had definitely collided right behind where they were. She hoped no one was hurt.

Then she heard someone shout what sounded like the word "grenade". People started to flee; they must have thought they heard the same word. But it couldn't be. Why would someone shout "grenade"? She turned around, towards where the two cars which collided had slithered to a halt, and that's when she saw something flying through the air towards her.

It took a second to register. It was small, round and a vivid shade of blue. And it was headed straight for her. It had obviously topped-out within its trajectory and was looping down towards her at a fast rate. Her brain assimilated everything in a milli-second. Then flight mode kicked in as she started to leap, but in a further milli-second her brain had also told her that it was hopeless. The grenade was only feet away.

As she started to jump, it hit the ground right in front of her. She couldn't take her eyes off it.

*

Vinnie watched the grenade as it hit the ground right in front of Christine. Then nothing. Nothing happened. The blue object bounced up into the air before hitting the ground for a second time. Still nothing. It just rolled to a stop. Vinnie screamed, 'Christine here, run.' He saw her head spin around, and through the thinned out crowd their eyes locked in mutual recognition.

Vinnie was out of the car by the time Christine arrived. He didn't know why the device hadn't gone off, or whether it still would. She flung her arms around him and he hugged her like he'd never hugged anyone in his life. No words were spoken. None were needed. Then a familiar cry brought him back to the initial matter in hand. 'Armed police; put your hands where I can see them, do it now.'

Vinnie turned to see several of the surveillance team's ARV crews with weapons drawn approaching the Nissan. The driver suddenly leapt from the Nissan and opened fire with a handgun before he grabbed hold of one of the last members of the crowd. He backed off across the road with his gun to the terrified man's head. Then Vinnie recognised the scared man from the crowd. It was Major Crompton, in civilian clothes. But he was playing along, shouting and wailing as one would expect. Three armed police followed the retreating McKnowle at increasingly widening angles, until his back was up against a wall on the opposite side of the road next to a small pub.

'Stand the fuck down or this twat gets it,' McKnowle shouted.

But the armed police continued until they were only twenty feet away, but covering a wide arc. McKnowle couldn't watch them all, and he must have known it.

'Just put your weapon down and no one needs get hurt,' the middle cop said.

'I knows how you fuckers work, I put the weapon down and yous kill me,' McKnowle said.

'Even if that was true, which it's not, would we do such a thing with all these witnesses?' the same officer said.

McKnowle looked as if he was taking in his environment for the first time. The crowd had re-formed, albeit at a safe distance. Amazing how bold the inquisitive mind could be, Vinnie thought.

McKnowle took the gun away from his hostage's head. Crompton was still playing his part, wailing and muttering. McKnowle said, 'Just so yous know who the feekin boss is here; I'll lame this fucker.' McKnowle then started to move his gun arm towards Crompton's right leg. The moment of impasse was clearly not one which the experienced soldier was going to let pass. He balked back, knocking McKnowle backwards into the wall with a look of genuine surprise in his eyes. He'd clearly not seen his hostage as a threat due to his excellent playacting.

Crompton kept himself bent double as he rushed forward, in a zig zag pattern. Vinnie watched as he saw McKnowle rebound off the wall before he started to raise his gun arm again, clearly trying to track Crompton's movements as his arm swung to and fro. Then two shots rang out and McKnowle went down. He'd given the police no choice, as the middle cop started to run to McKnowle's aid.

This had all gone off in seconds, but had seemed like minutes to Vinnie. He spun around to look for the Nissan, but it was gone, and so was Quintel.

Chapter Sixty-Seven

As Vinnie spun around to look for the Nissan, he also saw Christine approach McKnowle with her soundgirl and cameraman following on. He reckoned that they were recording as the light was on above the camera. He quickly pulled Christine to one side. 'Did you see where Quintel went?'

'Quintel?' she asked.

'He was just here in the Nissan.'

'Sorry, no I didn't.'

Two paramedics arrived and started to work on McKnowle, who was awake and swearing. Vinnie stepped forward. 'Will he be alright?'

The paramedic nearest to Vinnie said, 'Looks superficial, once we staunch the bleeding he'll be in no danger. He might need minor surgery to his wounds, but he'll live.'

Then Major Crompton approached and that reminded Vinnie of the unexploded grenade. 'The grenade?'

'Worry not Inspector, I'd been keeping an eye from beyond the gatehouse and saw the attack. But the fools used a training ground grenade. That's why they are painted bright blue – no explosives in them. One of my men has already recovered it; and before you say anything, it's preserved for forensic examination.'

'Thanks, Major,' Vinnie said.

'Looks like whoever sold that munition to your man knew he was not ex-military so ripped him off,' Crompton said.

'Brick dust,' Vinnie said.

'Pardon?' Crompton asked.

Vinnie quickly explained that if a heroin dealer thought he was dealing with a patsy he'd sell him brick dust instead of heroin, as it looked like the real thing.

'I thought heroin was white?' Christine said.

'Only on the telly, Vinnie said, 'or if it is pharmaceutically produced in a lab,' he added.

'Brick dust it was then,' Crompton said.

Vinnie realised he'd yet to ask Christine if she was alright, and did so apologetically.

'I'm fine, but it has been a hell of a few days, Vinnie Palmer, I can tell you that,' she answered.

Vinnie could see that the paramedics were preparing to take McKnowle away, so he grabbed one of the guarding armed cops and stepped forward. 'I understand you spent twenty years in a Locked-in Syndrome,' Vinnie started.

'What the fuck is it to you,' McKnowle answered.

'Well, you can now look forward to the next twenty in a locked-up syndrome,' Vinnie said and then spoke through the obscene response to let McKnowle know that he was under arrest for murder and conspiracy to murder, and that was just for starters. He cautioned him but didn't bother noting the indecent reply. He told the armed cop to stay with him, but as McKnowle was being stretchered towards the rear of the awaiting ambulance, fast movement caught Vinnie's periphery vision.

He turned to see McConachy making straight towards the stretcher. Before anyone could react he was there next to it. He looked down at McKnowle and reeled back with astonishment all over his face. 'You?' he said.

'Yes it's freekin me, who the fuck did you expect?' McKnowle replied.

'But why?' McConachy asked.

'Why do you think? For selling us out to the Brits, for sticking your brown nose up their arses; anything for power.'

'You stupid bastard,' McConachy started, his visage now one of rage. 'I wasn't selling out, I was playing the long game to return the six counties to the Republic, but thick gun-happy eejits like you could never see that. I'm not brown-nosing these; I hate the fucking Brits,' McConachy finished before standing back, apparently stunned by his own outburst. He then turned and pushed his way back through the enclosing crowd as his police escort arrived.

'What was all that about?' Vinnie asked of no one in particular.

'I think I know,' Crompton said, as Vinnie turned to face him. 'It's not exactly a secret, in fact it is on public record, as I only discovered thirty minutes ago,' Crompton said.

'What is?' Vinnie asked.

'No offence, Inspector, but I'll need to make a call first, in order to put some context to it. But if I'm right, it would explain a lot. I'll ring your superintendent later.'

'Fair enough,' Vinnie answered.

'You get all that?' Christine asked her crew just as Paul Bury joined them. They said that they had, and Vinnie asked Christine, 'what next?'

'I need to get back to Manchester, get this ready for broadcast and get going on the end of the documentary. After today, I could do with the documentary airing within the next 24 hours, whilst the events of today's broadcast are still current.'

Vinnie asked Paul if he'd take Christine back, which he readily agreed to. He then headed over to a plain BMW which was one of the surveillance gunships still with its three-man armed crew on board. He identified himself to them and told the driver to jump in the back. 'You're with me; we've got a Nissan and a nutter to find.'

Chapter Sixty-Eight

Quintel couldn't understand why McKnowle had run at the cops like a demented leprechaun, but he was grateful for the diversion. It was each man for himself now. He'd sped off behind the backs of the cops as all the attention was trained on the mad Irishman. The backed-off crowd, backed off some more as he accelerated through them and through the traffic lights outside the Barracks. He then went straight through the next set and as soon as he was out of sight he threw a right turn into a wide urban road that he noted was called Cromwell Road. A hundred metres in and he screeched to a halt, got out and ran to the boot. He shoved his handgun down the back of his waistband as he delved into the holdall.

He pulled the remaining grenade from the bag; it was one of the original two that he'd bought with Jason. It was green with yellow markings on it and he instantly realised why the other one had failed to go off. 'That Birmingham bastard,' he shouted out loud. Once he was clear and away he'd pay that fat, hairy lump of lard a visit, and clean him out of all his cash before killing him, and it would be slow. He was already out of pocket to the tune of a hundred and ten grand. All this effort and drama for absolutely nothing. He'd never felt madder as he pulled the pin from the grenade and lobbed it into the Nissan.

He then pulled his mobile phone from his pocket as he ran, and three seconds later he felt the heat of the blast hit his back as a deafening noise rang in his ears. He threw himself onto a grass verge between the road and the footpath, as small pieces of debris flew past.

A few seconds later he picked himself up and calmly kept on walking without looking back. He dialled a number into his phone, but couldn't hear the ringtone as he put it to his ear.

*

'Any of you see which way the Nissan went?' Vinnie asked as he started the BMW's engine. All three said that they hadn't. Then just as Vinnie was about to move off he heard an almighty explosion from somewhere in the foreground. It was followed immediately by a plume of dark smoke rising up above the rooftops. 'I'm guessing it went that way,' he said to himself, but before he could set off, his phone rang. It was Harry.

'Be quick, Harry,' Vinnie opened with.

'I'm in comms at Preston so monitoring, but listen,' Harry said, who then lowered his voice to a whisper before continuing, 'The line on Quintel's phone is now live, and he's just put a call into an unknown mobile demanding he be picked up. Says he's on Cromwell Road. I've got the surveillance team en route, you grab a gunship and go.' Harry then raised his voice to normal, and gave Vinnie directions.

'On it,' Vinnie said before ending the call, and putting the car into gear.

Chapter Sixty-Nine

Minutes later, Vinnie turned into Cromwell Road and could see the burning wreckage of the blue Nissan up ahead. A number of bystanders were starting to gather and he could hear distant sirens approaching. He had to slow to drive carefully past the blaze to ensure he missed any burning debris, which was scattered everywhere. After negotiating his way past the worst of it, he accelerated hard along the straight avenue.

'Boss, boss,' one of the armed cops in the back seat started, 'it's on the radio. The surveillance team have picked up their target in a Black VW Golf and are inbound from the other end of Cromwell Road. They are screaming for armed back up.'

'How long is this road?' Vinnie asked, as he floored the accelerator.

''Bout a mile,' the cop answered.

The BMW almost took flight as Vinnie hit seventy as the road rose up over a small hill. But as soon as he cleared the brow and all four wheels were back on the ground he had to stamp hard on the brakes.

Fifty metres ahead a number of plain cars surrounded a black VW which was trying to turn left into a side road, and they were forcing it to halt. Vinnie managed to bring the BMW to a stop in time as the cars ahead also stopped. He and his crew jumped out and all four of them drew their weapons as they approached the VW, which was only feet in front of them.

Vinnie immediately recognised the front seat passenger - it was Quintel, with Blister behind the wheel. He also saw a handgun on the dashboard. He shouted, 'weapon,' as he watched both Quintel and Blister make a grab for it.

Blister got to it first and pointed it at Quintel.

Vinnie's three armed cops moved in, but Vinnie held one back as Blister got out of the car and ordered Quintel to do the same.

As the two armed cops cautiously approached, Blister spoke, 'I heard the call so attended, saw the suspect so pretended to offer him a lift, I'm arresting him.'

'You little shite,' Quintel said, 'how fucking dare you?' he added. But before he could say anymore, the two advancing cops grabbed him, searched him for weapons and handcuffed him.

Vinnie approached as two police vans joined them from up ahead. 'Jack Quintel, I'm arresting you for murder, conspiracy to murder, God knows how many firearms offences and anything else I think of later.' And then he told the two cops to take him away and they led him towards one of the vans, as he continued to shout accusations towards Blister. Vinnie re-holstered his weapon.

'Good try,' Blister shouted back as Vinnie approached him. He touched the remaining armed cop's elbow, signifying to follow him.

He stopped in front of Blister, who said, 'Those fucking criminals will try anything to get themselves out of the mire, claiming I'm in on it indeed. As if?'

'Yeah, nice one,' Vinnie said as he pulled a plastic exhibits bag from his jacket pocket and put his hand out for Blister's gun.

'Oh yeah, of course. It's Quintel's; I had to wrestle it off him when the cars surrounded us,' Blister said as he handed it over.

'Very brave of you,' Vinnie said, as he made the gun safe before putting it into the bag, sealing it and putting it into his jacket pocket.

'I wouldn't be surprised if they don't give me a commendation and a promotion after this,' Blister continued.

Vinnie then punched Blister in the face as hard as he could before grabbing hold of him by his shirt and whispering in his ear, 'That's for Charlie and Christine, you bent pond life. You'd have sacrificed her, just as you were no doubt involved in the sacrifice of Charlie, just to gain brownie points with Quintel. You make me sick.'

Vinnie then stood back and told Blister out loud that he was under arrest for conspiracy to murder and for misconduct in public office, and for being a shit. Blister didn't answer, he just looked shocked.

'I saw you go for the gun, which was idly lying on your dashboard,' Vinnie said. He knew he couldn't reveal anything from the line, nor could any of it be used in evidence. So he used what he had just seen by way of explanation, for now.

Vinnie turned to the remaining armed cop and told him to take Blister away and lock him up.

'But sir, don't you know who he is?' the cop said.

'I know who he was; now just get him out of here.'

Chapter Seventy

Forty five minutes later and Vinnie was nursing his second mug of tea in the SIO's office at Preston as he finished briefing Harry on all that had taken place.

'Interesting you ended up on the quaintly named Cromwell Road, like a modern version of the English Civil War,' Harry said.

'Sorry?' Vinnie said, and then regretted asking. He'd forgotten that Harry was a bit of a history buff as he then went on to explain about the Battle of Preston in the 1600s between Oliver Cromwell's model army and the Royalists backed by the Scots. Trying to steer Harry back on subject, who to be fair was clearly starting to relax for the first time in days, for which he couldn't blame him, Vinnie said, 'What do we know about this McKnowle character? Other than he is one angry puppy.'

'Well,' Harry said, who took a sip of his tea before he continued, 'Apparently, he was a senior member of the IRA's ruling Army Council.'

Vinnie knew he was an ex-terrorist but little more. 'Well ok, but what's his beef with McConachy?'

Harry said he'd had one call from Major Crompton and was expecting a second, and then reminded Vinnie that Mathew McConachy was the First Minister of Northern Ireland.

'That's obviously why Christine and her crew were there. He's the bloke she has been doing her investigative documentary about,' Vinnie said.

'Quite. But what Christine doesn't – and can't know – is that according to the Major, McConachy is not only suspected of being the ASU Commander on that fatal ambush in West Belfast twenty odd years ago, when McKnowle was left in the lurch; but that he then went on to take over from him within the IRA's top brass, and led the organisation into the peace process.'

Vinnie nodded and said, 'No wonder he wanted McConachy dead, all that bitterness. But you said, "not only" is there more?'

'I'll come to that, but obviously as he wanted McConachy dead that's why he hired Quintel and Jason; he had to use unknown assassins.

Carstair and Reedly were just for starters, though it appears that their, or should I say Reedly's investigation, was straight.'

'I should think so; the bastards were about to murder an innocent man before the SAS intervened.'

'And his family, according to the major, if McKnowle had got his way,' Harry added.

Vinnie sat back in his chair and considered just how lucky they had been today, before he remembered what McConachy had said to McKnowle before he was taken away in the ambulance. He reminded Harry of it.

'Perverse, isn't it? Everything McKnowle thought that McConachy had become was wrong. They were on the same side but McConachy's approach was just more subtle.'

'True,' Vinnie said, adding, 'plus, I think he is obviously enjoying the power kick in being the First Minister.'

'Let's see how long that lasts once his real aims are aired via Christine's programme.'

'Should prove interesting viewing,' Vinnie said. He then asked Harry what Darlington thought.

'He hasn't got the whole story yet, but as you can imagine he's well-relieved, he should be here soon.'

'And what about that dirty bastard, or should I say, the soon to be ex-Chief Inspector Russell "Blister" Sharpe. Have we got enough evidence to charge him?'

As you know we can't use phone tap intelligence in court, but I think we'll have plenty. He's already started to sing, trying to say Quintel was blackmailing him,' Harry said.

Vinnie knew that was a good start; Blister was admitting his actions, so they just had to prove the real motive. A quick look at his bank account should help do that.

Then Harry's desk phone rang and Vinnie drained his mug as Harry listened for several seconds, before thanking the caller and putting the phone down. 'Looked serious?' Vinnie said.

'It was. That was Crompton. He's been granted permission to tell us officially why McKnowle was so extra bitter towards McConachy.'

'The "not only" bit?'

'Yes.'

Vinnie thought he'd already heard reason enough, but let Harry elaborate.

'Mathew McConachy is Bobby McKnowle's brother,' Harry started.

Vinnie was shocked.

'According to Crompton they were dead rivals within the IRA which is probably why McKnowle went on that fatal job, just to give his brother who was leading it, grief.'

'So is he some sort of step-brother?' Vinnie asked.

'Apparently not. Blood. But soon after McKnowle went into his Locked-in Syndrome, McConachy was promoted and could obviously see the way things were going, so changed his name by deed poll in 1998 before the Peace Process was signed. Crompton says he wanted to distance himself from his terrorist past.'

'Crafty bastard,' Vinnie said.

'Indeed,' Harry said, adding, 'It's on public record, but just not obvious, it was forgotten about during the transition from armed struggle to peace. But it's there if anyone cares to look.'

'That would have just made McKnowle worse, no doubt,' Vinnie said.

'And he's had twenty odd years to fester on it.'

They then agreed that Vinnie could tell Christine this last bit, as it was on public record, but would have to hold back the bit about McConachy being the ASU Commander on that fatal evening. That couldn't be proved, openly. Then Harry told Vinnie to get off home; he could wait until tomorrow before all the post arrest paperwork needed to be started. He'd already instructed two interview teams who had made a start on Quintel and Blister. McKnowle would have to wait until he was discharged from hospital of course.

Vinnie thanked his boss, and then put a quick call into Christine before leaving. She told him that Paul had dropped her off before heading to the airport, and she was relieved to hear of Quintel's arrest, but shocked to hear of Blister's. 'Look, I know you are dead busy, but I could do with seeing you tonight,' he said. He sensed a rejection coming from the pause that followed, so added, 'Two reasons, both very important.'

'Go on,' she said.

'One, that I need to buy you that dinner, and to avoid confusion I'll be treating it as a date.'

'You will, will you? Ok. But the second reason better be as good.'

'I think I have a superb ending for your programme, which you are going to want to hear, but not over the phone.'

Christine agreed, but said they should meet soon, as in a couple of hours' time, as she would probably have to go back to work after they'd eaten. He agreed and ended the call, and then remembered he didn't have a car, well, not one that was drivable. He turned back to face Harry. 'Just one last favour?'

Acknowledgements

As always, I wholeheartedly thank my advance readers who give up their time freely to read through an early draft of my work to advise me on the story itself. What they see from their objective positions really does make all the difference to the finished work. They volunteer as I never ask so thanks again to David Price-Williams, Chris Wells, Chris Hughes and Nick Wells.

You can find out more about me via my website: www.rogerapriceauthor.com for which my continued thanks goes to Ivor Wood for his techno-wizardry. You can find me on social media (links displayed on my website) or email me at rapricereviews@aol.com . Please do get in touch I'd love to hear from you. I could even add you to my email list, or you can subscribe direct via www.rogerapriceauthor.blogspot.co.uk so as to ensure you never miss out on updates or giveaways.

This book is the second in the new series following on from 'Nemesis' and I'm thrilled at the way that book has thus far been received, if you've not read it yet, why not give a try?

My thanks also go to my family and friends, some near, some far, for your continued support and interest.

And to all my readers from all the far flung corners of the globe, together with those closer to home, much love and gratitude; without you none of this would happen.

Finally, to all at Endeavour Press; from acquisition to editorial through to cover design, production and marketing, thank you for your total professionalism. When an author hands his book over, he entrusts a piece of him or herself. This book could not have been in better hands.

Printed in Great Britain
by Amazon

49996797R00163